In Search of a Love Story

Rachel Schurig

Copyright 2012 Rachel Schurig
All rights reserved.
ISBN-13: 978-1475252750
ISBN-10: 1475252757

No part of this book may be reproduced, or stored in a retrieval system, or transmitted in any form or by any means, electronic, mechanical, photocopying, recording, or otherwise, without express written permission of the author.

This is a work of fiction. Names, characters, places, and incidents are either the product of the author's imagination or used fictitiously. Any similarity to real persons, living or dead, is coincidental and not intended by the author.

For My Parents,
who live the truest of love stories every day.

ACKNOWLEDGMENTS

Special thanks, as ever, to Andrea and Michelle,
chick-lit gurus,
and beta readers extraordinaire (and pretty good
friends to boot).

Thank you to my family and friends for amazing
support,
particularly my siblings and parents.

Thank you to Shelley Holloway for editing services.
www.hollowayhouse.me

Book cover design by Scarlett Rugers Design 2012
www.scarlettrugers.com

Lastly, I am so lucky to have spent such a large portion of my life enjoying the beautiful woods and lakes of northern Michigan. My wonderful memories of these places helped inspire much of this book. I am so grateful to my Sheridan and Plaskon cousins, my mom, Aunt Judy, Aunt Joanne, and my grandmother Innabelle, for making me an up-north girl.

Chapter One

That's it. I'm done with men.

I mean it. I am absolutely, completely, one hundred percent finished with the male species.

I've come close to swearing off men before. Like after my break-up with Jacob. I was nearly ready to throw in the towel then. Or after my disastrous experiment with speed dating (you don't even want to know). But my optimistic side always won out in the end, and I would give dating another shot.

Not this time, though. This time I really am done. Finished. For good.

I explained my newfound determination to my roommate Ashley as I drove to work that first morning AD (After Dylan).

"You don't mean it," Ashley soothed, her voice crackling somewhat through my cell phone. "You're upset. You just got dumped!"

I made a face at the phone.

"I did *not* get dumped," I said. "I did the dumping."

Ashley was quiet for a moment. "Oh," she said. "I guess I just assumed…"

"Thanks, Ash," I said. "You really know how to make me feel better."

"Sorry, sorry," she said hurriedly. "So what happened?"

I had a mental flash of the night before, sitting in Dylan's kitchen, take-out from his favorite restaurant laid out on the table in front of me, an ill-advised surprise to celebrate our three-month anniversary. From the hallway outside the apartment, I had heard the muffled sound of voices and the rattle of keys, which surely signaled Dylan's arrival. Then I froze. Along with Dylan's deep, familiar voice, there was another sound. A high-pitched, giggling sound. A girl.

"There was someone else," I said to Ashley, forgetting to signal before I switched lanes. The driver behind me laid on his horn, and I fought back the urge to flip him off. "Another girl," I clarified to Ashley. "He showed up at his apartment with her last night."

On the other end of the phone, Ashley gasped. "The bastard!"

I felt myself flush as the mortification washed over me again. The cheating wasn't even the worst part. Much more humiliating was the look on his face when he saw me sitting there at his kitchen table in my stupid red dress. He didn't even have the decency to look scared or guilty. Instead, I caught a clear flash of annoyance in his eyes. That's all I was to him: an irritation standing in the way of his plans to get lucky with the wide- eyed bimbo behind him.

"I should have known," I told Ashley. "I mean, it was clear he was a bastard long before last night."

"Love blinds us," she said sagely, and I rolled my eyes. Typical Ashley. "Em, I'm so sorry I wasn't there when you got home," she continued. "You should have called me! I would have come back immediately."

The truth was, I felt a measure of relief when I got back to our apartment last night and found the note from Ashley letting me know that she'd be spending the night at her boyfriend Chris' place. Under her familiar handwriting, Chris had added a little note wishing me luck with my surprise dinner and seduction plans. The embarrassment had been too much, and I was grateful that I'd have an evening alone to nurse my pride (or at least drown it with wine) before I had to tell either of them about it.

"It's okay," I told her. "I wasn't up for much company anyhow."

"You poor thing," she said. From the other end of the phone I heard the muffled sound of a bell ringing, signaling the start of Ashley's day as a kindergarten teacher.

"You should go," I told her. "I'm almost to work anyhow."

"We'll have dinner tonight, whatever you want," she told me. "I'll call Ryan on my lunch break and tell him to come over."

Ryan was one of our closest friends, so I knew he would find out what had happened eventually, but I still groaned softly at the thought of her telling him all the details. "Em, he loves you," she said, obviously having heard me. "He'd want to be there."

"I know," I said, resigned. "Thanks for calling him."

She was quiet for a moment. "What about...um...Chris? Do you want...I mean, he would want to come too, I bet. But if you don't want him to—"

"Of course," I said, feeling slightly awkward. Chris had been our friend for years—actually he'd been my friend first, since we'd been lab partners back in eighth grade science. We had bonded over a joint refusal to dissect the frog Mrs. Carter had provided. But now that he and Ashley had finally figured out they were meant for each other and started dating, the boundaries of my friendship with him seemed a lot blurrier. "The more the merrier."

"Okay," she said, clearly relieved. "So we'll see you at home around six?"

"Sure," I said. "Thanks, Ash."

"Listen," she said hurriedly, and I could hear the sound of lots of little voices in the background. "Everything is gonna be fine, okay? You can call me any time, and I can have Jana cover my class if you need to talk—"

"I'm fine," I assured her. "Get to work. I'll see you tonight."

I ended the call and threw my phone into my bag on the seat next to me. I was almost to work now, and the thought of trying to make it through a long day with the remnants of my wine-induced hangover did nothing to improve my mood. I said a silent prayer that my patients would be easy as I pulled into the parking lot of the small outpatient facility where I worked as a physical therapist.

Friday was usually my favorite day to work—most people didn't want to spend the first evening of the weekend at therapy, so we closed at four. Since the schedule was usually light, there was only one therapist on duty. It was a nice change of pace from the usual crowded and noisy weekdays.

After gathering my things, I pulled down the visor and peered at myself in the mirror. My eyes looked a little on the puffy side, more from the wine than from any tears. I hadn't cried much last night. Hopefully I could get away without anyone noticing anything was amiss.

"Hey!" Sarah called from the front desk the moment I walked into the reception area. "How'd it go last night?"

Damn, I thought. I had totally forgotten that I had told Sarah about my anniversary surprise.

"Good morning," I said, plastering a smile on my face as I slipped behind the desk to hang up my coat.

Maybe I could deflect her. "You're here early!"

Fat chance. "I wanted to get in a few minutes on the bike," Sarah said, waving her hand dismissively. "Who cares about that, how'd it go?"

I cursed myself for telling her about my plans. I should have known she'd act like this. Despite her predilection for overexcitement, particularly when it came to boys and dating, I like working with Sarah. She is a bit younger than I am, still in college, but she is good at her job as a physical therapist assistant, and the patients seem to love her. But this morning I could do without her eagerness.

"It didn't go too great," I told her, deciding vague was the best policy. "I'm not really feeling it with Dylan, actually."

Sarah stared at me with wide eyes. "But he's so handsome and charming!"

I felt a little twinge, wondering just *how* charming he had been with her on the few occasions he had come to pick me up from work.

"Oh well," I said, shrugging. "Plenty of fish in the sea." She looked ready to argue the point, so I continued. "So what's on the schedule today?"

Sarah looked down at the appointment book. "We're pretty booked." I sighed. Of course we were. "You've got most of the regular crowd this morning. Mr. Brandon and Mr. Cowdin are coming in on their lunch breaks. And you have three evals this afternoon."

I stifled a groan. Evaluations were time consuming and tedious, requiring all of my attention and leaving no room for just going through the motions. This was exactly the kind of day I had been hoping to avoid.

"Well," I said, moving around the desk to head to the tiny office at the back of the room. "I'm gonna review my charts. You may as well start getting everything prepped now. The weights and resistance bands are looking pretty disorganized; will you take care of that, please?"

"Sure thing," Sarah said. "Let me just put the towels in the dryer..."

I made it to the safety of the small office and collapsed in my desk chair. For once, I wished one of the other therapists was here. Then I could foist off some of my clients and go home. There was a beep from my cell phone, and I pulled it out of my bag, looking down at the new-message screen. Ryan.

Ash just txtd me, it read. *Dylan is a prick and ur better off. I'm bringing vodka 2nite, C ya soon!*

I sighed. It was only 8:15, and already the news of my humiliation was going viral. I stared at my phone for a minute, debating. There was one person in the world that I was actually eager to talk to that morning, but it was early, and if I knew her, my best friend would be rushing to get to work. I pictured Brooke, her hair probably wet, maybe thrown back in a ponytail, a coffee most definitely in her hand, probably searching for her shoes in her notoriously messy bedroom.

The image, as clear to me as if she were really there before me, brought a sharp little pain to my chest. The thought of talking to her was just too tempting. I picked up my phone and dialed.

"Hello?" she said a moment later, her voice every bit as harried as I had imagined.

"Brooke?" I said, embarrassed to feel my voice catch slightly on her name. "It's me. Do you have a minute?"

"What's wrong?" she asked immediately.

"I'm having a crap day," I said, sighing heavily.

"Em, it's like, eight a.m. How could your day be

bad already?"

"I broke up with Dylan last night," I said quickly, wanting to get this part over as soon as I could. "He was cheating on me."

"Shit," she said. The curse almost brought a smile to my face—it was so typical of my brassy, loud best friend. "Did you kick him in the balls? Do you want *me* to kick him in the balls?"

"Might be kind of difficult from two hundred miles away."

"A four-hour drive to castrate the son of a bitch would be well worth it to me," she muttered. "God, Em. Are you okay?"

I closed my eyes. "I'm freaking out a little," I admitted. "I feel like I'm in a giant shame spiral right now."

"Shame spiral?" Her voice was sharp. "What do you have to be ashamed about?"

I didn't respond. How could I explain to Brooke what I had felt sitting there, watching Dylan and that girl walk through the door? I didn't think Brooke had ever had a moment of self-doubt in her life.

"Emily," she said, her tone softer now. "This had nothing to do with you."

"Of course it did," I whispered. "He didn't want me. He didn't even respect me."

"Because he's an asshole. Not because of anything you did or didn't do."

"It's just hard to not feel terrible about myself right now."

"Alright, let me ask you this," Brooke said. "Who do you trust more—Dylan or me?"

"You," I said immediately. "Obviously."

"Well I chose you to be my best friend. No one made me. It was my decision, and I chose you because you are funny and smart and loyal and all that other crap."

I snorted, and I could hear her laugh softly on the other end of the line. "I mean it, Em. I've known you since we were, what, six years old? His asshatness had nothing to do with you. I promise you that."

"Thanks," I said. "I know you have to get to work. I just needed a little pep-talk, I guess."

"Work can wait. I have time."

"No, it's okay," I told her. "I feel better already."

"God, I really am a spectacular friend, aren't I?" she said, and I laughed. "I mean that took like, what, five minutes for me to pull you back from the edge?"

"You are pretty amazing," I said drily.

"You sure you're okay?" Her tone was more serious. "I really can talk for a minute if you want."

"Thanks," I said. "I'm okay. I should get to work too."

"Alright. Well, call me anytime. Really."

"Okay," I said. "Thanks, Brooke."

"Bye, babe."

"Bye."

I ended the call, tossing my phone onto my desk. Talking to Brooke had helped, but I was still feeling like a hot shower and a shot of Jack Daniels would really do the trick.

"Emily?"

I looked up to see my friend Elliot standing in the open office door. He had two paper coffee cups in his hands, and I smiled. Elliot was the manager of *VitaLife*, the health store next to the clinic. He had become a pretty good friend over the last few year—even though he was always bugging me to start taking supplements. He often came over to have lunch with me in the office, and we had gotten into the habit of trading coffee-fetching duty most mornings.

"You are a lifesaver," I said, holding out my hand for the coffee. "I couldn't remember if you were working today."

"Bright and early," he said, smiling back. Elliot was usually smiling—he was one of the most genuinely happy, friendly people I had ever met.

"You gonna be around for lunch?" I asked.

"Inventory day," he said. "I'll probably be tied up for most of the day."

"Next week then," I said.

"You could always join us for a hike tomorrow," he said hopefully. In addition to trying to convince me to get on a vitamin regimen, Elliot also seemed to think that my life would be more satisfying if I joined his Adventurers Club for their weekly outings. You could tell Elliot was the outdoorsy type just by looking at him—his feet were almost constantly clad in hiking shoes, and he seemed like he'd be much more at home in faded jeans and Henley shirts than in his work uniform of khakis and Polos. His red wavy hair usually looked pretty messy, like he had just come in from a windy day. He even had a bit of a scruffy goatee thing going. Total mountain man.

"We're heading down to Lake Erie," he continued. "Supposed to be some pretty amazing bird-watching."

I laughed. "You really know how to tempt a girl, Elliot. Bird-watching? It's almost too exciting to imagine."

He laughed too. "You don't know what you're missing," he said.

"Maybe next time."

"I'll hold you to that," he said. "Alright, I'm off." He tapped the doorjamb twice, flashed another smile, and left.

I decided I'd spent enough time socializing. My first patient, Frank, would be here in fifteen minutes. I picked up his file and opened it, looking over the notes of his previous session. If I had to be here, I may as well get some work done. With any luck, it might keep my mind off things.

Chapter Two

When I got home that night, all I could think about was getting into a hot shower. Being busy had made the day go by quickly enough, but I was exhausted. I dropped my bag on the kitchen table and noticed a note propped up against the fruit bowl. *Went to get provisions—A.*

I smiled a little as I headed to my bedroom. I would put money on Ashley returning with at least three bulging bags full of ice cream, potato chips, and assorted junk food in which I could drown my sorrows. In Ashley's mind, the best way to get over a guy was to partake in some good old-fashioned wallowing, preferably with several close friends and an assortment of chick flicks. I was grateful for Ryan and his promise of vodka—in my opinion a much more effective form of self-medication.

Under the hot water, I tried to massage the tension from my shoulders. While at work, I had managed to keep my mind off the nightmare of the previous night, but now, in the quiet of an empty apartment, it was hard not to let it all back in.

I've always believed that there are defining moments in every life. I've had a few myself. Some were predictable, obvious, while others were more subtle.

The biggest, of course, was my mom's death. I mean, it goes without saying that when you lose your mom at the age of twelve, your life changes forever. Mom's death wasn't exactly a shock, since she'd had cancer for more than a year. Still, you never really get prepared for something like that.

For some of my defining moments, I *was* prepared, like leaving my small hometown in northern Michigan for the state's capital, Lansing, to attend one of the best public colleges in the country. Others came as a surprise—I never would have imagined I would end up with a life-long friend when I asked the new girl in Mrs. Philip's kindergarten class if I could play with her My Little Pony.

And never in a million years would I have guessed how much things would change when I made the decision to plan an anniversary dinner for my boyfriend. I had never been the type to plan elaborate surprises or romantic tête-à-têtes. Ashley liked to say that I was born without the romantic gene, and I couldn't exactly argue with her. But I had been with Dylan for four months, one of the longest relationships in my adult life, and I was determined to make this one work.

***

So on that Thursday in February, I decided to do something I had never done for a boy before—make dinner. Okay, that's stretching it; I didn't actually cook. But I did place a carry-out order at Dylan's favorite restaurant, and I spent an inordinate amount of time picking out the best wine to go with it. I even baked a batch of chocolate chip cookies. Serious stuff.

I left my apartment in Royal Oak with butterflies in my stomach. I had gone all out, putting on a dress (one of the two that I owned, which usually lived in the very back recesses of my closet) and curling my normally stick-straight blonde hair. Earlier that day, I had told Dylan I had a late evaluation at work and arranged to meet him later in the evening. I was banking on the fact that he would come home straight from work—and hopefully be happily surprised to find me waiting there with dinner.

I found the key to his apartment below his mat, just where it always was. I felt a little funny letting myself in. I had never been in Dylan's place without him before. It was dark and quiet, everything clean with Dylan's belongings put away in their proper place. Unlike me, Dylan was a total neat freak. The smell of his aftershave seemed to linger in the hallway, and I smiled as I slipped into the kitchen.

I found the dishes and silverware and got the table ready, transferring the food from the take out containers to a few Pyrex bowls I found in the bottom of the cupboard. In a flash of sentimentality, I had picked up a bouquet of daisies on the way over. I couldn't find a vase, so I made do with a large glass beer stein. I surveyed my handiwork and felt a rush of pride. Maybe Ashley was wrong—maybe I did have the knack for this romance thing after all.

I had finished just in time—I heard the sound of jangling keys in the hallway, followed by Dylan's muffled voice. He was home.

But of course, he wasn't alone.

When I saw the girl behind him, it took me a minute to understand what was happening. My first ridiculous thought was that she was a work colleague. But how many girls wore skimpy hot pink dresses to work at a mortgage broker's office?

"What are you doing here?" Dylan asked, his voice cold. It was only then that I got it—Dylan was on his own date.

"I...I brought dinner," I said, my voice shaking.

"I thought we were getting together later," he said,

looking at the girl out of the corner of his eye. "I'm busy now."

"Who's that?" I asked, pointing at the girl. She smirked at me.

"A friend," she said, her voice high and girlish. God, it was such a cliché. She took a step closer to Dylan, her smirk growing wider.

"Are you kidding me?" I asked, still not quite believing that this was happening.

Dylan sighed. "Look, Em. You're great and everything, but we never said we were exclusive. I'm at a point in my life where I just need to have fun. I thought we were on the same page."

It was clear from his face that, at that moment, he found me anything but great. I finally realized what I was seeing in his eyes—it wasn't guilt, or fear that he had been caught. It was irritation. He was annoyed that I was there, ruining his plans. I meant nothing to him, nothing at all. I felt a rush of shame so strong it made me nauseous.

"But...it's our anniversary," I whispered, more to myself than anyone else.

The girl giggled next to Dylan, and it hit me like a slap in the face. She was laughing at me! This blonde bimbo who was about to sleep with my boyfriend, on our anniversary, was laughing at me. The anger that had been absent up until this point arrived with force, mingling with the shame and embarrassment. I quickly stood up, grateful for once for my nearly six-foot-tall height. I could *squash* this girl if I wanted to. Instead, I turned to Dylan.

"We're done," I said, looking him straight in the eye. "Don't ever call me again."

"Fine, Emily," he said, the indifference in his voice and face clear as day.

I had a brief moment of panic that I wouldn't be able to get out of the apartment without wobbling. I wasn't exactly an expert at wearing heels, and now seemed like an unlikely time to become proficient. But somehow my legs and feet managed to cooperate, and I made it to the doorway of the kitchen before turning. Dylan and the girl were both standing there, looking at me—his face impassive, hers amused.

"Enjoy your dinner," I said quietly, then turned and fled the apartment.

***

I felt a bit more revived after my shower. Back in my bedroom, I pulled on a pair of soft yoga pants and a worn T-shirt bearing the logo of a charity 5K race I had run in several years ago. As I pulled my wet hair into a ponytail, I heard voices from the kitchen. Ashley and Chris must be home.

"Hey," I called out as I left my room.

"We're in here!"

I entered the kitchen and shook my head slightly at the sight before me. Ashley and Chris were pulling an assortment of snacks out of the last bag, setting them on the counter where they joined a massive pile of ice cream cartons, candy bars, potato chips, and frozen pizzas. "Is all of this really necessary?"

They both looked up at the sound of my voice. "Em!" Ashley said, dropping the Doritos bag in her hands and rushing toward me. She pulled me into a tight hug. "Are you okay?"

"I'm fine," I said, pushing her away. "Seriously."

She just looked at me with raised eyebrows, clearly skeptical.

"Well, I think we got enough food to feed a small army," Chris said, smiling at me across the room. I grinned back.

"For real, Ash," I said. "You do realize that there are only four of us, right?"

"You can never have too much comfort food," she said seriously, returning to the counter and handing Chris the pizzas. "In the freezer, please."

There was a buzz from the intercom in the front room. "That'll be Ryan," I said, turning to go let him in.

Ryan didn't mess around with hugs. Instead, he offered me a fifth of vodka. "Where are the glasses?" he asked, deadpan.

I laughed in spite of myself. "You know perfectly well where the glasses are," I told him, leaning forward to peck him on the cheek. "Seeing as how you're here on a weekly basis and all."

"True," he said, squeezing my arm. "So are the lovebirds in there?" he nodded his head in the direction of the kitchen, and I gave him a stern look.

"What do you think?"

Ryan let loose a dramatic sigh. "Are they being all kissy and disgusting?"

"Ryan, come on. You know they aren't like that."

"It's not fair, that's all I'm saying. A person gets used to life a certain way and then his friends decide to go ruin it. I mean, come on."

I laughed. Typical Ryan drama queen. "How are they ruining anything? Besides, if you didn't foresee this ages ago, then your radar is seriously off."

"Oh, I forgot," Ryan said, slipping out of his leather jacket and laying it across the back of the couch. "You had them pegged ever since what, freshman orientation?"

"Not quite." I linked my arm through his and led him toward the kitchen. "But pretty close."

Ryan, Chris, Ashley, and I had all gone to school together at Michigan State. Most of my friends were staying closer to home, but having won a full-ride scholarship to State for track I didn't have a lot of opportunity to make my choice based on social reasons. So I had been incredibly relieved when my friend Chris also got a scholarship to State, for scientific merit, or something nerdy like that. Regardless, it made me feel loads better to know I'd have a familiar face accompanying me to the much bigger city.

I'd met Ashley my first day, in the lobby of our dorm building. She was struggling to carry a large box up the stairs, as the elevator had conveniently chosen move-in day to break down. After I helped her lug her box up the stairs, she invited me to sit down and have a Coke. Neither my roommate nor I had been able to spring for a mini-fridge for our dorm, so I was suitably impressed.

Ash and I hit it off right away, soon spending much more time together than we did with our own roommates—mine a ditzy, frat party type, hers a socially awkward brainiac who put tape on the floor of their closet to encourage Ash to keep her shoes on her own side.

On our second night in the dorms, I took Ashley two floors down to meet my old friend Chris and his roommate Ryan. Meeting Ry for the first time, I was a little worried. It was pretty clear from the get-go that he was gay, and I wondered how Chris would react to that. Not that he had ever acted bigoted, or anything, but you never know about guys that age. Chris surprised me by clearly not giving a damn—he and Ryan were best friends from day one.

Chris looked up as we entered the kitchen. "Bro,"

he said, hitting Ryan on the back. "How's it going, man?"

"Glad it's Friday," Ryan replied. "How have you been? You never made it to basketball on Wednesday. We waited for you."

I saw Chris glance briefly at Ash before telling Ryan, "Sorry, something came up. I should have called."

Ryan noticed the glance too. When Chris turned his attention back to the counter, where he appeared to be adding ice to the blender, Ryan gave me a meaningful look, and I stifled a giggle.

Though I had detected a spark between Chris and Ashley almost immediately after they'd met, Ryan claimed not to see it. As the four of us became a close unit, Ashley and Chris seemed determined not to rock the boat by admitting to anyone that they had feelings for each other. When they finally got together a few months ago, my overwhelming reaction was relief. Ryan, however, felt differently.

"They'll ruin the group," he moaned to me on more than one occasion. "They'll break up, and the four of us will never be able to hang out again."

"You don't know that," I would tell him patiently, every time.

"Well, that could be even worse," he would counter. "What if they stay together forever? Before we know it, they'll be spending all their time together. Then they'll get married and have babies and leave the two of us behind."

There was no use arguing with him when he got going. Deep down, there was a part of me that was worried my relationship with Ash would change now, but I tried not to let it bother me. After all, she was one of my closest friends, and I was very happy for her.

Really.

"Whatcha making?" I asked Chris, peering over his shoulder to get a look at the blender. "Daiquiris?"

"Yup," he said, as he pressed the start button, filling the kitchen with the sound of blending ice.

"Are we hungry?" Ash asked over the noise. "Should we start with pizza?"

We decided to put the pizzas in the oven and get started with the daiquiris. Chris ordered us all out to the living room. "I'll bring them out in a minute," he said.

I settled into my favorite chair, a comfy Papasan I had kept since Ashley and I moved in together sophomore year. Ashley sat on the loveseat, curling her feet under her, while Ryan plopped onto the battered old recliner. Because Ashley and I had the biggest place, the four of us spent most of our time here, even though Ryan had much newer, stylish furnishings. He worked in recruitment at some big office downtown. I wasn't quite sure what he did day in and day out, only that he wore expensive suits and drove an Audi.

"Here you go," Chris said, following us out and handing us our daiquiris. "Should we toast?"

"To what?" I asked, feeling some of my bitterness return. "This isn't exactly a happy occasion."

"You're wrong," Ryan said, looking at me sternly. "It's a very happy occasion. You got yourself free of a loser guy who was dragging you down. I say that's definitely worth toasting."

"Hear, hear," Chris said, raising his glass. "To Emily. Who is far cooler than Dylan could ever hope to be."

The other two raised their glasses as well. "To Emily!" they chorused.

I couldn't help but smile. Ryan was right—Dylan was totally a loser, and I was better off without him. I had these great friends, a good job, and tons of junk food only steps away.

Besides, I was done with men now. I really, really was.

Chapter Three

Two hours, and four or five drinks later, I was feeling very blurry around the edges. We had moved from daiquiris to wine, and were almost done with that. Ryan decreed it was time to make use of the vodka, and he went to pour us all some shots, only stumbling slightly on his way to the kitchen.

"I should have known," I said to the room at large. My voice sounded very loud in my own ears, and I wondered if the others could tell. "I mean, I should have guessed he'd do something like this. He was always so flirty with everyone. Charming, that's what Sarah said. Charming."

"Who's Sarah?" Chris said, his head flat against the back of the couch, his eyes closed.

"At work," I muttered. "But it doesn't matter, 'cause she was right. He was that way with everyone. Accept...expect...except me." Hmm, talking had started to become difficult. I thought about slowing down, but decided to hell with it. I had nowhere to be in the morning. Besides, if you can't get sloshed when your boyfriend cheats on you, when can you?

Ryan brought out the shot glasses, and I downed my first immediately.

"Bad luck," he said, pointing at me. "We never do shots without cheersing."

"Is that even a word?" Ashley asked. She had moved from the loveseat to the floor, where she was now leaning up against Chris' legs. "Cheersing?"

"Who cares," Ryan said, pouring me another shot.

"The point is we do it."

I obliged and held my glass up, clinking it against his before downing the liquor inside it. This one went down easier, my throat already feeling a little numb as the liquid warmed my chest.

"Men are bastards," I said. "Sorry, guys, but it's totally true."

"She has a point," Ryan said, flopping back down in his chair. "I don't know why I mess with them."

"Well, I'm done," I said emphatically. "For real. I'm over it."

"That's silly," Ashley said, sitting up and looking at me. Even through my own fuzzy gaze, I could tell she was trying to focus on me, and I giggled. "You can't give up on love."

Ryan snorted. "Maybe love is a crock."

"You don't believe that," Ashley said. "I know you don't. If you did, you wouldn't spend so much time trying to find your dream guy."

"In my experience, love has very little to do with it," he said drily, and I giggled again. *Man*, I thought, as the world spun around me. *Maybe I should slow down.*

"I just don't think you should be making any decisions based on Dylan," Ashley said, turning her attention back to me. "I mean, he was so clearly a Wickham kind of guy, of course he was gonna screw around on you."

"A Wiccan?" I asked, confused. "He was Catholic."

"No, not Wiccan," she said, rolling her eyes. "Wickham. You know, George Wickham. *Pride and Prejudice*? That kind of guy."

I just looked at her blankly, but Ryan gasped. "Oh my God," he said. "He so was. Wow, I never saw it, but you're totally right."

I looked at Chris, but he merely shrugged his shoulders. "I have no idea what you guys are talking about," I said.

"How have you never read *Pride and Prejudice*?" Ashley asked me, sitting up straighter to look at me. The expression on her face could best be described as shock. "Or at least seen one of the movies?"

"Yeah, Colin Firth is in that one," Ryan said. "Yummy."

"Sorry," I said, leaning back in my chair. "You know those sappy movies are not my thing." It was true—when Ashley was in the mood for a chick flick she was much more inclined to ask Ryan than me. My tastes were more similar to Chris'—comedies, action movies, and the occasional thriller were much more my style.

Suddenly, Ashley gasped. "But that's it!" We all stared at her blankly. "I just had an...an epipif...an epifininy. You know, one of those things."

"An epiphany?" Chris asked.

"Yes, one of those!" Ashley actually jumped up from her seat on the floor and started pacing the room excitedly. "It all makes so much sense now."

"Ash, what are you talking about?" I asked.

"Your bad luck with guys. You," She stopped pacing and pointed at me, "are clueless about romance."

That stung a little. I might not have always been the most sought after girl in the world, but I'd had my fair share of boyfriends over the years. "I've done okay," I muttered. "It's not like I'm some nun, you know."

"That's not what I mean," Ashley said dismissively. "Em, tell me who Julia Roberts ends up with in *Pretty Woman*."

I just stared at her. Ashley sighed. From his seat in the recliner, Ryan sat up straighter, narrowing his eyes. "*Gone with the Wind* then, who are the main love interests in that story?" he asked.

"Uh…" I felt like I should know this one, but I was drawing a complete blank. "Scarlett someone, right? And, uh…"

"See?" Ashley said, turning to Ryan. "She *doesn't know*!"

"So?" I asked. "What the hell does *Gone with the Wind* have to do with anything?"

"Emily," she said gravely, "I think you're striking out with guys because you never learned what you should be looking for. You never watched romantic movies like the rest of us did. You never read romantic books. Any girl in her right mind should have known right away that Dylan was a Wickham, and not a Darcy. But you didn't. I bet you don't even know who Darcy is."

When I didn't respond, she pointed at me again. "See? I told you!"

"I still don't understand what the hell you're talking about," I said rubbing my forehead. A slow headache was starting to build. I needed another drink.

"Listen," Ryan said. "I think Ash might have a point. There are certain things you should know to look out for. Stereotypes, you could say. The guys who are good and the guys who should be avoided. Most of us learn about this from books and movies, but you never did. So now you're making all these mistakes because you don't know what you should be looking for."

I stared at him for a minute, then burst into laughter. "Are you serious?" I asked, trying to control myself. "You seriously think I have bad luck with guys because I never watched Julia Roberts movies?"

"Oh, you can laugh," Ashley said darkly. "But I'm so right. What about Jacob, huh?"

I stared at her. "What are you talking about?" I asked, feeling a little lurch in my stomach at the mention of Jacob. He had been my high school boyfriend, and we had broken up just before going to college. It had been pretty traumatic, in that teenager kind of way, and Ashley had heard me moan about it many times over the course of our freshman year. I was a little pissed at her for bringing him up now.

"He's the classic high school sweetheart," Ashley said. "The guy you should have hung onto, but let get away."

"Ah," Ryan said sagely. "The one that got away. There's like, a million romantic comedies with that exact set-up."

"Dude, how do you know all of this?" Chris asked sleepily, not even opening his eyes.

Ryan raised an eyebrow. "I may be into sports," he said, "but I do like boys. Of course I know about chick flicks."

"But that's...that's like two examples. You can't base an entire theory off of two examples."

"What about Nick?" Ashley asked. "We all told you that you should go out with him."

"But, that was..." I spluttered. Nick had been a really nice, somewhat soft-spoken guy who had asked me out freshman year. Unfortunately, his timing was terrible. I had been training for a really big race at the time. When I refused him, he was so embarrassed he never asked me out again, which in turn made me too embarrassed to ever do anything about it either. Last I heard, he was living in Chicago.

"He was totally a hidden-depths kind of guy," she said seriously. "The guy every girl knows she should hang onto, if she's lucky enough to find him. Like Ross on *Friends*—someone perfect for the girl, but she never notices because he isn't flashy. Nick was just like that, but you let him slip by because you didn't know the difference."

"This is silly," I said, even though a pit of fear was starting to grow in my stomach. Could any of this actually be true? Was I seriously setting myself up for heartbreak because I picked John Grisham over Jane Austen?

"Chris," I said, almost desperately. "You agree with me, right? You think this is ridiculous?"

Chris was sitting up now, a thoughtful expression on his face. "I don't know, Em," he said. "What about Thomas?"

"Who's that?" Ashley asked quickly.

"Em's boyfriend in junior high. He ran track for a different school. They ended up breaking up because all of their friends were mean about it, them being on competing teams and everything. I mean, now that I think about it, isn't that kind of like that one Shakespeare play, the one with the fighting families?"

"Star-crossed lovers!" Ashley cried. "*Romeo and Juliet*! You're so right!"

"See?" Ryan said, triumphant. "Even Chris gets it!"

I was definitely feeling panicked now. "Do you guys seriously think I'm sabotaging my love life because I'm clueless about romance?"

"Sweetie," Ryan said, coming over to sit on the edge of my chair. "All I'm saying is you could avoid a lot of heartbreak if you had a better idea of what to look out for. I mean, there are certain guys that you should just know are bad news. And other guys you should know to hang on to, if you're lucky enough to find them."

"But how am I supposed to know?" I wailed. "Isn't it too late now?"

"No," Ryan said. "Of course it's not! All you need to do is a little research."

"Research?"

"Oh my God, project!" Ashley cried. "We totally need to help you bone up on your Romance 101."

I looked at Chris helplessly, but he only shrugged. "Can't help you, sweetie. I mean, maybe they have a point. What do I know?"

"Look, all I'm saying is you could stand to know a little bit more about the great love stories of our time," Ashley said. "I mean, at this point, it couldn't hurt, right?"

I thought back to last night. Of the pain and humiliation I had felt in that moment, knowing that I picked the wrong guy, knowing that he couldn't care less about me. Could I possibly have avoided that if I'd known who this Wickham guy was? Suddenly, I felt like I would do anything never to feel that way again.

"Okay, I said, looking up at Ashley and Ryan. "Just tell me what I need to do."

***

The next morning I woke up with a massive hangover. It felt like my eyelids had been sewn shut, like a ten-pound weight had taken up residence in my skull and was determined to break free.

"Oh God," I moaned. The light shining in from my bedroom window seemed to seep between my closed eyelids, attacking me. I pulled the cover up over my head, but then found I couldn't breathe.

"Water," I muttered. "I just need to get up and get some water."

Somehow I managed to open my eyes and get my feet firmly planted on the floor, though my stomach gave a massive lurch when I did so. I hadn't had quite so much to drink in a while—I forgot how terrible it made me feel the next day. Wondering what state the others were in, I wobbled down the hall to the kitchen.

Ashley was sitting at the table, drinking coffee and writing something in a notebook. Her hair was wet from a shower, and she had already applied make-up and had dressed in a soft grey cardigan and expensive-looking, dark-wash jeans.

"She lives," Ryan said, grinning at me from the stove, where he appeared to be making pancakes. He, too, was showered and dressed. Which must have meant—

"Did you already go home?" I gaped at him.

"Of course," he said, smirking at me. "We can't all stay in bed all day. We have lots of work ahead of us, you know."

"Can I just have some coffee? Please?" I asked, sinking down into a chair at the kitchen table and burying my head in my hands. "I don't understand how you guys are functioning so well."

"Most of us stopped after two shots," Ashley pointed out, sliding a mug of coffee toward me.

"I wish you would have stopped me," I muttered, taking a huge swig. I sighed in relief. What was it about coffee that instantly made you feel better?

"You'd had a rough week," Ryan said, setting a plate of pancakes in front of me. Shit. It all came rushing back to me now. Dylan, the bimbo, the horrible spiral of humiliation that kept rearing its head at me ever since Thursday.

"It's okay, we have a plan," Ashley assured me, patting my hand. "You just eat; we're on it."

I took a bite of pancakes. Dripping in butter and syrup, they were the perfect hangover food. Plus, Ryan was a really good cook. I was enjoying them so much that it took me a minute before I registered what Ashley had said.

"Wait...what do you mean you have a plan?" I asked.

She raised her eyebrows at me. "Our plan. Like we discussed last night."

"You're gonna have to refresh my memory," I said. Just trying to remember anything after the wine hurt my brain.

"Your romance research project," she said. "Remember?"

I gaped at her. It sounded vaguely familiar...

"Em," she said in her disapproving teacher voice. "We went over this. We all decided that your horrible luck with men can be traced to the fact that you are clueless about romance. So Ryan and I are going to help you do some research. Remember?"

"Oh my God," I said, shaking my head. "This is because I didn't know who Hugh Grant was, isn't it?" Snippets of memory were coming back now—Ryan and Ashley lecturing me about my lack of knowledge in all things romance. But there was no way, no way at all, that I had agreed to do anything about it.

"Hugh Grant was only the tip of the iceberg," Ashley said. "Though I still can't believe that you never saw *Four Weddings*."

"You guys," I said, putting down my mug and looking at the pair of them. "You don't honestly think that my relationships don't work just because of the kinds of movies I like. I mean, that's asinine."

"It's not just that," Ashley said, looking uncomfortable. "I mean, I do think we learn a lot about love and relationships from books and movies. That's just natural. But there's also the fact…we think it also might be…" She trailed off, clearly uncomfortable.

"We don't think it helped much that your mom wasn't around," Ryan said bluntly, coming to sit with us at the table.

I felt a lurch in my stomach, the way I always did when my mom's name came up. She had been gone for thirteen years now, but it was the kind of pain that never went away, even if I could manage to forget about it for a while.

"You didn't get much of that girl experience as a teenager," Ashley said gently. "I know your dad did an amazing job with you—"

"He did," I said fervently.

"I know," she said, nodding. "But he's not really the feminine type. Don't you think there might have been some things he didn't know how to teach you?"

"And you think I should have learned all of this from books?" I asked. I was feeling an empty sort of ache now. I knew there was some truth to what they were saying. When I was younger, I had really missed a lot of those girl things I saw my friends do with their moms. I had never had anyone take me to get my nails done, or take me shopping. There had been no one to talk to when I had questions about boys.

"Look, there's nothing wrong with it," Ryan said quickly. He was looking at me in a concerned sort of way, and I wondered vaguely what my face looked like. "I just think a little crash course in the ways of romance and dating could help you."

"It certainly couldn't hurt, right?" Ashley asked.

"I guess," I said, taking another sip of my coffee. I wondered if they really did have a point. Was I stunted because I hadn't had a girly past? I tried to take a look at the facts. I had been raised by a single father. Even before the cancer had taken my mom, I was always a daddy's girl—the apple of his eye. I would do anything to please him. So instead of ballet, I signed up for soccer. Instead of watching soap operas, I sat by his feet while he watched the Tigers and the Red Wings.

Then, after mom was gone, I threw myself into my sports and activities with a vengeance, eager to distract myself from the quiet, lonely little house that had become my reality. In high school, I played soccer, softball, and ran track, for which I would eventually get my scholarship. A chance to move away from the tiny little town where I saw my mom everywhere I looked. Where everyone knew her and wanted to tell me just how much I was looking like her the older I got.

Had my efforts at blocking it all out turned me into someone who couldn't be successful in love? The thought of living my life that way, of never finding someone, of never having a full family all of my own—it terrified me.

"So, what exactly does this all entail?" I asked.

"We'll do all the work!" Ashley said, relieved that I was caving in. "I promise! Look, I've been making a list." She pushed the paper toward me, and I saw that it was a list of movies and books. "This is just a start!" she promised, and I gaped at her. A start? There had to be two dozen titles on that page.

"I already own a lot of these," she murmured, looking down at the list with her pen between her teeth. "And Ryan picked some up from his apartment today. The rest we can get on Netflix, I'm sure. I think what we have is enough to be starting with."

"How...how many is enough?" I asked, feeling overwhelmed already.

"Oh, about fifteen or so," Ashley said, unconcerned. "Why don't you hop in the shower, and Ryan and I will get everything organized?"

"We're starting today?" I asked.

"There's no time like the present!" Ashley trilled.

Ryan burst into laughter.

"What?" I asked.

"You should see the look on your face. It's like you're about to face the firing squad." He smiled at me. "This will be painless, Em. I promise. It's just a few chick flicks."

I sighed, and stood, downing the last of my coffee as I did so. "Okay," I said. "Let's get this over with."

Chapter Four

Mondays were always busy days at the clinic. Most of our evaluations were scheduled on Mondays, and many of our patients liked to get at least one of their sessions done early in the week, particularly our elderly patients, most of whom were on three-day-a-week schedules. We usually had two or three PTs on duty, and we were all kept busy from open to close.

"Hey, Sarah, can you get Mrs. Zinder all set up?"

Sarah looked up from her magazine and gave a little start. I liked the girl, but, man, did she have a tendency to flake out sometimes.

"Sure," she called out, jumping up and heading to the reception area to get my next patient. I turned my attention back to Frank in front of me. He was lying flat on his back on a therapy table with a stretchy band around his knees and a sour expression on his face.

"That's perfect, Frank," I said, encouraging him. "Do you think you can give me five more like that?"

He winced, but didn't argue. Slowly, carefully, he brought both knees several inches away from each other, stretching the band out. I noticed a bead of sweat pool on his forehead. "Don't overdo it," I cautioned. "Remember what I told you about pain."

"Sweetie, I've dealt with worse pain than this," he grunted, continuing with his exercises. "You wanna talk about pain? You try getting shot in the keister in some damn trench in Korea."

"So you're saying this is a cake walk?" I asked, reaching down to untie the stretchy band. I smiled at him, and he winked at me.

"With a pretty thing like you to look at all day?" he said, winking again. "You better believe it."

"Frank, you are a shameless flirt," I said, shaking my head. He only grinned.

"Okay, fifteen minutes on the exercise bike, then I'll come over and work on you, sound good?"

"You got it, darling."

I couldn't help but grin as I walked away. Flirting patients were nothing new to me, but it was hard not to love Frank. He was in his late seventies, but every bit as energetic as I imagined him having been as a young man. He'd led an interesting life, that was for sure. Sometimes it was hard not to get caught up in his stories about serving in the army in Korea, or working on the line at Ford, or each and every one of his three wives. A ladies' man till his dying day.

Sarah had led my next patient, Mrs. Zender, over to an empty therapy table and was helping her get comfortable there. "How's the shoulder feeling today, Mrs. Z?" I asked her.

"Oh, dear," she said in her characteristic raspy voice, a hint of southern drawl just evident below the surface. "It's been acting up all night."

I ran my hands over her shoulder and the surrounding muscles. Mrs. Z flinched—it was clearly tender. I sighed. "It's not progressing as fast as I'd like."

She raised one exquisitely penciled on eyebrow. "Tell me something I don't know, darling. I live with this pain every day."

I smiled at her. "You've been through a lot. I guess we'll both have to be a little more patient."

Mrs. Z settled back against her pillows. "Easy for you to say. I've had just about enough of being cooped up. I have such a hankering to go dancing, I can't even tell you."

Over her head, Sarah rolled her eyes at me. Mrs. Z was quite a character. In her early sixties, she still operated under the impression that she was the belle of the ball, the most eligible girl in Cobb County, Georgia, where she had left forty years ago for the bright lights of New York City. She traipsed around every room she was in, as if she owned it, and my therapy office was no exception. She flirted with all the men here, regardless of their age. Speaking of which...

"Is that you, ZiZi?" Frank called out from the bike. "Where've you been?"

"Oh, hey sweetie!" Mrs. Z called back, her southern accent suddenly becoming much more pronounced. "Emily switched me over to mornings last week. How've you been?"

Across the room, Frank got off the bike and ambled slowly over, clearly trying to mask his limp. Mrs. Z sat up straighter and fluffed her hair our. I suppressed a sigh. Sometimes it seemed like I was running a senior rec center, rather than a therapy center.

"You look lovely today," Frank said, approaching the table. "Is that a new hairdo?"

"Ooh, do you like it?" Mrs. Z crooned, batting her eyelashes at him. "I was hoping you would. Now where is that Philip? I haven't seen him in days."

"Whaddaya need Philip for?" Frank asked. "He's an old sour puss. What you need is a man who can show you a good time." He winked at her and she giggled.

Oh, dear Lord, I thought to myself. "Alright, enough social hour," I said, taking Frank by the shoulders and steering him back toward the exercise bike. "We all have work to do."

Frank grinned at Mrs. Z over his shoulder, and she giggled again. "Talk to you soon, sweetie!" she called after him.

"Sarah, ultrasound therapy, then the wet heat pack on that shoulder, okay?" I instructed, before turning back to Frank. "Mr. Carter, why do you insist on flirting with all of my patients?"

"Honey," he said, leaning toward me conspiratorially, "when you're as old as I am, you take it where you can get it."

I snorted, and pushed him gently toward the bike. "Get on with it."

A tinkling bell sounded, signaling the opening of the front door. I looked up to see Michael, one of the other PTs, enter the building. I waved as he headed past me to the office. Seeing that all the patients were duly occupied, I followed him back.

"The troublemakers are out in force today, I see," he said, grinning at me as he dropped his bag on the desk.

"It wouldn't be a Monday afternoon if we didn't have the geriatric dating society going strong," I muttered, making Michael laugh. The truth was, we were crazy about our patients. Sure, they got on our nerves sometimes, but they were also entertaining as hell. Between Frank's stories about playing farm ball for the Tigers back in the 50s and Mrs. Z's tales of her four clueless ex-husbands, there was rarely a dull moment.

"Speaking of which, I have a favor to ask you," Michael said, grimacing a little in anticipation. I knew immediately where he was headed.

"Oh, please, don't," I said. "I haven't even had lunch yet, don't make me."

"You're the only one he works for," Michael said. "Last week he told me to eff off, I'm not even kidding you. That kind of language should not come from a man that age. Come on, Em. You know you're his favorite."

"A fat lot of good being his favorite gets me," I muttered. "Fine, I'll take Philip. But you're finishing up with the flirt patrol out there."

"You're a life saver," Michael said. "I owe you one."

"Don't think I'm going to forget that," I said, turning to leave. I headed out to the main exercise area. Sure enough, I could see Philip sitting in chair over by reception, his walker next to him and a scowl clear on his face, even from this distance.

"Hello, Mr. Jackson," I said politely. "How are you feeling today?"

"I'm feeling like someone who had a hip replaced," he muttered.

"Well, why don't you head back here with me, and we'll see what we can do to get you better."

"Fat chance," he muttered, just loud enough for me to hear. I decided to ignore him, instead helping him to get into his walker, an action that earned me a chilling glare. I pointed to the nearest therapy table and helped him get settled on his side. Philip had been coming in for out-patient therapy three times a week for the past four weeks. His recovery had been slow, which wasn't uncommon for men his age. Personally, I felt his attitude was doing little to help him heal, but he wasn't the kind of man who would take kindly to suggestions about mental health affecting his physical health.

"Philip! Helloooo!" Mrs. Z called from the other side of the room. Philip's scowl became more pronounced. "Nothing worse than a bold woman," he muttered.

"Watch out there, Mr. Jackson," I said. "You happen to be talking to a pretty bold woman."

He snorted. "Don't see you throwing yourself at married men."

I felt a little pang in my chest at his words. Philip often referred to himself as married, though I knew from his file that his wife had died five years ago. Determined to make his appointment as pleasant as possible, I pulled the curtains around his table, blocking the others from his view.

"Any new pains since you were here last?" He shook his head. "Would you say it feels better, worse, or the same since your last visit?"

"'bout the same."

"Alright, I'm gonna go get the ultrasound machine. That might help a bit with your inflammation. Then we'll have you do some simple exercises, work on getting that strength back. Sound good?"

"You're the boss," he muttered. I patted his shoulder and stepped out from behind the curtain.

"Emily, dear, how is that young man of yours?" Mrs. Z called from her table. She was leaning back against her pillows, her hair arranged perfectly around her, looking for all the world like a queen on her throne. I sighed. It hadn't even been a week since our break-up, so I suppose it was only natural for my stomach to still drop every time Dylan came up. I hoped it would pass soon.

"We actually broke up, Mrs. Z."

She gasped and held her hand to her heart. "Why on earth? He was so handsome!"

"He wasn't quite right for me," I said. I noticed

that every eye in the place was on me now and felt my cheeks start to burn. I grabbed the ultrasound machine and moved back toward the safety of Philip's curtains. Not fast enough.

"Are you sure that was such a good idea?" Frank said, walking over from the bike again. "You young girls all seem so picky. You're not getting any younger, you know. What are you now, twenty-eight? Don't you think it's time you were settled?"

"I'm twenty-five, actually," I said, a touch of acid in my voice. "And it turned out Dylan was an adulterous bastard. Still think I should have settled for him?"

"Oh! Oh, you poor dear!" Mrs. Z cried. I cursed my momentary lapse of judgment in telling them. The gossip around this place could be worse than in a junior high cafeteria. So not what I needed.

"You did the right thing, of course you did," Mrs. Z continued. "I mean, just look at me—four husbands. Four! All of them good for nothings. You can never settle, dear. Life is too precious to be tied down to trash."

"Thank you, Mrs. Z. I should get back..."

I edged toward the curtain, trying to ignore the loud stage whispers coming from Mrs. Z and Sarah. "I can't *believe* it," Sarah was saying.

"Wonder who he was cheating with," Frank said.

I sighed and pulled the curtain back around Philip's table. He lifted his head and locked eyes with me for a moment. "Gossipy old bags," he muttered.

I grinned at him. Maybe Philip wasn't so bad after all.

***

"Want some company?"

I had finally managed to take my lunch break and was just settling down in the office with a book when I heard Elliot approach. I looked up from my book and saw him standing in the doorway of the office, a blue insulated lunch bag in his hand. I smiled at him, moving over to make room for him at the small desk.

"By all means," I said.

Elliot sat down and immediately began pulling his lunch from his bag. It was typical Elliot fare—sandwich on whole grain bread, fruit, carrot sticks, and water.

"You're such a health nut," I said, looking down at my frozen meal.

"I know unprocessed food is pretty foreign to you," he said, tucking a strand of his wavy, red hair behind his ear. "But you should really try it sometime."

"Don't start," I warned, but he ignored me.

"Vitamins would be good too. Maybe a nice B-12 complex to perk you up."

"Elliot," I said firmly. "No selling in here. We've talked about this."

"I'm not trying to sell," he said, picking up his sandwich. "I'd be happy to give it to you for free. Anything to see you take better care of yourself." He glanced at my reheated mac and cheese and gave a little shudder before taking a big bite of his sandwich.

"So, whatcha reading?" he asked, after he had chewed.

I felt a little flash of embarrassment as I turned the cover of my book so he could see it.

"*Pride and Prejudice*?" he asked, clearly surprised. "That's a bit of a departure for you, isn't it?"

I felt a blush start to rise on my cheeks. "I'm branching out a little bit," I told him, shrugging.

He looked at me closely. "Okay, what's up?"

"What do you mean?"

"You're not telling me something, I can tell."

I blushed harder. I so did not want to admit to Elliot what I was up to.

"Emily," he said, "just spill it."

"Fine," I tossed the book back onto the desk. "Ashley and Ryan convinced me that the reason I'm such a joke with men is because I've never been into all this romance stuff."

A funny look came over Elliot's face, but he didn't say anything.

"So I kinda let them talk me into this project."

"Project?" he asked. "What kind of project?"

"Kind of a research project, I guess."

"What exactly are you researching?"

I pointed at the book. "Romance novels. Chick flicks. Love songs. That kind of thing."

"So it's a romance research project?" he asked, his mouth flickering with the beginnings of a smile.

"It's supposed to help me figure out what guys I should be looking for," I said. "Apparently there are patterns."

Elliot tried to cover a snort, and I had to smile. "You probably think this is pretty stupid, huh?" I asked.

"No," he said, his smile wide now. "Bat shit insane is probably a better term for what I think."

"Thanks a lot!" I said, laughing.

"Emily, come on. Do you seriously think you're going to have better luck with men because you read *Pride and Prejudice* and listened to a bunch of sappy songs?"

"Don't forget the chick flicks," I reminded him, grinning. He had a point, of course. It was pretty ridiculous.

"Oh, yes, of course," he said drily. "The chick flicks will make all the difference. Come on, why are you doing this?"

"Elliot, at this point, it can't hurt," I said, sighing. "I'm a total mess when it comes to men. I clearly have no idea what I'm doing. So I might as well listen to Ryan and Ashley, right?"

"Maybe you just haven't met the right man," he said.

"Well, yeah," I agreed. "That's kind of the point. I haven't met the right man because, apparently, I have no idea what kind of man I'm supposed to be looking for."

"And you think you'll find out what 'kind of man' is right for you by reading and watching movies?"

"Who knows." I shrugged. "It's worth a try, isn't it?"

He looked at me closely for a minute, before smiling slightly. "Sure," he said. I felt a funny little dip in my stomach as my eyes met his. *Must be embarrassment,* I thought to myself. "So," Elliot continued, moving onto his carrot sticks. "What have you learned so far?"

"Apparently, Dylan was a classic Wickham," I told him, pointing down at the book. "The guy who seems so charming and perfect but is really a huge jerk. According to Ashley, I should have noticed this straight off."

"If it was so obvious, why didn't Ashley warn you?" he asked drily.

I laughed and grabbed one of his carrot sticks. "Good point. Anyhow, what I'm supposed to be looking for is a Mr. Darcy, but from what I can see so far, he's kind of a jerk."

"So according to your research you should ignore

the guys who seem great and go for the ones that act likes jerks?"

I laughed again. "I'm hoping it becomes clearer before the end of the book."

"I hope so too," he agreed.

"Then tonight I guess we're watching *Pretty Woman*, which Ash and Ryan assure me is essential to my education."

"Awesome, now you'll be on the lookout for men who hire prostitutes."

"There's supposed to be a larger theme," I said, snatching another carrot.

"Want to finish them?" he asked, holding out the bag. "Clearly your body is trying to tell you something—you need more fresh produce in your life. And I didn't even need to watch a Julia Roberts flick to show me that!"

I grinned, taking the bag from him. "If only true love was so obvious," I said.

I thought I saw a reddening of the tips of Elliot's ears, but he stood up before I could be sure. "Alright, I guess I better get back to work. Good luck with the research."

"Thanks," I said. "Good luck with the vitamins."

"I meant it about the B-12," he said seriously, looking down at me. "Stop by any time."

I winked at him. "We'll see about that. Bye, Elliot."

"See ya, Emily."

Chapter Five

"This is one of my favorites," Ashley sighed, setting a giant bowl of popcorn on the table and taking her seat on the couch. "It's so romantic."

"What's the premise?" I asked, leaning back into my own seat. Ryan walked by, handing me a wine glass. "Thanks."

"It's about a poor orphan girl who goes to work for some rich landowner," Ashley said, taking her own wine glass from Ryan. "They fall madly and passionately in love, but there are complications, forces set on pulling them apart."

Her eyes were lit up with excitement, a dreamy smile on her lips. I was torn between a flash of affection for her and a desire to roll my eyes. She was silly, but there was something endearing about how seriously Ashley took all of this.

"When did this remake come out?" Ryan asked, studying the *Jane Eyre* DVD cover.

"Just a few years ago," Ashley said. "It's very good. Michael Fassbender is gorgeous."

"Then let's get it started," Ryan said.

I was surprised to find that I liked the movie quite a bit. I found the heroine to be independent and smart, and I was impressed that she didn't come across as a doormat or a swooning, silly love-struck girl. She was strong, and I liked that.

But I couldn't for the life of me tell how it was going to help me with my project.

"What was I supposed to learn here?" I asked

Ashley once the credits started to roll.

She looked at me in surprise. "That true love conquers all!"

"And that you shouldn't judge a book by its cover," Ryan said. "At first she thinks that Rochester is cruel and rude and ugly. But then she gets to know him and finds he's her perfect match!"

I raised my eyebrow at him. "Her perfect match who's hiding his real wife in the attic," I clarified.

"Minor detail," Ryan said, waving his hand dismissively.

"So I'm supposed to be looking for a guy who seems kinda like a jerk and fall in love with him, and then forgive him when I find out he was lying to me about another woman?"

Ashley sighed. "It doesn't have to be so black and white."

"But the not-judging-a-book-by-its-cover thing does work," Ryan said. "So maybe focus on that part of the story."

This was the fifth movie I had watched with Ryan and Ashley since they'd convinced me to participate in their little plan. So far, they'd had an answer to every one of my objections. Any time I pointed out some flaw in the story—a heroine who acted like a wet dish rag, an implausible plot, a leading man who seemed better suited to a Neanderthal folk tale—they had drawn me back to some larger theme. I wasn't sure yet if I admired their persistence, or thought they were nuts.

"Okay, what's next?" Ryan asked.

"We have a choice between *When Harry Met Sally* and *An Affair to Remember*."

"Both very good choices," Ryan said. He looked at me. "Are you in the mood for another classic, or a more modern day love story?"

I picked up the two DVD cases, studying their covers. "Is this Billy Crystal?" I asked.

"Yup," Ashley said. "Not exactly your typical leading man, but it works."

"Let's go with this," I said, handing her the case. I figured at least Billy Crystal would be funny. I wasn't sure I had the patience for another overly sentimental film that night.

Before Ashley could get up, my phone rang. I plucked it up from the coffee table. "It's Brooke," I said, immediately standing. "I'm gonna go take this."

"Might as well get some wine refills," Ryan said, plucking up our glasses and heading to the kitchen.

I accepted the call as I walked to my bedroom. "Brooke?" I said.

"Hey, babe," she replied. I smiled at the familiar sound of her voice. Sometimes I missed her so much it was like having a stomachache.

"How's it going?" I asked.

"Oh, you know," she said, and I pictured her rolling her eyes. "Not a whole lot is new in hopping Alpena, Michigan."

I laughed, but felt a little pang all the same. I understood why Brooke disparaged our tiny hometown, and I had certainly jumped at my chance to hit the road, but I sometimes still envied her for being there.

"How're your folks?" I asked. "How's the inn?"

"They're good," she said. "Taking a cruise next month, if you can believe it."

"Wow, that's kind of amazing," I said. Brooke had been helping her parents run their little inn on the shores of Lake Huron since we had graduated from college. She had spent two years at the community college at home before she had saved up enough money to transfer to Northern Michigan, a smaller public university in the Upper Peninsula. I had hoped she'd be interested in one of the schools down state, so she'd be closer to me. She was just happy to finally be away from home.

She'd majored in business management, a subject that I found totally boring. It suited her though—Brooke had always been a logical, no nonsense kind of girl. It was probably why we got along so well. There was no guessing with Brooke, no secret, girl code words that I had to try to navigate. She always told you exactly what she thought and precisely how she felt.

Three months before graduation, just as Brooke was trying to make a decision about what grad school to attend for her MBA, her father fell and broke his hip. Her parents were both getting up there in years—Brooke had been a later-in-life surprise. They managed to cope for a few weeks, her mother doing the bulk of work around the inn. It wasn't until Brooke went home after graduation that she realized how bad things were.

Her mom was barely able to keep the place afloat. Business was way down. Her dad did what he could, but with hip replacement surgery on the way, he wasn't much help.

I knew what Brooke would do before she had even decided herself. Sure enough, two days later, she announced that she was moving home. She would run the inn until her dad was back on his feet, and defer her MBA for later.

Three years later, things hadn't quite turned out that way. Though her dad hovered around constantly and drove her crazy, his role was greatly diminished in the actual running of the place. Brooke was just so good at it—business was way up, and the inn had even been listed in a statewide tourism campaign. Despite her complaints, I think Brooke really loved her job, even if it might not have been exactly how she pictured her life.

"He's actually okay leaving you alone there?" I asked. "I can hardly believe it."

"I know," she said, her voice dry. "It's a miracle."

"How's Robbie?" I asked.

"Eh," she said. "I just can't tell if he's worth my time."

I laughed. Brooke had neither the time nor the inclination to mess around with unworthy men, of whom there always seemed to be many, vying for her affections. To start, she was gorgeous, a total knock-out. Her dark hair hung in a riot of curls half way down her back. Though she didn't come close to my 5'11" height, she was tall. And where she didn't match me in height, she far exceeded me in curves. Add to this a wicked sense of humor and an air of being completely uninterested in most men, and her appeal was complete. As my dad liked to say, she beat off the boys with a stick.

"What about you?" she asked. "Did you get right back out there after He Who Must Not Be Named?"

I squirmed a little bit. For some reason, I didn't want to tell her about being the subject of Ryan and Ashley's project. I had a feeling it wouldn't sit well with her.

"Nope," I said. "Still footloose and fancy free."

"That's the spirit," she said. "It's high time you saw men for what they really are—a chance for a little fun. Nothing more."

I heard Ryan calling me from the living room, and I sighed. "Need to go?" Brooke asked.

"Yeah, Ry and Ash are holding a movie for me," I said.

"Alright, I should probably go start turn-downs anyhow," she said. "Call me tomorrow?"

"You got it," I said. "Bye, Brooke."

"Talk to you later, Em."

I walked out to the living room, where Ryan and Ashley were both waiting for me expectantly. I thought about what Brooke had said about guys, and stifled a laugh at the thought of her arguing the point with these two.

"Okay," I said, reclaiming my seat on the couch. "Let's get this over with."

Chapter Six

"You ready?"

I looked up from my notes to see Chris standing at my office door.

"Hey!" I stood up to give him a hug. "How's it going?"

"I'm good," he said, hugging me back. "How are you?"

"Same old, same old," I told him, stacking my files neatly on the desk. "Haven't seen you in a while. Why haven't you been by the apartment?"

"Chick flick over load." Chris straightened his glasses and grinned at me. "Sorry."

"Sure, leave me alone with the wolves." I hit him on the shoulder and picked up my bag. "So, you ready to get going?"

"Whenever you are."

I led him out of the office and out into the therapy room. "Michael," I called out. "I'm out of here."

"Have fun!" he called back. "See you tomorrow."

"So how was work?" I asked as we stepped out into the parking lot. I braced myself for his answer—Chris did some kind of research at the university downtown, and when he got to talking about his work, I had a hard time not zoning out.

"It was fine," he said, smiling at me. "I won't bore you with details."

"Thank God," I told him, slipping my arm through his. "It's good to see you. We haven't had a chance to hang out much lately."

"Are you about to go all Ryan on me?" he asked, opening the passenger door of his Explorer for me. "All I hear from him lately is how I'm an awful friend for ditching him for a woman."

"No, I'm not complaining." I jumped up into the seat, and Chris shut the door for me. When he got in on his side I continued, "just saying that it's nice to see you. And Ryan doesn't mean all that, you know. He's just being dramatic."

"Imagine that," Chris said, his tone dry. "So, where to first?"

"I think we should just hit the mall. Gives us the most opportunities."

"You're the boss."

Chris pulled out into traffic, and I settled back into my seat. "Do you have any ideas of what you'd like to get her?"

"I don't know...jewelry?"

"Jewelry would be nice," I said, nodding. "A little predictable..."

Chris sighed. "Why does this have to be so complicated?"

"It doesn't." I patted his arm. "Just get Ash something you think she'll like, and she'll appreciate the effort. Promise."

"It's the first birthday she's had since we got together," he said, pushing up his glasses again—a sure sign he was starting to get anxious. "I want it to be special. Romantic, you know. So she'll be happy."

I turned my head to look at him. "If it comes from you, it will be romantic. Trust me."

"Speaking of romance," Chris said, turning from the road to grin at me. "How's the research project going?"

"It's actually not that bad." He coughed loudly,

and I laughed. "Seriously, Chris. Some of these movies are fun. And the books are pretty good. I can't believe I never read Jane Austen at school."

"Do you think it's going to help you at all?"

"Probably not." I said. Chris snorted. "But as Ashley keeps saying, it can't hurt."

"You know, I never thought you were that hopeless with men," Chris said. "I mean, you've had plenty of boyfriends over the years."

"Yeah, but none of them ever went anywhere."

"Em." Chris looked sideways at me. "You're twenty-five. Where should these relationships have gone?"

"I don't know." I shrugged, feeling uncomfortable. "I just...There's never been any serious connection, you know?" I wasn't sure how to explain to him how I felt about my relationships. About how different they had seemed from the things my friends had described. "It's not that I think I should be married, or anything. But I feel like I've never...I don't know. I don't know how to describe it."

"You've never been in love."

I stared at Chris. "That...that's not what I was going to say."

"It's okay, Em," Chris said. "I've known you since you were what, thirteen? We talk about everything. You've never once been all giddy or moony about a boy. I've never once heard you talk about the way you felt, not even about Jacob."

I frowned. Pathetic as it was to admit, my relationship with Jacob had been one of the most serious of my life. We had dated for years. Was it possible that I had never told any of my friends how I felt about him? How *had* I felt about him?

"I wasn't giddy about Dylan?" I asked. "'Cause I

thought things might have been different with him."

Chris shook his head. "The only thing you ever told me about Dylan was that he had his life together. You said it made you feel grownup to be with him."

"God, I said that?" Chris nodded. "That doesn't sound very romantic at all." I was quiet for a moment. "I really am hopeless with romance then, aren't I?"

"I didn't say that," Chris said quickly. "All I am saying is that I don't think you've been in love. So maybe that makes you feel like something's lacking."

"I guess that's true."

"But maybe you just haven't met the right guy yet."

I smiled at him. "*That* actually sounds kind of romantic, you know."

Chris laughed. "Maybe Ashley is rubbing off on me."

We pulled into the mall parking lot, a monstrous three-level garage that I could picture myself getting lost in for days. Chris drove up and down the aisles, finally finding a spot up on the third level. As we got out of the car, I heard him chuckle.

"Do you remember what it was like to go to the mall at home?" he asked.

I laughed too. "A little different from this, huh?"

The Somerset Collection, where Chris and I were hoping to find a present for Ashley, was enormous, made up of two separate buildings connected by a glass-enclosed walking bridge. In addition to upscale department stores like Nordstrom and Saks, there were dozens and dozens of high-end little boutiques. There was a Michael Kors shop here, for God's sake. When Brooke had first visited me down here, I took her to The Collection—she was so awed she could barely talk (a first for Brooke in all the years I had known her). It was as far from the tiny, single-level mall in Alpena as you could get.

I led Chris into the mall, figuring we could start at one of the department stores and go from there. As we passed a marble-fronted shop, Chris stopped suddenly. "What about that?"

"Tiffany and Company?" I asked, surprised. "You want to try Tiffany's?"

"Isn't that supposed to be, like, *the* place for jewelry?"

"Sure, if you have a boatload of cash."

"Let's try it." Chris looked excited. "I bet Ash would flip *out* if I brought home one of those blue boxes."

"If you say so," I said, shrugging. I followed him into the store, where we were immediately met by a gorgeous woman in a taupe suit. Her hair was up in a sleek chignon and her make-up was impeccable. And though shoes were much more Ashley's area than mine, I was pretty sure she was wearing Jimmy Choos—the pair, in fact, that Ashley had been mooning over for weeks.

"How can I help you today?" the woman asked, her voice smooth with just a touch of condescension. I saw her eyes flick over Chris, probably cataloging his cargo pants, hoodie, and well-worn black pea coat. Apparently, her inspection did not do him any favors—I detected a slight raise of her eyebrows as she looked at him.

"I'm looking for a present for my girlfriend," Chris said, clearly not noticing her appraisal. "For her birthday. It's not for a few months, but I really want to get her something special."

"Then you've come to the right place," the woman said, her voice ever so slightly colder than it had been before. She led Chris to a glass display case. Even from a distance, I could detect the sparkle of diamonds.

"What did you have in mind?" The woman asked. "We have some lovely watches, very appropriate for a gift. Or maybe bracelets? A ring?"

"Not a ring," Chris said quickly. "I don't want her to get the wrong idea." He laughed a little nervously. "Maybe a bracelet? She would probably like that."

"Here's a lovely piece," the woman said. "A classic silver bangle, with three rows of diamonds. It can be worn with just about anything. Very nice for a gift."

"Wow," Chris said, pushing his glasses up. "That's really nice. Ash doesn't have anything like it, does she?" He turned to me, and I shook my head, silent. I had a feeling Chris was about to get a very nasty surprise. "How much is it?"

The woman's eyebrows raised another nearly imperceptible notch. Was asking for the price too gauche for her, or something?

"It retails for fifteen."

"Fifteen?" Chris asked. "I thought those were diamonds?"

I suppressed a laugh, but just barely. The woman's eyes flicked to my face, a hint of irritation in her expression now. "Fifteen *thousand*," she said, her voice low.

"Holy shit!" Chris said, clearly shocked, and I did laugh then. The woman glared at me, then back at Chris again.

"Our pieces are the highest quality." Her voice was tight now, all pleasantness long gone. "Perhaps you'd like to see something without such high-end gemstones?"

Chris nodded, a dazed expression on his face. The woman led him down the display case to another row of bracelets.

"This cuff is very nice," she said, pointing to a plain silver band. "It's stamped with the Tiffany logo. Very classic and sophisticated." She sniffed. "And much more reasonably priced at two hundred and twenty-five."

"Two hundred dollars?" Chris still sounded shocked. "But...but...it doesn't even have any jewels on it! I could buy her an iPod for cheaper than that!"

The woman looked downright pissed now, and I had a hard time not laughing again. "Maybe this store is a bit out of your range," I said. "Everything is lovely," I said to the woman, trying to be polite. "But maybe not quite right for this occasion."

"Yeah," Chris said, shaking his head. "I think you're right."

"Thank you anyhow," I said to the woman. "For all of your help."

She nodded curtly and turned to the other side of the store, obviously eager to get away from us. I grabbed Chris' arm and ushered him away from the counter and back out into the mall. Only then did I allow myself to laugh.

"Oh my God. You should have seen your face when she told you the price!"

"It's obscene!" Chris said, still shaking his head. "A bracelet for fifteen thousand dollars? That's like, a Ford Focus!"

I tried to get my breath. "You thought she meant fifteen dollars!" I cracked up all over again. "God, that was amazing!"

"Shut up," he said, finally smiling as he shoved me. "How the hell was I supposed to know? I thought she was joking." Suddenly he froze. "You don't think Ashley is expecting me to get her something like that, do you?"

"No," I said firmly. "I guarantee she isn't."

"Okay." Chris looked slightly doubtful, so I took his arm and propelled him down the concourse.

"You know, that wasn't a total waste," I told him. "You actually gave me a really good idea. Here, let's take the escalator. We need to go over to the other side."

I led Chris up to the second level where we could take the glass walkway to the other building. It had moving sidewalks, just like at the airport, and I didn't even try to hide my excitement. "It doesn't matter how many times I go on this thing," I told Chris. "I'll always think it's cool."

"It's a little high up for me," he said, staring straight ahead so he wouldn't see the traffic moving quickly on the road below us.

Once we were on the other side, I led him back downstairs, stopping in front of a glass-enclosed store bustling with activity.

"The Apple store?"

"You said you could get her an iPod," I told him. "That's actually a really good idea. She just has that really old Nano, remember? And the battery always runs down so fast. You could get her a fancy new one, like the Touch. She would love it."

"Don't you think that's kind of impersonal?" He frowned.

"You could download a bunch of music for her," I told him, taking his hand to pull him inside. "Everything you know she loves. Then you could arrange it in playlists for her—like, work-out songs and love songs, and songs that make you think of her. She would think it was so sweet."

"That's actually a really good idea. Thanks,

Emily!"

Twenty minutes later we were up in the food court, a new iPod Touch and an iTunes gift card in a white bag on the table, sharing a small pizza.

"What are your plans for the birthday extravaganza?" I asked, taking a swig of my Coke.

"I figured we'd start the weekend with a friend's outing that Friday night, all of us together," Chris grabbed another slice of pizza. "Then on Saturday, I'm going to surprise her with a trip up to Port Huron. I booked a room right on the lake, and there's a cute downtown area with stores and a bunch of places to get good food."

"Impressive," I said, nodding my approval. "She's a lucky girl."

"You had your chance," he said, grinning at me. "I asked you to be my girlfriend in eighth grade, remember?" He waved his hand across his body and face. "All this could have been yours."

I snorted. "I liked you way too much to ruin it by dating you."

"And thank God for that," he said.

"Hey!"

"You know what I mean." He wiped a drop of sauce off his lip with his napkin. "It would suck if we weren't friends anymore."

"True," I said. "That would be terrible."

We ate in silence for a moment, my mind wandering to all the good times I had shared with Chris over the years. He had been such a good friend to me, and to Brooke. There was a part of me that had been so scared to go away to school; having Chris there had been like having a piece of home with me all the time.

My phone rang, dragging me from my thoughts. I

fumbled around in my purse, pulling it out to see my dad's number flashing on the screen. "My dad," I said to Chris. "I should get it."

"I'm gonna go to the bathroom," he said, standing up. "Then I'll get us some refills."

"Hi, Dad!" I said.

"Hi, sweetie." His voice, warm and familiar, sent a little pain into my chest. It had been too long since I had been home.

"How are you?" I asked. "How's work?"

"Business has been good." I heard him cough, a raspy sound.

"Have you been sick?" I asked, immediately on my guard.

"No," he assured me. "I had a cold last month, and the cough doesn't seem to want to hit the road."

"You need to rest more," I said, a flash of fear running through me. I couldn't deal with it if my dad got sick.

"I'm fine. Promise. How are *you*? How's work been?"

"Work is going good. It's been busy too."

"Good, good."

There was a moment of silence. My dad and I had never been all that chatty with each other. Don't get me wrong, I love him more than just about anyone on the earth. But sometimes it was hard for me to think of things to say to him. He just wasn't much of a talker. After my mom was gone, the house got a whole lot quieter.

"Did you catch that Wings game last night?" I asked, reverting to our old standby conversation—sports.

"Yeah," he said eagerly. "Great game. Lidstrom is just unstoppable, isn't he?"

We talked about hockey for a few minutes, fully exhausting the topic before lapsing into silence once more.

"The kids are good?" my dad asked finally. "Ashley and Chris doing okay?"

"Everyone's good," I told him. "I'm actually out shopping with Chris for Ashley's birthday present."

"Oh, I won't keep you then," he said, sounding almost relieved. I felt another little pang. I wouldn't change a thing about my dad, I really wouldn't. But it would be nice if he was just a little more communicative.

"Alright, Dad," I said. "Look, I'm gonna get up there for a visit again real soon, okay? I promise."

"I hope so." The gruffness of his voice seemed to slip for a minute. "I miss you, Em."

"I miss you too, Dad," I said softly. All of a sudden I could feel a lump in my throat. "I promise I'll be home soon."

"Take care of yourself, sweetheart."

"You too," I said. "Rest, Dad. Okay?"

"I will," he said, laughing a little. "Don't worry about me. I'm fine."

After we hung up, I stared down at the table for a minute, thinking about my dad. Sometimes the thought of going home made me feel anxious, almost panicked. There were just so many memories there, so many things to remind me of the past. Other times I missed my dad so much I felt like I might go nuts. I hated the idea of him there alone.

The lump in my throat grew a bit. I felt frustrated and confused, and I couldn't even say why. I sighed.

"Everything okay at home?" Chris asked. I looked up to see him standing in front of me, two fresh Cokes in his hands. He handed me one.

"Yeah," I said, forcing a smile onto my face. "Ready to get going?"

Chris reached out a hand, pulling me to my feet. For one second he held onto my hand tightly, looking me straight in the eye before letting go. I knew that he understood, at least a little bit, what I was feeling right then.

It wasn't much, but it helped.

Chapter Seven

"Okay, I think you've done super tonight," Ashley said in her best teacher-explains-things-to-little-kids voice. "What do you think we've learned so far?"

I glared at her. "I'm not seven, Ash."

"Sorry," she said, looking sheepish. "Force of habit. Anyhow, what *do* you think you learned?"

I looked at Ryan helplessly, and he smiled. "What did you think of Hugh Grant in this one?"

"Well, he seemed like the obvious choice," I said, scrunching up my nose as I considered it. "But it was pretty clear early on he was all talk. That Mark guy was much better."

"Good!" Ashley said. "Did either of them remind you of anything?"

"Well...Mark's last name was Darcy, right? So, like, was that on purpose? Was he supposed to be like Darcy in *Pride and Prejudice*? And Hugh Grant was like that Wickham guy?"

"Yes!" Ashley said, clearly thrilled that I had caught on. "*Bridget Jones* is a modern day retelling of *Pride and Prejudice*!"

"Yeah, I can see that," I said, nodding. "You know, that's actually kind of cool."

Ashley beamed at me.

"So I guess what I learned..." I thought for a moment. "Is that you can't always judge a book by its cover? Sometimes the quiet guy has a lot more going on underneath the surface than the obvious choice?"

"Look, Ash," Ryan said, putting his arm around

her. "Our little girl is finally catching on."

I rolled my eyes. "Okay, so can we add that to the list?" I asked, pointing at the notebook on Ryan's lap.

"Guy...with...hidden...depths..." Ryan muttered as he added the description to the notebook. "Okay, let's see what we have so far..."

Ryan and Ashley had been leading me through a litany of movies and books over the last two and a half weeks. I had watched classic black and white films, Disney cartoons, and modern-day romantic comedies. I had found many of them silly, and a few downright offensive in their portrayal of woman. But I could grudgingly admit that I had liked a few. And I was definitely starting to pick up on some patterns.

"Okay, first we have *When Harry Met Sally* and *30 Going on 30*," Ryan said. "Which showed us..." They both looked at me expectantly.

"That old friendship can turn into true love," I said dutifully.

"Good," Ryan said, giving me an approving smile before turning back to his list. He quizzed me for another five minutes, and I was able to satisfactorily remember what they had told me about the boy next door, the bad boy, the one that got away, and the boy that you love to hate.

"You know," Ryan said, leaning back in his chair. "I think you've got it."

"You don't have to look so surprised," I muttered. "I do have a master's degree, you know."

"Has a master's degree, yet she doesn't know the first thing about guys," he shot back. I glared at him.

"We're proud of you," Ashley said, giving Ryan a warning look. "And I think you're ready for the next step."

"Next step?" I said, immediately alarmed. "What

next step?"

"Your makeover!" they cried in unison.

"Oh, no," I said, feeling panicked. "No, no, no. I never agreed to any makeover!"

"You said you wanted our help," Ryan reminded me. "You agreed to listen to us."

"I agreed to learn about the classic romances! I never said you could give me a makeover."

"Em, it's not a big deal," Ashley said. "We're not talking anything drastic here. We just think you should pick up some more feminine clothes."

"What's wrong with my clothes?"

Ryan burst out laughing. "Oh, sweetie. Please. You live in track pants and T-shirts."

"I'm a physical therapist," I said testily. "What exactly am I supposed to wear to work, heels?"

"No," he said calmly. "But you also don't need to wear your work clothes all the time. Like on weekends. And when we go out."

"I don't wear track pants when we go out."

"Yeah, 'cause your ratty jeans are so much better."

I started to argue with him, but Ashley held up a hand. "Look, all we're saying is that it would be nice for you to get a few new things."

"And maybe a haircut," Ryan added. "And some makeup."

"No," I said flatly. "I put my foot down at the makeover."

Ryan sighed dramatically but Ashley only smiled. "We'll revisit this later."

"Revisit what?" Chris asked, entering the room. He had been hiding in Ashley's bedroom ever since we turned on *Bridget Jones*. I had asked if I could please join him, but Ryan and Ashley were firm that I watch the entire movie.

"Emily's impending makeover," Ryan said.

"Why does she need a makeover?" Chris asked, squinting at me. "She looks like Emily." I beamed at him.

"She could stand to look like a better version of Emily," Ryan explained.

"We just want to soften her up a little bit," Ashley said.

Chris took a look at my face and burst out laughing. "Good luck with that," he said.

"Can we drop this, please?" I asked. "I know I agreed to this and everything, but I think I'm going to scream if we have to talk about makeovers or gooey love stuff for another second."

Chris looked at his watch. "It's still pretty early. We could go out for a while."

"Dancing?" Ryan asked, his face lighting up.

"I was thinking more like finding some good beer somewhere," Chris said.

"Oh God," Ashley moaned. "You're gonna make me spend the rest of the night in some pretentious micro-brewery where everyone goes on and on about the inferiority of anything that costs less than twelve bucks for a six pack, aren't you?"

Chris looked hurt. "I thought you liked it when I explained good beer to you," he said.

"Sweetie, that was before we were dating," she said patiently. "Back when I was trying to get you to like me."

Chris sputtered incoherently for a moment. I decided to put him out of his misery and change the subject. "How about we go to the WAB?" I suggested. The Woodward Avenue Brewery was one of the few bars we could all agree was awesome.

"Good call," Ashley said. "I'll go get ready." She

stood up and started toward her bedroom, before turning to look at me expectantly.

"What?" I asked.

She glanced pointedly at my (admittedly) ratty jeans, and I sighed. "Fine. I'll go get ready too."

***

Predictably, the WAB was crowded on a Saturday night. I had always liked coming here; it was a large, multi-storied bar, with a decent food menu, and a very laid back, comfortable vibe. It was a good compromise for our group. When we let Ryan pick the place, we typically ended up in a super swanky, posh nightclub—the kind of place that would make me feel underdressed no matter what I was wearing. When Chris was in charge of planning the outing, we'd inevitably spend hours in a microbrewery where the staff looked at you like you had three heads if you dared ask for a Miller Lite. At the WAB, we could all just be ourselves.

Chris went up to the bar to get our beers while the three of us hunted for a suitable table. Eventually we found a high top near the back wall. It was a little cramped, but it would do. I surveyed the room—it was a typical mix of couples and groups like ours. Not seeing anyone I recognized, I returned my attention to my friends.

"He doesn't look too bad," Ashley was saying to Ryan, squinting over his shoulder. Ryan turned in the direction she was looking and made a face.

"No way," he said, his voice dismissive. "He's way too short for her."

"What are you guys doing?" I asked, suspicion immediately kicking in.

"Just checking out your prospects," Ryan said, not

looking at me as his eyes scanned the bar.

"Oh, come on," I said. "Can't you give it a rest?"

"You need to get back on that horse sometime, metaphorically speaking," Ryan said. "We're just helping you out."

Chris returned from the bar with our beers, and I was happy for the distraction. But he, too, seemed bent on bringing the focus of the evening back to my love life.

"Emily," he said, setting my beer in front of me. "You are never gonna believe who's over at the bar."

"Who?" I asked, grabbing the beer and immediately taking a sip. It was cold and good and helped calm my irritation.

"Jacob Bower."

Ashley gasped, clearly remembering who that was. I felt my heart rate pick up, a pit of nervousness lodging itself in my stomach.

"Jacob?" Ryan asked, scrunching up his face like he was trying to remember something.

"Jacob. Remember? He and Emily went out in high school... The one that got away," Chris explained as I sipped my beer, trying to calm the racing of my heart.

"I knew that name sounded familiar," Ryan said, smacking his hand on the table. "So what was the whole deal with that? I want backstory."

"On and off for a year," Chris continued. "Everyone thought they were so perfect for each other."

"They were both soccer captains for their teams," Ashley said. "They had everything in common."

"You didn't even know him," I muttered, but Ashley was undeterred.

"Then Em broke up with him before they started

college," she continued. "She didn't want to try the long distance thing."

"And she's regretted it ever since," Chris said dramatically. I gave him a shove, nearly knocking him off his bar stool.

"I have not," I said. "It was totally the right decision at the time."

"But he was the last guy you were ever really serious with," Ashley pointed out.

"Wow. If that's not a recipe for a great love story, I don't know what is," Ryan said.

"You guys," I moaned. "I thought we were dropping it."

"Oh, come on, Em," Ashley said, excited. "That's been the whole point of this, right? To help you make better decisions about your love life. And this is a classic romantic set-up. The high school sweetheart? The one that got away? Reunited after all these years. It couldn't be more perfect!"

"So what am I supposed to do?" I asked. "Just walk over there and ask him if he wants to star in a real-life romantic comedy with me?"

"No," Ryan said, sighing. "You walk over there and say you can't believe it's him, after all this time, and then start up a conversation like a normal person."

Hmm, when he put it that way, it did sound like a no-brainer. I sipped my beer, thinking about Jacob. Regardless of Ashley's over-dramatization, I had always liked him. There had been many nights, alone in my dorm freshman year, when I'd wished I had made a different choice. Was this my chance to try again?

"I'm gonna go say hi," I said, making my mind up suddenly and standing.

"You are?" Ryan said, sounding shocked.

"Yup," I said. I downed the rest of my beer for courage, then headed across the room to the bar.

I recognized Jacob right away. He was sitting with a small group of guys, his bleached blond hair a dead give away in the dim light of the bar. The last few years hadn't changed him much. To me, he still looked pretty much like my first love—tall, wiry, with a shock of messy hair.

"Jacob?" I said, standing beside him. He turned in my direction, and his entire face lit up as he recognized me.

"Emily!" he said. "What are you doing here?"

"I live down here now," I told him. "I have since I graduated, actually. What about you?"

"Visiting some buddies," he said, gesturing at the boys next to them. They all had a similar look—jeans and tight T-shirts, most wearing baseball caps. It was a little frat-boyish for me, but who cared? This was Jacob!

"Have a seat," Jacob said, gesturing to the stool next to him. I hopped up, and Jacob raised his hand to the bartender. "What are you drinking?" he asked.

"Miller Lite," I told him. When the bartender approached, Jacob got a refill for himself and ordered my beer.

"It's on me," he said, smiling. "Man, I can't believe you're here!"

"So what have you been up to?" I asked, taking a sip of my new beer.

"I live up in Oxford," he said, naming a pretty rural town an hour or so north of the city. "With my brothers," he continued. I remembered Jacob's family: a sweet, quiet mom and four rowdy, athletic boys, plus their father, who could have easily passed for one of his sons.

"In fact, Mikey is over there somewhere." He gestured over his shoulder at the guys behind him, who appeared to be having a paper football competition. I caught the eye of one of them—a stockier guy with that trademark Bower white-blond hair. He smiled at me, and I waved. Seeing me, Jacob turned around and grinned. "Hey, Mikey," he called to the guy. "Look who's here!"

Mike got up and came to stand behind us. "Is this little Emily Donovan who broke my brother's heart?"

"Hey, Mike," I said, smiling at him politely before I saw his eyes dart obviously down to my chest. Real classy.

"So what do you guys do in Oxford?" I asked, turning back to Jacob so I couldn't see Mike's gaze.

"We fix up dirt bikes," Jacob said. "And snowmobiles and four wheelers. Pretty much anything people like to ride for fun."

I grinned. Jacob had always been into thrill riding back home. "I can picture you in Oxford," I told him. "You were always such a country boy."

"Yeah, it's a good fit for me," he laughed. "But I come down here pretty often. All the good bars are in Royal Oak and Ferndale."

"That's true," I said.

"So is Brooke here with you?" Mike asked.

I shook my head. "She still lives in Alpena," I said.

"Shame," Mike replied, shaking his head sadly. "She was always one hot little piece of ass."

I felt a shiver of revulsion down my spine. I wished Jacob had never waved Mike over, he was totally creeping me out, and he'd barely been there for five minutes.

"Alright, you old pervert," Jacob said, slapping his brother's arm. He didn't look too put out though, his expression was more amused than anything. "You're grossing Emily out. Go sit back down."

Mike laughed, and, before I could stop him, reached out and grabbed my hand. "It was really, really nice to see you again, Emily," he said quietly, once again looking down at my chest. I wanted to punch him.

"Sorry about him," Jacob said, a smirk on his face as he watched Mike walk away. "He thinks he's a real ladies' man." He took a sip of beer as a bit of awkwardness enveloped us. Mike had put a damper on seeing Jacob again. I couldn't put my finger on it, but there was something different about him. But I supposed that was only natural after seven years, and decided to give him the benefit of the doubt as he started describing his work in the bike shop.

After a few minutes, his chatter moved on to sports talk. Apparently Jacob and his brothers sometimes raced their dirt bikes in competitions. As he went on and on describing his latest third-place finish, it dawned on me that he had yet to ask a single question about me. Why I lived here now, what work I did. It was annoying.

When the conversation moved back to high school friends, however, I finally had enough. Jacob asked me if there was anyone I still kept in touch with, so I told him that I had remained close with Chris and that he was, in fact, there with me that night. Jacob smirked. "That guy was always such a pansy," he said.

"Excuse me?" I asked, the irritation that had been slowly simmering below the surface suddenly erupting into full-blown anger.

"He was always so dorky," Jacob went on, clearly not sensing that he was on dangerous grounds. "With his nose in a book. And those glasses. What a loser."

I stood so abruptly that my stool fell back into the bar. "I have to go," I said, my voice cold. My hands were practically shaking, I was so pissed. Who did this asshole think he was?

"Really?" he asked, looking disappointed. "I was hoping we could really catch up."

When his gaze, too, slid down to my chest, I decided I had been standing here way too long.

"Sorry," I said, feeling disgusted. I threw a few bills down on the bar. I didn't want him paying for anything for me. "Bye." Before he could respond, I had turned on my heel and walked away as quickly as I could.

As I strode across the room, I tried to get control of my anger. Had Jacob always been like that? Had I just never noticed? I thought back to how he had been in high school. Yeah, he had always been a jock, but he had also been sweet and kind and a little quiet. Maybe it was because he was the youngest and probably spent more time with his mom than with his older brothers. Now that he was grown, though, and out of the house, it was clear he had changed for the worse.

"How did it go?" Ashley asked me excitedly as I approached the table.

"Terrible," I said flatly. "He turned into a total ass. And his brother practically sexually harassed me. Big fat waste of time."

Ashley's face fell. "Man, I was really hoping it might turn out. It seemed so romantic."

"This is real life, not a movie, Ash," I said, snatching Ryan's beer from in front of him and taking a long sip. "And in real life, men are pigs."

Chapter Eight

"Is that what you're wearing?" Ryan asked the second I walked out of my bedroom.

"What's wrong with what I'm wearing?" I asked, looking down at my jeans and black sweater.

Ryan sighed. "Have we taught you nothing? Haven't you noticed anything about the heroines in the movies we've been watching?"

"They all let sappy love stuff control their lives?" I asked.

He glared at me. "They all dressed like females," he said.

"Hey!" I was offended. I may be a tomboy, but I think he was pushing it. It wasn't like my clothes were super baggy or masculine—you could still tell I was a female, for God's sake.

"Don't you have anything in your closet that shows a little skin?" he asked. "A dress would be nice."

"Ryan, can we just go?" I asked. "I didn't even want to go to this party, and now you're hassling me about my clothes."

"Em, the entire reason we're going to this party is so you can meet some guys. What's the point if you don't put some effort into it?"

I sighed loudly. I was getting very tired of both Ryan and Ashley. Following their advice had seemed like a good idea at the time—or, at the very least, like something that couldn't possibly hurt me. But lately all I felt was hassled and annoyed. And, if I had to watch another stupid chick flick, I was pretty sure I was going to start pulling my hair out.

Ryan must have noticed the look on my face. "Look," he said, his voice sweeter now. "Let me just go take a look in the closet. You don't have to wear anything you don't want to."

"Fine," I said, turning on my heel and walking back into my bedroom. Once I'd crossed the threshold, I realized Ryan wasn't with me. I peeked out into the hallway and saw him walking into Ashley's room.

"I never said *your* closet," he said over his shoulder.

"Oh dear Lord," I muttered, following him into Ashley's room. "You do realize that I'm about five inches taller than her, right?"

"I'll figure something out," he muttered. A few minutes later he had pulled several options out and draped them over his arm. "These should work," he said, holding up a pair of black leggings. "They're stretchy, so they should fit your freak legs."

"Real nice, Ry," I muttered, taking the leggings from him. "What else?"

He handed me a grey top that looked fairly shapeless to me. "Really?" I asked.

"Just try it on," he said. "And then you can wear your leather boots, and I'll find you a necklace." He saw the look on my face and raised an eyebrow. "Brooke bought you those boots, which are totally hot by the way, two years ago, and I've only seen you wear them once."

"They pinch my feet."

"Beauty is pain," he said. "I get regular waxings, I should know."

Ten minutes later I had put on the outfit Ryan had put together. I had to admit, it looked pretty good on me. The leggings, despite being stretchy, were still a few inches short on me, but the boots covered the gap. The grey shirt that had seemed so shapeless to me, actually draped asymmetrically across my shoulders and chest in a really flattering way. He finished the look with a long chunky silver chain and several silver bangles on my wrist.

"Admit it," he said, looking over my shoulder at my reflection in the floor-length mirror. "You know you look good. And you like it."

"I do feel pretty good," I admitted. "I'm almost not dreading this night."

"Look at it this way," Ryan said, throwing an arm around my shoulder. "At the very least, you get to spend an entire evening with me."

"Lucky me."

***

The party was at a loft downtown. The expansive space was sparsely furnished, with exposed brick walls and stainless steel appliances and fixtures. It felt a little cold to me, but Ryan was in transports of delight over it.

"This is so cool," he babbled excitedly in my ear. "Don't you love the play on function and form here? The blending of the hard lines with the stark space. Really impressive."

"It looks like a yuppie's overpriced loft," I muttered. He ignored me.

For a while, Ryan stayed by my side, leading me around as he mingled with his friends. But it wasn't long before he zeroed in on a prospect—not for me, but for himself. The guy looked to be about twenty years old, thin as a rail, and dressed in baggy pants and a white undershirt—totally *ick*, in my opinion. But then, it wasn't very often that Ryan and I agreed on men.

In no time at all Ryan had cornered the kid by the bar, laughing uproariously at his every comment. "Pathetic," I muttered, grinning to myself as I watched from the other end of the granite counter. Ryan was, without a doubt, the most shameless flirt I had ever met.

"Emily?" A familiar voice said behind me. I spun around and was pleasantly surprised to see Elliot standing at the bar.

"Hey! What are you doing here?" I asked.

"I came with a few friends," he said, gesturing over his shoulder at a group of people near by. "What about you?"

"My friend, Ryan," I said, pointing him out. "Who has abandoned me to go flirt with some twenty year old. An art student."

Elliot laughed, pushing the sleeves of his shirt up onto his forearms. *Nice arms*, I thought automatically, noting the trail of goldish red hair dusting across his skin. I looked him over briefly. He was dressed in a pair of dark-wash jeans and a black long sleeve T-shirt. I realized that I had rarely seen him in anything other than his khakis and *VitaLife* Polo shirt. He looked good in normal clothes.

"Do you need a refill on that?" he asked, pointing down at my empty beer bottle.

"You're not going to lecture me?" I asked, feigning shock. "Not gonna give me some long diatribe on the way alcohol chokes off the nutrients in my body?"

"Beer *is* an essential nutrient," he said, winking at me. He took the bottle from my hand and set it down on the counter, picking up a fresh beer and handing it to me. "So Ryan abandoned you, huh? That's kind of lame."

"What's lame is that I didn't even want to come

here in the first place," I said. "I was looking forward to a night home alone when Ryan called and told me he was dragging me here."

"Why didn't you just say no?"

"He can be very persuasive," I muttered, glancing down the bar at my friend, who was now leaning in close to art school boy, whispering something in his ear.

"I can see that," Elliot said drily.

"It's a shame," I continued. "Tonight was supposed to be the first night in ages I didn't have Ryan or Ashley forcing me to watch some stupid romantic comedy."

"Ah, the research project," Elliot said, and I thought I detected a slight grimace on his face before he took another pull of his beer. "How's that going?"

"I've about given it up," I said. "I knew it was silly from the word go."

"But Ryan can be very persuasive?"

I laughed. "Yeah. And so can Ashley."

"Let me guess, he dragged you to this party so he could help you put some of your research into practice?"

"You got it," I said. "But as he seems to be otherwise engaged, I guess I'm off the hook."

Something in Elliot's face seemed to ease a bit; his smile seemed much more normal when he asked me if I wanted to find a place to hide out in case Ryan should remember his purpose for bringing me.

"You're a lifesaver," I told him.

"Just follow me."

We ended up sitting on the floor, leaning against the exposed brick wall in a quiet corner of the loft. With a large group of obnoxiously loud hipsters in front of us, I was reasonably sure we would be safe from Ryan's observation for the foreseeable future.

"Do you know the guy who owns this place?" I asked.

"No, my friend Kyle does; they work together. What do you think of it?"

I looked around. From our vantage point in the corner I could see most of the loft—it was one of those open floor plans where there aren't even full proper walls between the bedrooms and the living space. The ceilings were high with exposed ductwork and one entire wall was windows—overlooking an overgrown field and not much else.

"It's okay," I said. "I mean, if you like this kind of thing."

"Not your cup of tea?" he asked, smiling at me.

"I just think people try too hard to be urban sometimes."

"Did you know this used to be an old department store?" Elliot asked. I shook my head. "The company went under, and the building was abandoned for a while before David Barker's people came in and refitted everything. They kept all the original stonework and the wooden fixtures in the lobby, but made the space into something usable."

David Barker was a big-time developer in the city. I knew he had a reputation for doing a lot to revitalize some of the harder hit neighborhoods in the city. "I guess that's pretty cool," I said.

Elliot laughed. "You're so not a city girl, are you Emily Donovan?"

"Oh, you're one to talk!" I said. "Mr. I Go Camping and Hiking Every Weekend."

"You're right," he said, smiling. "I just think architecture is pretty cool. So I dig that they kept this place true to its original form."

"Point taken."

"So what is it about city life that you don't like?" he asked.

"I like the city," I argued. "It's just very different from where I grew up."

"And where was that?"

"Alpena," I said, checking his face for any recognition. When none came (not surprising), I went on. "It's a little city up north. Right on Lake Huron."

"Hmm," he said, scrunching up his face. "I don't think I've heard of it. Is it close to the Upper Peninsula?"

"Not really," I said. "It's down the coast a bit. On Thunder Bay."

"What's it like?"

I thought about that for a minute. When I had been a teenager it had been easy to dismiss my home as small town and boring, the ultimate backwoods, middle of nowhere, podunk town. But with distance came a recognition of all the things I missed.

"It's nice," I said. "Quiet. It's actually kind of a big town by northern Michigan standards, but there's not much around. Farms, woods, that kind of stuff. Being so near the lake was awesome."

"I bet," he said. "Lake Huron is really beautiful, at least from what I've seen."

I nodded eagerly. "It really is. And there's a bunch of smaller lakes and a pretty big river near by. We used to spend so much of the summer on the water."

I felt a little pang. I was referring to my high school friends, but it was hard not to remember the long summer days when my parents and I would take the sailboat out into the bay. Dad and I would handle the sailing while Mom lounged around reading. We would stay out until we could watch the sunset over the trees before we would head back home, where Dad would grill burgers.

"Emily," Elliot said softly. I looked up, feeling a little dazed. "You went away there for a minute," he said, smiling. "You okay?"

"Yeah," I said, shaking my head a bit. "Just thinking."

"I'm surprised you won't join the Adventurers Club," he said. "Seeing as how you seem to miss living out in the woods so much."

I grinned. "Who says I miss it?"

"Your face just did," he said.

"Well maybe you have a point," I said. "Okay, what am I missing by not taking part in the Adventurers thingy? That's a totally lame name, by the way."

Elliot nodded sadly. "We used to be the Outdoorsmen," he said. "But our female membership didn't like it much."

"I don't blame them."

"We do all kinds of stuff," he said. "Hiking, kayaking, snowshoeing in the winter. We do some camping when it's nice out. We'll go down to Lake Erie when it's warm, have cookouts, and go swimming. That kind of thing."

I suddenly realized that, as we had been talking, we had moved slightly closer together, to better hear over the hipsters arguing the merits of some band I had never heard of. It wasn't entirely uncomfortable to be sitting so close to Elliot. There was something so easy about being in his presence. Like I didn't have to try.

"I think you would like it," Elliot was saying. "You should really come out sometime."

"Maybe I will—"

"Emily!"

I looked up to see Ryan pushing his way toward us, an excited look on his face. "I found him!"

"Who?" I asked, totally confused.

"The guy! For you to go hit on."

"Oh dear God," I whispered. Next to me, Elliot laughed softly.

"I'm talking to my friend right now, Ry," I said emphatically. "You remember Elliot, right?"

"Sure," Ryan said. The two had met at my clinic a few times over the past year. "Hey, dude," he said, nodding at Elliot before turning his attention back to me. "Em, though, seriously, this guy is totally perfect for you. You have to come meet him. He's really handsome and quiet. I think he totally goes along with what we were talking about before."

"Here it comes," I muttered.

"You know, how we watched all those movies where the guy had hidden depths? I think Bruce totally does. Come on!"

Beside me, Elliot was shaking with suppressed laughter.

"I better go, or he'll never leave me alone," I told him.

"Of course," he replied, managing to keep a straight face. "Research calls, and all that."

"Thanks for keeping me company," I told him, standing up.

"It was my pleasure," he said, some of the amusement slipping from his face. I wondered if he was annoyed that Ryan had interrupted us.

"See you Monday?"

"Yup," he said, smiling again. "See you then."

Ryan led me across the room to a large water feature—it appeared to be made of old pieces of chrome and bent pipes. My first thought was that it was pretentious, but I tried to remember Elliot's attitude. Maybe it was made from like, recovered bathroom fixtures from old abandoned houses, or something like that.

"Hey, Bruce," Ryan said, pulling on my arm gently to keep me from walking past the man. He was drinking from a coffee mug on a modern, armless, white and chrome couch that had probably cost about four months of my salary. He appeared to be alone.

"Emily, this is Bruce. Bruce, this is my friend, Emily."

"Hello," I said, trying to smile through my growing embarrassment. Could Ryan be any more obvious?

Bruce smiled slightly and nodded in my direction, before directing his attention back to his coffee cup. He was good looking, in an artistic, lanky sort of way. Even seated I could tell that he was tall, maybe even taller than me, with dark hair and wire-rimmed glasses. Not exactly my type, but not at all bad.

Next to me, Ryan raised his eyebrows and mouthed, "Cute!" I made a face at him, but Ryan was determined. "Bruce comes from Traverse City, isn't that amazing?"

"Um, yeah," I said, bewildered. "It's pretty there."

"And you're from Alpena!" he continued. "Isn't that a coincidence?"

I just stared at him. Besides the fact that they were both in the northern half of the state, Traverse City and Alpena were really nowhere near each other.

"Anyhow," Ryan said. "I thought you guys should talk. Bruce looks so lonely sitting over here all by himself, doesn't he?"

Bruce gave that same, vague smile. *Lonely?* I thought to myself. *More like socially awkward.*

"So," Ryan said, edging away. "I'll just leave the

two of you to talk."

I glared daggers at him, but he only smiled in return. As he slipped past me he murmured in my ear, "Hidden depths."

I sighed and sat down next to Bruce. I may as well give him a few minutes of my time. Then I could make my excuses and go find Ryan to demand that he get me out of here. *Or maybe find Elliot again...*

Bruce gave me another of his vague smiles before taking another sip of his coffee. We sat in silence for a minute—me feeling awkward, Bruce smiling and drinking coffee. This is the guy Ryan would pick for me? Seriously?

Hidden depths, he had said. Maybe he knew more about Bruce than I did. I mean, there must have been some reason that he would think I should give it a try. Ryan was nothing if not picky when it came to men, for either of us. And we had watched an awful lot of movies where the main guy was more than what he appeared. It seemed to be a popular theme. It wouldn't hurt to at least put some effort in.

"So, Bruce," I said, my voice as bright and pleasant as I could make it. "What do you do?"

"I'm working on my novel," he said seriously, the vague smile disappearing at once.

Hmm, a creative type. Could be promising.

"What's it about?"

"It's about the dark, unspoken truths of the average American life journey," he said, with an entirely straight face. "All the nightmarish monstrosities that exist just below the surface in every man's soul."

I stared at him. Was this guy serious?

"Wow," I finally said. "That sounds...intense."

"I'm a very intense person," he said, his flat voice

the farthest thing from intense I could imagine.

"Wow," I said again.

"I could send you some chapters, if you like," he said.

"Um…sure. That would be great." I had a horrible feeling that I might burst out laughing. I made myself take deep breaths.

"Ryan tells me you're a physical therapist?" Bruce asked.

"Yeah," I said. "I work at a small outpatient facility in Royal Oak."

"And do you enjoy that job?"

"I do," I said. "I like helping people and trying to find the solution to their physical problem."

Bruce nodded sagely. "Ryan was right. We do have a lot in common."

"Um…"

"You serve people in their physical state, helping to heal the body. I work to help heal the soul. Through my words."

"Oh, my," I whispered, again feeling like I might burst into laughter. I wondered what Elliot would think of this guy, and the thought made me almost lose it. I hid my smile behind my bottle and took a long sip of the beer, trying to compose myself.

Bruce looked down at his watch. "I need to get going," he said. "I have to be up early tomorrow."

"Oh," I said, feeling a huge wave of relief. I wouldn't have to make an excuse after all.

"Listen, Emily," he said, turning to me. "I would really enjoy continuing our conversation. I feel like we might have quite a lot to say to each other. Would you like to have dinner this week?"

I was so shocked, I couldn't even think of a response. Did he really think the last five minutes had been in any way pleasant? What could we possibly have to say to each other?

I was about to tell him no, the excuse about being swamped at work already at my lips, but at that moment I looked up and saw Ryan, standing several feet away from us, his arms crossed and a stern look on his face.

Hidden depths, I could practically hear him say. *Give it a chance.*

I looked back at Bruce. He was smiling in that vague way again, and his glasses had slipped down his nose a little. He looked cute, in a bemused, dorky sort of way. Maybe we *would* have a lot to talk about. Maybe I shouldn't be judging this book by its cover—or his novel by its ridiculously pretentious synopsis.

What do you have to lose?

"Okay," I said, smiling back. "That would be nice."

Bruce suggested a restaurant, and we arranged to meet there the following Tuesday. With another slight smile, and a final sip of his coffee, he got up, leaving me alone on the uncomfortable, expensive couch.

"Well?" Ryan asked, appearing at my side so quickly I was sure he'd been watching the entire exchange.

"We're going out this week," I said, still not quite sure how I felt about this development.

"Good job!" Ryan said, throwing his arm around me. "I knew you could do it!"

"How do you know him?" I asked.

"He's a friend of Phoenix, that guy I was talking to? He's supposed to be a totally brilliant writer."

"He was telling me about his book," I said. "I'm not sure it's really my thing."

"Emily, you only read John Grisham novels," he said, rolling his eyes. "Hardly high-minded literature.

This guy is totally smart and creative, a real artist. He could be really good for you."

Maybe Ryan had a point. Creative and artistic were not exactly words that anyone would use to describe me. Maybe I could use a little of that in my life.

And okay, so Bruce had freaked me out a little. His detachment, coupled with his description of his book, had seemed down right creepy to me. But maybe that was just how artists were. I was just a washed up jock—who was I to judge?

"Maybe he could be good for me," I said. "Who knows?"

Chapter Nine

"Alright, that's it," I said the moment I'd walked through the front door.

Ryan, Ashley, and Chris all looked up from their movie. "I'm done with this whole research project thing." I pointed at Ashley and Ryan, who were sitting next to each other on the couch. "And I sure as hell am done taking advice from the two of you."

"What happened?" Ryan asked, pointing the remote at the television to mute the sound.

"That was the worst date of my life," I fumed, throwing my bag down on the ground and flopping into the arm chair. "I mean it. There were no hidden depths. Nothing below that book's cover. He was actually as boring and lame as he appeared to be!"

From his spot lounging on the floor, Chris coughed loudly. I glared at him. If he laughed at me now, after the night I'd had, I might actually hit him.

"Come on," he said, sitting up and looking at me. "What did you expect? When you met the guy, you thought he was too quiet. You thought he was dull. I think you even used the word 'creepy'. But you actually went out with him because these two nut-jobs convinced you it would be like some movie? Seriously, Em?"

"You're right, you're right," I said, putting my head in my hands.

The night had been just awful. Bruce had spent the entire time talking about his book (groundbreaking), the books being written by members of his critique group (absolute dross unworthy of being discussed alongside his own), and the crap that was being published (evidence of the complete decline of our culture). When he wasn't talking about his book he was staring off into the distance, a blank expression on his face. He hadn't asked me about myself once, and the one time I tried to bring up my job he interrupted me to ask what I thought about *Faust*.

What a nightmare.

I groaned into my hands. "It's all my fault," I said, my voice muffled. "I never should have gone along with any of this crap. It's all too ridiculous for words."

"Hey!" Ashley said, reaching down to smack the back of Chris' head. "That's totally not fair. I think we've given you great advice."

I looked up at her, incredulous. "Are you kidding me? Since you guys started this whole thing I've had zero luck. I've had two terrible encounters with the guys you said I should go for. Nothing that you've told me is coming true in real life."

"Rome wasn't built in a day," Ryan countered. "You didn't really expect to meet 'the one' on your first date, did you?"

"Why wouldn't she?" Chris muttered, apparently undeterred by the smack. "Listening to you guys, all she had to do was watch some crappy movies and she'd be swept off her feet by week's end."

"We never said that," Ashley said. "These things take time. But every date, good or bad, is an experience that can be used to help you along on your quest for true love."

"Okay, enough," I said, standing up. "I'm going to take a bath and try to forget that this night ever happened. When I get done I'm going to come out here and watch the most violent movie I can find." Ashley started to object, but I raised my hand. "I mean it. I'm taking a break from the gooey love stuff. No argument."

"Fine," Ashley said, settling back on the couch. "A break is fine. But I'm not giving up on this, Emily."

"Me either," Ryan said.

"Good for the two of you," I muttered as I left them sitting in the living room.

***

"Where are you off to?"

I looked up from my bag, which I had been busily stuffing files into, to see Elliot standing in the doorway to my office.

"Taking off a little early today," I told him. "Which means I have to take some work home with me."

"That sucks," he said, wrinkling his nose in sympathy.

"Oh, well," I said. "I'd rather go through files in my PJs watching TV than do it sitting here."

"Good point," he said. "So, can I interest you in lunch? There's a buffet special at that Thai place today. I mean, if you're leaving early and all."

I stopped what I was doing to look at Elliot. He seemed a little on edge today, more tense than usual. Then again, Elliot was usually as laid back as a person could be, so maybe I was reading too much into it. Regardless, I was running late.

"Sorry," I told him, picking up my bag and swinging it over my shoulder. "I'm ducking out early 'cause I have plans."

His face seemed to tighten, and I wondered if there really was something the matter.

"Let me guess, you hit it off with the hidden

depths guy?"

"Oh God, no," I said, effecting a mock shudder. "He was absolutely terrible. Nothing hidden about him whatsoever. No, I'm meeting up with some old friends from college downtown."

"That sounds nice." His voice was lighter now, but it still seemed like something was bothering him. I promised myself I would ask him about it the next time we had lunch together.

"I really should go," I said, looking at my watch. "I'll pick up the coffee tomorrow, okay?"

I patted his shoulder as I left the room, shouting out a goodbye to Michael and Sarah. Once I was in the car, I pulled out my GPS and typed in the address of the restaurant. I hated to admit it to anyone, but I found driving in and around Detroit incredibly confusing. There were so many one-way streets and missing road signs. Then there were all the freeways that were called different names in different parts of the area—like, half the time people called the M10 the Lodge, and the M8 the Davison. I could never figure out why. I once spent twenty minutes looking for the Jeffries, only to find that I was already on it but it was really called I-96.

I had lived in the metro area for three years now, but I still got lost anytime I ventured too far from Royal Oak. I tried to hide this from my friends—Ryan would just laugh and tell me to head back up to the farm.

My GPS got me to the restaurant in one piece, and only five minutes late. I had been looking forward to this lunch for a long time. It wasn't everyday I got to see my old track friends from college, especially now that more and more of them were settling down to get married or moving away from Michigan.

"Emily!"

I smiled as I entered the restaurant. Several of the girls were waving and calling my name from their table near the window.

"Hi!" I said, setting my purse on the table so I could hug my friends properly. "It's so good to see you!"

"You look great!" Marybeth said, once I had settled into my chair. "You're still in such great shape."

"Oh God," I said, waving my hands dismissively. "I haven't run a race in ages. I would get destroyed if I tried to actually compete with someone."

"At least you don't have fifteen pounds of baby weight to get off," she muttered, rubbing at her stomach. "Collin is almost a year old. I can't believe I'm still carrying this around."

"Join the club," Ginny said drily. "Danny is three, and I'm still not down to my pre-baby weight."

Ginny had been a year ahead of me at school. She was that gorgeous, cool girl that Marybeth, Kaitlin, and I had looked up to when she was a senior. Not too long after leaving school she had gotten pregnant—which I bet was totally traumatic for her, because she was single and unemployed at the time. But she was married now and seemed really happy—and was clearly insane, as she looked every bit as thin and gorgeous as she had running track back in college.

"How's Danny?" I asked. "I had hoped you might bring him along."

"He's with his auntie Jen today," Ginny said.

"You're so lucky to have help," a girl named Bonnie said. "All of my family lives on the other side of the state. I feel like I'm going crazy with twins around the house."

I looked around at the group of girls as they

continued to talk about babies, and it suddenly struck me that I was in the minority here. Four of the girls were married now, three of them with children, and another two were newly engaged. Somehow, without me noticing it, all of my old friends had settled down, started families of their own. As the conversation swung around to the two upcoming weddings, I felt a lump form in my throat.

"You okay, Em?" Kaitlin said, close to my ear so no one else would hear. "You seem pretty quiet."

I turned to smile at her, but found my mouth didn't want to work. All of a sudden, I felt like I might burst into tears.

"What's wrong?" she said, more loudly. Most of the other girls broke off their respective conversations to look at me, and I felt my face redden.

"I'm sorry," I croaked, reaching for my water glass to keep from crying. "I've just had a rough few weeks. I...I broke up with my boyfriend, and it's been kind of hard."

There was a general outcry of sympathy. Kaitlin put her arm around me, and several of the other girls patted my arm.

"Do you want to talk about it?" Marybeth asked.

"No, it's okay," I said. "I'm sorry to get all upset, I seriously don't know what's wrong with me."

"It's fine to get upset," Ginny said, smiling at me from across the table. "Break-ups suck. Especially when you have to listen to a bunch of girls gabbing on and on about their husbands." She leaned across the table at me and winked. "I promise it isn't all it's cracked up to be. And I can tell you from experience that things tend to fall into place precisely when you stop worrying about it."

I smiled back. I knew Ginny had been through a

lot to get to where she was, happy now with her husband and baby. But in that moment I felt so envious of her it made my stomach hurt. No matter what I had said to Ashley and Ryan about being over the romance scene, I wanted what these girls had. Love. A family.

Ginny steered the conversation to safer waters, and before long I was joining in as they reminisced about our days at State. The meal passed pretty pleasantly after that, but at the back of my mind, I still felt disconcerted. What was wrong with me?

I left the restaurant after lunch feeling more confused then ever. Listening to Ginny talk about her family had made me feel an almost overwhelming desire to find someone I could love. I had never quite realized how strongly I felt, but now at least my reaction to Ashley's romance theory made more sense. When she had told me I was screwing up my chances by being clueless, I felt something akin to panic. It was that fear that I'd be alone that made me go along with their romance project.

But now I was pretty sure that the whole thing had been a waste of time. I knew Ryan and Ashley had my best interests at heart, but I also knew they both had a flair for the dramatic. Ryan had been searching for his dream man since the day I met him—doing lots of his own research in dating and hooking up as he went. Despite his flirtatiousness—and okay, downright promiscuous reputation, I knew that at heart he was a big old softie.

Then there was Ashley. She was a daydreamer, always had been. She was the poster child for the phrase Hopeless Romantic. I thought back to all the serious relationships she'd had since we met in college. Most of them were promptly blown right out of proportion. How many times had she assured me that whatever new guy she was dating was different? How many times had she told me, in all seriousness, that she was absolutely positive that this one was really the one?

Yet these were the people that I had allowed to get me all confused and worked up. I mean, I loved them, don't get me wrong. They were some of the best friends I had ever had in my life. But taking advice from them had been seriously, seriously stupid.

I had parked a few blocks down from the restaurant, and as I began to walk in the direction of my car, a steady rain began to fall. "Great," I muttered, pulling my coat up over my head. As I approached the last intersection between me and the safety of my dry car, my phone beeped in my pocket. I glanced down at the display to see a text from Brooke flashing back at me. I decided it could wait until I was out of the rain.

Brooke, I thought, shaking my head as I stepped out into the street. What would Brooke say if she knew how silly I had been? She would probably laugh her head off. Or, more likely, be seriously disappointed in me. This was just not the way either of us had ever—

Suddenly, I heard a loud horn blow about ten feet away. I looked up from under my jacket, startled, to see a huge truck barreling toward me. Before I could even react, two hands had grasped my shoulders and pulled me back, roughly, toward the curb. The momentum of the pull propelled me off my feet, and I felt my back hit a broad body behind me. As I slammed into him, I felt him lose his balance too, and soon we were both stumbling down to the pavement, right at the edge of the road.

"Oh my God," I gasped, my heart racing. It had all happened so fast, I couldn't even be sure of what I had just experienced. I looked behind me and felt a flash of embarrassment mix with the adrenaline coursing through my veins. The man who had pulled me back was now sitting on the pavement, my butt in his lap, his hands still gripping my shoulders tightly.

"I'm so sorry," I cried, trying to right myself. "What a stupid idiot I am, you could have gotten hurt!"

He grinned at me, rather dazed, and said, "You were the one that could have gotten hurt. That truck would have flattened you."

"Thank you," I said. "God, I don't know what I was thinking."

I realized that he had not let go of me yet. My back was still leaning against his shoulder, and he felt strong and solid below me. I looked up into his eyes and realized with a jolt that he was totally gorgeous.

"Sorry," I said again, pulling back so I could try to stand. With one swift motion, he pulled me up as he found his own feet. He turned me slightly so I was facing him full on; only then did he release my shoulders.

"Don't worry about it," he said, beginning to brush off his pants, which I could now tell were an expensive wool. Under his black overcoat, I could just make out a suit jacket and tie. His outfit probably cost more than my entire wardrobe. He smiled down at me. "It's not every day you get to save a pretty girl from getting squashed by a truck."

"You did save me," I said, looking up into his face. He really was very handsome. And it wasn't often that I met a man who towered over me like he did. It made me feel feminine, somehow, even though I was sure I looked like a wet mess. "How can I thank you?"

"Please don't worry about it," he said. I noticed that his hair was getting positively soaked in the rain.

Up on the curb, there was an open umbrella lying on the pavement. He must have thrown it aside when he saw me step in front of the truck.

"You're getting wet," I told him.

"We both are," he agreed, then he put a hand on the small of my back, pulling me with him as he stepped out of the street. He opened his umbrella and held it up over both of our heads. "Now, do you think you're all right? Does anything hurt you?"

"I'm fine," I told him. "Just embarrassed. I don't even know what I was thinking, not looking before I crossed."

"Don't be embarrassed," he said, smiling down at me. Under the umbrella, he was standing very close to me. I could practically feel the body heat radiating off him. "The rain makes us all do stupid things."

Something about his tone made my stomach lurch in a pleasant sort of way. Was he flirting with me?

"Like save silly girls from getting flattened," I asked, smiling back.

"Yeah, like that," he agreed.

"Look, I really do owe you one." I felt another flash of embarrassment as I realized again how dumb I had been. "You'll need to get those dry cleaned." I pointed down at his pants, which were clearly wet and muddy. "Let me pay for them."

"Don't be ridiculous," he said. "It's no big deal."

"I'm very grateful," I pressed. "I'd like to pay you back."

"Well, if you insist," he said, taking a tiny little step closer to me. "Why don't you buy me a drink sometime?"

"Yeah?" I said, surprised. Why would someone like him want to spend any more time with someone like me? He must think I was some silly, stupid ditz after watching me walk blindly in front of a moving truck.

"If you don't object," he said. "I know I would enjoy it." I felt a blush rush to my cheeks, which only seemed to make his grin wider. "What do you say?"

"That would be great," I said, forcing myself to meet his gaze even though my stomach was now squirming. "Do you have a card or something? I could call you."

"What's your number?" he asked, pulling a cell phone from his pocket. "And your name, for that matter."

I laughed. "I'm Emily."

"It's very nice to meet you, Emily," he said, smiling down at me again. "My name is Greg."

I told him my number, and he dialed. I heard my phone ring in my pocket. "There," he said, snapping his phone shut. "Now you have my number, and I have yours. If you haven't called me by tomorrow night, I'll call you to demand my drink." He winked at me as he put the phone back in his pocket, and I felt the butterflies in my stomach multiply.

"Now," he said. "Where were you heading? I think I'd better walk you there, make sure no other rogue trucks attack you."

I heard myself giggle, an unfamiliar girlish sound, as I pointed toward my car. "Right over there."

He put his hand on the small of my back once more and led me back to the street. After making a big show of looking both ways (I giggled again—what *was* I doing?), he gently maneuvered me across the street to my car.

"Here you go," he said, leading me right to the driver's side door. "Are you sure you're okay to drive?"

"Yeah, I'm good," I said, pulling out my keys. I

looked up at his dark eyes. "Thank you, Greg. I really, really appreciate it."

He smiled in return. "It was my pleasure." Then he pulled the door open behind me and held it while I climbed into my seat. "I hope to hear from you soon." With one last smile he shut the door and stepped away from the car.

I took a deep breath, feeling giddy and exhausted as the adrenaline drained from my body. As I started the car and pulled out carefully, I could see Greg in my rearview mirror, standing at the curb under his umbrella, watching me drive away.

Chapter Ten

I told my friends what had happened over dinner that night. Predictably, Ashley was enthralled.

"It's perfect," she breathed, when I had finished my recap. "He rescued you. That's like, *classic* love story right there."

"Let's not jump to conclusions," Ryan said, taking a sip of his wine. "What did he look like?"

I rolled my eyes. "He was pretty cute."

Ryan just stared at me. "That's all you've got? Unacceptable, Em."

"Fine, fine," I said. "He was tall, much taller than me. Maybe six-three? Dark hair, dark eyes. Kind of gave me a Cary Grant vibe."

"Not bad," Ryan said, nodding in approval, whether for my description or the fact that I remembered who Cary Grant even was. "And what was he wearing?"

"Suit and tie," I said, squinting as I tried to remember. "And a black overcoat, I think."

"So he's a professional of some kind," Ryan murmured. "Better and better."

"I'm sorry to interrupt," Chris said. "But if we're gonna start guessing his bank account size next, I'll just excuse myself now."

I laughed as Ryan glared at him. "This is important," he said.

"It's a date," I said. "It's not a huge deal."

"It could be." Ryan pointed his fork in my direction. "You don't know, Em."

"That's what you said about the last two guys," I reminded him. "You got me all worked up that I was living some romantic fantasy, that these situations were straight out of a chick flick, and I was going to fall madly in love. And look at how that turned out."

"But this *is* straight out of a romantic story!" Ashley said, leaning toward me, her eyes bright with excitement. "I mean, just think about it. How many of the great love stories started with a guy rescuing the girl? And he's handsome and rich to boot? This is just too good!"

I stared at her, aghast. I had always known that Ashley and I were different when it came to men, but this was just too much.

"There are so many things wrong with that statement, Ash, I don't even know where to start."

She looked hurt. "What do you mean?"

"First of all, I only said he was in a suit. You're going to extrapolate that into him being rich? Don't you think that's getting a little bit carried away?" She started to respond, but I held up my hand. "But that's not the worst part. Do you really think that, in order for love to happen, a girl needs to be rescued by a guy? Is that an essential part of a relationship? Because if it is, I don't want anything to do with it."

Ashley just sighed. "You're taking this way too seriously," she said. "I know you can take care of yourself, okay? But what's wrong with having a knight in shining armor? Don't we all need some help sometimes?" When I didn't respond, she shook her head. "I think it's romantic. Call me old-fashioned, or whatever."

"I wish a cute guy would come on his white horse and rescue me," Ryan said, looking dreamy as he closed his eyes. "I wouldn't complain one bit."

"Do you know what I think?" Chris asked. "I think if you like this guy, you should go out with him. See how it goes. See if there's a spark." I was surprised to realize that Chris, normally so laid back and easy going, was clearly annoyed. Like, really annoyed. Something about this conversation had apparently irritated the hell out of him. "I don't see why it has to get turned into this big deal, why we have to read so much into it."

He stood up from the table abruptly. "I'm gonna get another bottle of wine," he said, his voice flat.

As he walked to the kitchen, Ashley looked at me, wide-eyed. "He seems pissed," she said. I nodded. She sighed, and stood too. "I'll go see what's up."

Alone with Ryan, I raised my eyebrows. "Think he got grossed out by me talking about cute guys?" he asked.

"Give me a break," I said. "You know Chris isn't like that. Besides, you talk about guys all the time. Like, constantly."

Ryan smiled. "You do have a point there. I wonder why he's pissy then."

I was quiet for a moment, thinking. "I wonder if all this romance stuff is bringing him down," I finally said. "The way Ash talks..."

"Maybe it's a lot of pressure, ya think?"

"Yeah," I nodded. "Like, maybe it makes him wonder if he lives up to all these ideals she's going on and on about."

"Perhaps we should cool it with the research talk," Ryan suggested.

I clapped my hands together. "Can we really? Yay!"

He tossed his napkin at me. "Quiet. We've given you a wealth of helpful knowledge about men and relationships. You just haven't realized it yet."

"Yeah, right. So far your tutelage has helped me so much."

"Just wait," he said, smiling smugly at me. "You haven't gone out with Greg yet. I still think your perfect love story is just over the horizon."

***

Greg surprised me by calling that very night.

"Sorry," he said, after we'd exchanged hellos. "I know we said you would call me, but I couldn't stop thinking about this afternoon." I felt a rush of pleasure color my face, and I was glad he couldn't see me. "I figured I'd better go ahead and set up our date before some other guy saved you from something even more impressive."

I laughed. "Like what?"

"Oh, I don't know. A stampeding elephant, maybe?" He laughed too, and I decided that I liked the sound. It was warm and deep and made me think about how tall he was. It was a manly sound.

"So, about that date," he pressed. I noticed that he was no longer referring to it as "drinks." That set my butterflies off again.

"When's good for you?" I asked.

"I'm free this weekend," he said. "How about Saturday night?"

"Saturday night would be perfect," I replied.

"Good," he said, sounding pleased. "What would you think about dinner? I mean, if we're getting together anyhow, we may as well eat, right?"

"Sure," I said. "Dinner would be nice."

"Have you been to The Lark, in West Bloomfield?"

"I don't think so," I said. Greg chuckled a little.

"Oh, you would remember it if you'd been there,"

he said. "But I think you'll like it. What do you say I pick you up around seven?"

"Sounds perfect," I said. After giving him directions to my apartment, we said good night and hung up the phone. I immediately opened my laptop, leaning back against the headboard of my bed as it powered up. When my Internet browser had loaded, I did a quick Google search for the restaurant he had mentioned. The website had a few pictures, and really good reviews. It appeared to be a fairly nice place—then I clicked on the menu tab. As I browsed the offerings, I could practically feel myself going pale.

"Shit," I muttered. I scrambled off the bed and rushed down the hall to Ashley's room. I said a silent prayer Chris wasn't in there with her before knocking.

"Come in," she called out.

I threw open the door. She was sitting on her bed, books and papers spread out around her, apparently in the middle of planning a lesson.

"Ash, I need your help," I gasped.

"What's the matter?"

"Greg wants to take me to the most expensive restaurant I've ever heard of," I said, still breathing heavily. "I just looked it up online."

"So?" she asked. "Maybe that means he really likes you."

"Ashley, you don't understand," I said. "I've never been to a place like that before. I have no idea what to wear, or how to act. I won't fit in at all. What am I gonna do?"

"Emily," she said firmly. "Relax." She picked up her phone and typed out a quick text. When she was finished, she looked up at me, smiling. "Ryan and I will take care of everything."

Chapter Eleven

When Ashley said they would take care of everything, she really meant it. Friday night found the three of us standing outside a salon in Birmingham, one of the ritzier suburbs in the metro area.

"I can't believe I'm going through with this," I moaned.

"Be brave," Ryan said, putting his arm around me. "I promise it won't be so bad."

"We won't let them cut much," Ashley assured me. "Your hair is beautiful. It just needs some layers so it will move more."

"Not too short?" I pleaded.

"Not too short," she agreed.

"Don't worry," Ryan said, rolling his eyes. "You'll still be able to throw it back in your beloved messy ponytail for work."

"Okay," I said, taking a deep breath. "I'm ready."

It wasn't really as bad as I had imagined. Though I found the staff inside the salon very intimidating (and really snobby), Ryan and Ashley did most of the talking. I just had to sit there. As they conferred with my stylist Sasha—a tiny, pixie-like girl with purple spiky hair and a lip ring—I noticed her assistant bringing over some plastic bottles and a pile of foil squares. When I realized it was hair dye, I had a minor panic attack.

"It's just some highlights!" Ryan insisted. "It's not a big deal."

"I've never dyed my hair," I cried, plastering my

hands over the top of my head. "You said nothing about dye."

"Are you saying this is your natural color?" Sasha asked, lifting up a strand of my hair and letting it run through her fingers.

"Yes," I said. "I've never done anything to it."

"Not even the roots?" she asked. I shook my head. "That's amazing. Your hair is in wonderful condition for someone your age." *My age?* I thought. I was twenty-five, for God's sake. "I wouldn't change the color one bit," she went on. "The bleached blonde look is really big right now, and if you can achieve it without dye you'd be crazy to mess with it."

I felt a rush of affection for Sasha.

"Fine," Ryan said. "But you *are* getting a bikini wax."

I glared at him, but Ashley intervened. "We can talk about that later," she said quickly. "Let's just see how you feel after your haircut."

***

An hour later, I was paying the front-desk receptionist eighty dollars. (Eighty! For a haircut!) I was pleased with what Sasha had done—she hadn't taken off too much length, just added some layers around my face. It swung easily down my back and felt smoother than normal. Ryan wasn't as satisfied. He was still trying to get me to agree to the bikini wax, but I had put my foot down quite firmly.

"No one is going to be seeing anything that even resembles my bikini area," I told him.

"It's more for you than for him!" he argued. "It will make you feel sexy and sleek."

"I don't need to feel sleek and sexy. I just want to feel normal."

In the end, Ashley convinced him to drop it, saying they needed to marshal their forces for the inevitable fight over my clothing choices.

After the salon, we headed to the mall where they dragged me to several stores, insisting I try on a variety of dresses before we made a final decision. Everything they put me in felt about the same to me—black dresses with shorter than I preferred hemlines. According to Ashley, the differences in fabric, silhouette, and cut were essential. I had no idea what she was talking about, so I decided to take her word for it.

In the end, they chose a sleek design that we found on clearance at Macy's for sixty bucks—marked down from one fifty. Even I could tell that this dress was a step up in fabric and cut. A cocktail dress with wide tank straps, the neckline came down into a low vee. The dress was ruched at the waist, giving my normally straight frame the illusion of some curves. It fit me perfectly, and the black satin had a substantial, weighty feel to it.

"It plays up your long legs and makes your waist look miniscule," Ryan said, staring at me in the full-length mirror. "Plus it looks elegant and appropriate without being too fancy."

"I have a silk wrap at home you can wear with it," Ashley said. "But none of your shoes will do."

So off we went next to the shoe section, where they had me try on and walk around in a seemingly endless parade of heels. After a while, it started to feel almost normal to teeter around an extra three inches off the floor.

"Red?" I asked, when I saw the pair that they had decided on. "I can't wear red shoes."

"Why not?" Ashley asked, clearly amused.

"Because people will think..." I looked behind my shoulder to make sure no one was listening before hissing, "Because people will think I'm a slut!"

Ashley only laughed. "You're going to be dressed all in black. A pop of color at your feet is totally appropriate."

"Besides," Ryan said. "These aren't red, they're burgundy."

"I've never worn red shoes before," I muttered, still not convinced.

"You promised you would trust us," Ashley reminded me. "Don't you think I want you to look gorgeous and classy on this date? Do you really think I would send you out there in anything that made you look slutty?"

"I guess not," I said.

"Then buy the freaking shoes," Ryan said.

***

By six thirty the next night, my nerves were threatening to overwhelm me, but I was ready to go. Primped and groomed to within an inch of my life was more like it. I was wearing my new dress and shoes, plus the black silk wrap Ashley had lent me. My hair, which she had carefully blown out, hung down around my shoulders. She had also taken great pains with my makeup, somehow managing to make me look a million times better than normal, without making it look like I was wearing much of any makeup at all. Ryan had even pitched in, carefully manicuring my nails—a feat at which he seemed altogether too skilled.

"You look great," Ashley said, looking me over one last time. "Gorgeous."

"You really do," Ryan said, reaching out to smooth a lock of my hair behind my ears. "Never better."

"What if I don't know what to talk to him about?" I asked, my nervousness rising. "Or what if I don't know how to act in such a fancy restaurant?"

"You'll be fine," Ashley said. "You know what a salad fork is, right?"

"Yes," I said. "At least, I think I do."

"Just follow his lead if you get confused," she advised. "And don't worry about the conversation. You're interesting and funny, no matter the setting."

"Yeah, personality has never been your problem," Ryan agreed. I smiled at them both, feeling marginally better.

Just then, my phone rang, the noise making me start. "You really are jumpy," Ashley said. "Just relax!"

I picked up the phone, noticing Greg's name flashing on the screen. "Hello?"

"Hi, Emily," he said, his voice every bit as deep and sexy as I had remembered. "I'm downstairs. Will you buzz me in?"

"I can just meet you downstairs," I said, already reaching for my purse.

"Oh, no," he said. "I would feel impolite if I didn't come to your door."

"Oh, okay," I said, feeling immediately wrong footed. The night hadn't even started yet, and I was already doing the wrong thing. "Give me just one minute."

I walked to the door and hit the buzzer, hearing it echo on the other end of the phone. "Thanks," Greg said. "I'll be right up."

"He wanted to come to the door," I said to my friends, who were watching me with interest.

"Awesome, we'll get to meet him," Ryan said, rubbing his hands together.

"I would rather you go hide in the bedroom," I

muttered.

"Fat chance."

Just then there was a knock on the door, and we all froze.

"Geez," Ashley said. "Even I'm nervous now!"

"Get the door!" I hissed.

Ashley rushed to the door, pulling it open to reveal Greg. Either he looked better out of the rain or I had forgotten just how good looking he really was. I felt my stomach lurch dangerously.

"Hello," he said, smiling at Ashley. "I'm Greg."

"I'm Ashley, Emily's roommate," she said. Her voice had gone all high-pitched and girly. I would have laughed if I wasn't feeling so terrified. "Come on in."

As Greg stepped into the tiny foyer, I felt a pang of embarrassment—why hadn't I thought to tidy the place up a little bit? He spotted me across the room, and his smile deepened, causing my stomach to lurch even more.

"Hello, Emily."

"Hello," I said, my voice sounding stiff and formal in my own ears. Out of the corner of my eye, I saw Ryan, edging forward toward Greg, a broad smile on his face. "This is my friend Ryan," I said.

"Hello, Greg," Ryan said in his most confident, smooth, I-can't-get-enough-of-myself voice. I fought back a smirk—he was such a flirt.

"Hi, Ryan," Greg said, holding out his hand. "It's nice to meet you." Ryan held onto his hand for just a fraction too long. I was amazed that he refrained from winking at the guy.

Ashley was staring at Greg in a most unflattering way, as if she couldn't believe someone so good looking was gracing our apartment. Fearing that one of them might soon do something to embarrass me, I hurried to get my purse. "Should we be going?"

Greg glanced at his watch. "We should." He grinned at Ashley. "Sorry to dash, but I made reservations."

"No problem," she breathed. "Maybe next time."

"Absolutely." Greg held out his arm to me, and I stepped toward him. In one smooth motion his hand was behind my back, gently pushing me toward the door.

I glanced over my shoulder at Ash and Ryan. They were both staring at me, wide-eyed. I felt a little flash of amusement. Maybe they wouldn't be quite so quick to tease me about my hopelessness with men.

Then again, I thought, as Greg led me through the open door, the night had barely started. Plenty of time for me to screw it all up.

Chapter Twelve

Amazingly enough, I didn't screw it up. Not even close. My date with Greg was one of the nicest that I'd had. Like, ever in my life.

The restaurant was great. Even though it was clearly nicer than any place I had ever been in, it was comfortable and unpretentious—I had absolutely no problem determining the correct fork. And the food...well, I had never had food like it before. It was absolutely amazing, every one of the full five courses. Greg ordered the filet mignon (I tried hard not to gasp when I saw the price), and I chose the somewhat less expensive sea bass. Even this made me feel guilty. I had never let anyone spend so much money on me before. My internal objections were silenced after the first bite. The buttery fish practically melted in my mouth. It was all I could do not to moan aloud.

Greg was completely polite to me the entire night, warm even. He was interested in my work, and laughed when I told him about the geriatric brigade at the clinic. He asked me a million questions about what it had been like to grow up in Alpena. He seemed genuinely interested in hearing about Ashley and Chris and Ryan and how we had all met.

I quickly found that I was interested in him as well. Greg worked as a real estate broker, his market focusing on the northern suburbs, though he had been doing more and more work downtown. Judging from his impeccable suit, the Jaguar he had picked me up in, and his insistence on paying the entire bill, I assumed he was pretty successful. Greg had grown up in the area and remained close with several friends from high school, to whom he was clearly deeply loyal.

We talked about our shared love of sports. He was very excited when he found out I was a runner, even suggesting we train together sometime; he was preparing for the Detroit Marathon in October.

But it wasn't until the topic of our families came up that I felt we truly bonded. After hearing a story about his older brother, Daniel, I asked after his parents.

"My father is great," he said. "One of the best men I know. He's remarried and lives in Florida now." His voice grew soft. "My mother passed away five years ago."

I gasped. "Oh, Greg. I'm so sorry to hear that," I whispered. As he stared down at the table, unmoving, his face looked so tortured, the pain exposed and naked. I reached my hand across the table and covered his with my own. "I lost my mother too."

He looked up then, his eyes wide. "Really?"

I nodded, feeling tears start to prick my own eyes. I rarely ever opened up about my mother to anyone. When the subject did come up, I would typically try to brush it off, as if it was no big deal anymore. I had spent the last ten years pretending I was over it. But sitting there with Greg, I knew I didn't have to pretend, not when it came to this.

"How old were you?" he asked, turning his hand over so our palms were now touching. In spite of the terrible subject matter, the contact still sent a little thrill through me.

"I was twelve," I said. "She had cancer."

"Mine too," he whispered. "That must have been terrible for you, being so young."

"No more terrible than it was for you, I'm sure. Your mother is your mother, no matter how old you are."

He nodded, now folding his fingers over mine so we were fully holding hands. I didn't feel nervous anymore, like I had every other time he had touched me. Now it just felt right.

"I think we may be kindred spirits, Emily," he said, smiling at me.

I smiled back. "I think you're right."

***

The entire next day I felt like I was walking on air. For all of my scoffing at Ashley and her romantic obsessions, I honestly felt like I was Cinderella. Who ever would have thought that such a good-looking, interesting guy would be so nice? And even more, that he would be interested in me. It was, to be honest, like something out of a fairy tale.

"I told you," Ashley said, over and over again as we partook in our Sunday morning ritual of reading the paper at Delmar, our favorite diner. "I told you this could be something."

Even her smugness couldn't put a damper on my mood. I spent most of the meal ignoring my paper and my bagel, staring out the window as I thought about Greg. My coffee even got cold before I had finished, which never happened to me.

"You're starting to freak me out," Chris said finally.

"Why?" I asked, pulling myself away from my recollection of the way Greg had insisted on walking me all the way upstairs before kissing my lightly on the cheek. He was so romantic, such a gentleman. And when he had leaned in close like that, I could smell the delicious aroma of his cologne, some musky scent that just screamed masculinity.

"Oh my God, you're still doing it," Chris said, tossing his napkin at me. "You're officially mooning now, Emily Donovan. I never thought I'd see the day."

"Sorry," I said, grinning sheepishly. "I just can't help it. It went so well."

"We know," Ryan said, not even looking up from his paper. "You told us. Several times."

"You're one to talk!" I cried. "You were the one that was so into this, convincing me it was a big deal. I would think you'd be a bit more interested in how successful it was."

"Don't mind him," Ashley said. "He's just jealous. After you left, we went out dancing, and he struck out with all the guys he hit on."

"Sorry, Ry," I said. "Do you think if we sat down and watched some romantic comedies you might have better luck?"

"Ha ha," he said, his voice flat. "So funny."

"Don't be upset," Ashley said. "Maybe if you're very good, Emily will bring her new man over to hang out at the apartment. Wouldn't that cheer you up?"

"He's hardly her new man," Chris said, looking up from his paper. "I mean, they've had one date."

"That's very true," Ashley said. "But I have a good feeling about this one."

I couldn't help but return her smile. It might be silly, but I had to agree with her. I'd never been out with someone like Greg before. Maybe this would be different.

"Oh, no," Chris said, staring at my face. "You've gone all crazy girl on me, haven't you?"

"What are you talking about?"

"You're gonna turn into one of those girls that is

convinced she's found The One after a single good date. One of those girls that starts calling obsessively and driving by the guy's house." He gave a mock shudder. "Next thing we know, you'll be doodling your married name on a piece of paper and checking out wedding dresses online."

"Give me a little credit!" I cried, my neck turning red. It was a total coincidence that I had, in fact, had a dream that I was wearing a wedding dress just the night before. I mean, that wouldn't have had anything to do with Greg. It was only our first date! Besides, you can't control what your brain does while you're sleeping.

Ryan was looking at Chris with an incredulous expression. "What experience do you have with obsessed women?" he asked. "Did I somehow miss the part of the last seven years where they were breaking down your door?"

I laughed along with Ashley, but Chris seemed unperturbed.

"I just want to make sure you don't get carried away," he told me. "Look, it's only been a few weeks since all that shit went down with Dylan. And I know how sensitive you are, Em. I just don't want you to get hurt if this doesn't turn out. You barely know the guy."

"You're right," I said, the little bubble of happy certainty in my chest deflating slightly. It was silly to be so sure that anything more would happen with Greg. He had said he would call me, and I would have put money down that he was interested in me, judging from his behavior the night before. But God knew how wrong I had been about guys in the past. Who was I to judge how he was feeling?

"He probably won't even call back," I said, sitting up taller and arranging my face in what I hoped was a more detached expression. "Regardless, it was a fun date. It doesn't have to be more than that."

"Don't say that!" Ashley looked scandalized. "You have to have hope that it will work out!"

I shrugged, determined to be in control. "If he calls, great. If not, I'll live."

Chris gave me an approving nod before retuning to his paper. I did the same, telling myself that I really meant what I had said.

Two minutes later, my phone beeped, and the bubble in my chest doubled in size. It was a text from Greg. Opening the message under my paper, I tried to keep the smile off my face as I read it. *Had a great time last night. I'm thinking about you.*

"What's it say?" Ryan asked. I looked up to see them all staring at me. Apparently, I was fooling no one.

"He's thinking about me," I said, and I knew my grin was as wide as my face.

"Oh God," Chris muttered under his breath.

I returned my attention to my phone, wondering how I should respond.

"Tell him you're thinking about him too," Ashley advised. "And that you had a great time."

"Tell him you couldn't sleep because you were so happy," Ryan said. "Then tell him what you're wearing."

"Yeah, I'm so gonna do that," I said. I thought for a moment than typed out a quick response. *I had a wonderful time, thank you again! I woke up with a smile on my face this morning.*

I looked at it with satisfaction before hitting send. It was nice with just a hint of flirtation. Hopefully just what the situation called for.

A moment later, my phone rang. I looked at the

screen and almost spit out a mouthful of coffee. I gulped the coffee so fast I started coughing. "It's Greg!" I sputtered.

"Answer it!" Ashley hissed.

I quickly accepted the call and held the phone up to my ear. "Hello?"

"Emily?"

Greg's voice sent a little fission right into my stomach. How could someone even *sound* handsome?

"Hi," I said, aware of the three faces turned in my direction. I got up and made my way through the maze of tables until I was standing in the café's small entryway. "How are you?"

"I'm good," he said. "Your text made me happy."

"Good," I said. "I'm feeling pretty happy myself."

He laughed softly, the sound feeling intimate in my ear. Oh, I was falling fast for this guy. I knew the realization should scare me—cause me to put my guard up a little, but I just couldn't make myself do it. Particularly not after his next words.

"I hope this isn't too pushy of me," he said. "But I'd love to see you again. Soon. Could you have dinner with me this evening?"

"That would be great," I said automatically.

"Wonderful," he said, and I could just tell that he was smiling on the other end of the phone. "How about something low key? Do you like sushi?"

"I've actually never tried it," I admitted, feeling almost embarrassed. How unsophisticated could you get?

"You'll love it," he said. "I'll pick you up at seven?"

"Perfect."

"Good. I'm really looking forward to it, Emily."

"Me too," I said, unable to wipe the smile off my face.

After we hung up, I headed back to the table. I had a feeling I was about to get more ribbing from my friends for mooning. I couldn't care less.

Chapter Thirteen

"Five more, Frank," I said, patting him on the shoulder. "Just keep doing exactly what you're doing now."

I walked away from the standing leg station where Frank was carefully completing a set of leg lifts. On the other side of the room, Mrs. Z was propped up against a stack of pillows with a heat pack on her shoulder. I made my way to Zachary's table, a teenage kid who had broken his leg in three places playing football. He was determined to be back to game shape by the following fall, and I usually had to slow him down a few times a day to keep him from overdoing things.

"How's that feeling, Zach?" I asked. "Ready for your ice pack?"

"I can do another set," he said, grimacing slightly. I made out a thin sheen of sweat on his face, and shook my head.

"I think you're done," I said firmly. "I'll get you your ice pack."

I headed to the back hallway and pulled the pack from the freezer. Returning to the therapy area, I saw Sarah helping Philip up onto his table, a typical grouchy expression on his face. When she clasped his arm for support, he glared at her so intensely she actually looked scared. I grinned to myself and continued across the room.

When I got back to Zach, he was hurriedly trying to complete an extra set, a grimace of pain clear on his face. I pulled the curtains around his table, feeling like a private chat was in order.

"Enough," I said, placing my hand on his leg. "You're not gonna do yourself, or your teammates, any favors by getting reinjured."

"You don't know how frustrating this is," he muttered. "It's bad enough I'm missing basketball right now."

"I played sports," I told him. "And I had my share of injuries. I know exactly how frustrated you are." I adjusted the pack on his leg and leaned over so I was closer to his face. "But I also know how pissed you'd be at yourself if you screw up your recovery. So do what I tell you, okay?"

"Okay," he said, smiling sheepishly.

I patted his leg and winked at him. "Now if only I could get some of my other patients to put in half your effort, I'd be able to discharge the lot of them in no time."

I pulled the curtains back and found myself face to face with Elliot.

"Hey," he said, holding up two cups of coffee. "Got your caffeine fix."

"God bless you," I told him, accepting the cup gratefully. I took a sip and sighed in relief. "Thank you."

"You're very welcome."

"Elliot!" Mrs. Z called from her table. "Yoo-hoo! Elliot!"

He gave me an expression of mock horror before turning to Mrs. Z. "Hey," he said, a teasing tone to his voice. "You're particularly lovely today, ZiZi. I swear, you look younger every day."

"Don't encourage her," I muttered, but Mrs. Z was laughing happily.

"You like to tease an old woman," she said.

"Not at all. You really do look great." He lowered his voice to a loud stage whisper. "But you're going to have to stop flirting with me. You'll make Frank jealous."

"Ha!" Frank said, abandoning the standing leg station to join Mrs. Z and Elliot. "Why would I be jealous of a child?"

"Oh, he's no child," Mrs. Z said, looking Elliot over with a lascivious leer on her face. The tips of his ears reddened, and I laughed.

"You asked for it," I said. "I told you not to encourage her."

"Hit on someone your own age," Frank said. "Like Emily there, she could do for a bit of flirting."

I gave him a warning look. "I'm quite fine, thank you."

"Hell you are," Frank said. "I know you haven't found yourself a man since that Dylan. What are you waiting for, eh?"

"Actually," Elliot said, a smile forming on his face, "Emily had a date just last week, didn't you? What was that guy's name again? Bruce, was it? Didn't you really hit it off?"

I flipped him the middle finger, making Frank howl with laughter.

"That's the spirit, dear," Mrs. Z said. "Don't you let him tease you."

"Is Bruce the guy you went out with last night?" Sarah asked from Philip's table. Out of the corner of my eye, I saw Elliot's head snap in my direction.

"No," I said, glaring at her. The last thing I needed was for Frank and Mrs. Z to start grilling me about my new relationship.

"You had a date last night?" Mrs. Z said, sitting up eagerly on her table. I sighed. "Who was it? Did he take you somewhere nice? Tell us, tell us!"

"You are a bunch of old gossips," I told them, shaking my finger at them. "Don't you all have work to do?"

"Work can wait," Mrs. Z said, waving her hand dismissively. "I want to hear about this date!"

"Yeah," Frank said, grinning at me. "Did you do any necking?"

"Frank!" I cried. "Necking? Are you kidding me?"

"We just want to hear about him," Sarah said. "All you told me was that you had a nice night."

I sighed. "Fine, if I tell you about my date will you all stop with the chatter and get back to your recovery?"

"Yes, promise!" Mrs. Z said.

"Cross my heart," Frank said, his face solemn.

"Okay. His name is Greg Cook. He's a real estate broker, and he's very nice. We went out on Saturday and again last night. We had a great time. End of story."

"Hang on, hang on," Sarah said. "You went out twice in one weekend?"

"Yes," I said, shrugging. "We hit it off, so we decided to see each other again."

"That sounds serious," Sarah breathed. "Wow, Emily."

"Is he handsome?" Mrs. Z asked, her eyes shining. "Oh, I bet he's handsome!"

"Don't tell me he's one of those namby-pamby boys. One of those, whatchamacallit? You know, one of those metro-sexy boys."

Laughing, I turned to Elliot, sure he would share in my amusement. But Elliot wasn't laughing—he was staring out the window, a detached expression on his face. Before I could ask him if he'd heard Frank, Sarah was grabbing my arm and pulling me over to sit on Mrs. Z's table with her.

"Okay, you have to tell us what he's like. Come on! I haven't been on a date in months! I need to live vicariously through you!"

"Fine," I said, laughing. "I'll tell you about him."

"Oh, good," Mrs. Z said. She closed her eyes and smiled dreamily. "It's been far too long since I've been out with a younger man."

"Okay, so Greg is very handsome," I told them. "He's taller than me, and has dark hair and eyes. And he dresses very well."

"Mmm," said Mrs. Z. "He sounds perfect. He's in real estate? Does he make a lot of money?"

"ZiZi!" Sarah said, looking shocked. "You can't ask that!"

"Why not?" Mrs. Z asked. "Money is important! My second husband, Alex, lost all his money on the horseracing and then expected to live off me. I ditched his good-for-nothing bottom so fast!"

"So how 'bout it, sweetie," Frank asked. "Is he loaded? Drive a nice car?"

"He seems to be very successful in his business," I said, standing up. "And that's enough of this talk, now. I need to get back to Philip, and the rest of you need to get back to your exercise. And I'm sure Elliot needs to get back to the store."

"Yeah," Elliot said, turning to go. "Everyone have a nice afternoon."

I watched as he walked out the door, wondering what was wrong. He had seemed a little odd the other day, before I left for lunch. I hoped he wasn't having problems at work.

I turned my attention back to the group at Mrs. Z's table. "Seriously, you guys," I told them. "Back to work."

Back at Philip's table, I removed his heat pack. "Let's get you on your side," I said, as I rummaged through a drawer in search of a bottle of warming lotion for his massage. "Then I can work on those muscles." When he didn't move, I looked up from what I was doing. He was staring at me, an incredulous expression on his face.

"What?" I asked, feeling self-conscious.

He just shook his head. "Blind woman," he finally muttered.

"What's that supposed to mean?"

Philip just shook his head again, but finally turned onto his side, pulling up his flannel shirt a bit to expose his hip. I took that as my cue to get started. As I worked, I wondered again about Elliot's strange mood. He usually seemed so even-keeled about everything, the type of guy you couldn't upset if you tried. I promised myself I would talk to him tomorrow at lunch.

From my pocket, I heard my cell phone beep. I hesitated for a moment—I had a very strict policy about not texting in front of patients. But Greg had mentioned he would be in touch today... After the second beep, my curiosity won out, and I slipped out my phone, checking it surreptitiously under the massage table. *Drinks after work?*

I grinned, and went back to Philip's massage. The day was definitely looking up.

Chapter Fourteen

"Ash!" I wrapped my robe around myself and stuck my head into the hallway. "Ashley?"

"Yeah," she called, appearing in her doorway. "What's up?"

"I'm ready for you to do my hair," I said. "And will you look at my makeup. I *think* I did okay..."

Ashley joined me in the bathroom, peering closely at my face. "Not bad!" she said. "You've been paying attention."

"It would just be nice to be able to get myself ready," I muttered. "So that I don't have to feel like a five year old every time I have a date."

"At this rate, you're gonna get lots of practice." She pushed me down onto the closed seat of the toilet. "What is this, your third date in a week?"

"Fourth," I said, grinning happily. I still couldn't get over the fact that Greg had taken such an interest in me. In me! I wondered if it would ever make sense to me.

"You really like him, don't you?" Ashley said, looking down at me.

"He's so great." I grinned even wider. "He's so handsome and charming, Ash. And nice to me. And he's sophisticated, you know? Not like any of the guys we know."

"That sounds great," Ashley said. "Is he a good kisser?"

I could feel my face getting warm. For the millionth time, I cursed my propensity to blush at the slightest thing. "He actually hasn't kissed me yet."

"What?" Ashley stopped in the act of pulling bottles and brushes out of the cabinet to stare at me. "Three dates, and he hasn't even kissed you?"

"He's kissed my cheek." I blushed harder. "He's such a gentleman."

"Wow," she said, still staring at me. "That either means he really likes you or there's something wrong with him."

I stuck out my tongue at her.

"So where's he taking you tonight?"

"The casino." I felt a little tingle of apprehension. Greg had advised me to dress up, saying that he wanted to show me some high-roller VIP room. I knew I would be out of my element. I closed my eyes and took deep breaths, reminding myself there was no reason to worry.

The nice thing about Greg, which I would never admit to anyone, was that he had a habit of taking control of any situation we were in. I assumed it was just second nature to him, what with his successful career and everything. But it was nice for me because I never felt put on the spot. All I had to do in a scary situation (whether it be a posh restaurant or a VIP lounge at the casino) was relax and follow his lead.

"What are you wearing?" she asked.

I pointed at the back of the door, where my dress was hanging. I had stopped at Somerset on my way home from work, and I was rather proud of myself for being able to handle it without Ryan or Ashley. Granted, I had explained the situation to a sales associate and asked her to help me, basically letting her pick out the dress in the end. But, still.

"Nice," Ashley said, peering at the strapless midnight blue sheath. "Your hair is going to look fantastic against that color. We should definitely leave it down."

She ran her fingers through my wet hair, thinking. "Let's go straight," she said finally. "Straight and sleek to go with the sleek dress."

"I wear it straight every day." I made a face at her. "I could do that myself."

Ashley rolled her eyes. "You let it air dry every day then end up pulling it up into a ponytail. I had something a little more sophisticated in mind."

"Whatever you say," I said, deciding to trust her. She hadn't done me wrong yet.

Ashley worked quickly, rubbing some kind of serum into my scalp and blowing my hair dry with a wide paddle brush. When she was done with that, she squirted something else into her hands before running them through my hair again. Finally, she plugged a hair straightener into the wall and set it on the side of the sink to get hot.

"You're straightening my hair?" I asked. "It's already straight!"

"Trust me," she said. "This will be completely different than what you're used to."

And when she had finished, I had to admit that she was right. My hair hung in a sleek curtain down my back, definitely smoother and shinier than I had ever seen it.

"Wow," I whispered. "How'd you do that?"

"Next time I'll show you how." She looked down at her watch. "You should get dressed."

Ten minutes later I was ready to go. I stood in the kitchen sipping a glass of wine to soothe my nerves while I waited for Greg. It was hard to sit in the dress, and I was worried about wrinkling the silk, so I leaned against the counter.

"Are those the shoes you're wearing?" Ashley asked, frowning at my feet.

"What's wrong with these shoes?"

"They're a little low," she said. "And that heel is way too clunky."

"And that's bad?"

Ashley sighed. "They're dowdy. You look like a librarian."

"They're the only other heels I own." I was starting to feel a little panicky. I couldn't wear the red heels Ashley and Ryan had picked out with this dress. Why on earth hadn't I thought to get new shoes? At that moment, I heard the sound of the buzzer from downstairs. Greg was here. I looked at Ashley, sure she could see my nerves from a mile away.

"Relax, I have a pair," Ashley said, turning to the doorway to buzz Greg in. "They'll be tight on you," she called over her shoulder. "But you'll just have to deal with it."

I had just managed to squeeze my feet into the way too small heels when I heard the knock on the door. "God," I moaned. "These hurt like hell. Are you sure I can't wear my other ones?"

Ashley gave me a quelling look. "Fine," I muttered. "Will you just get the door?"

She dashed to the door, pulling it open to reveal Greg standing in the hallway. He was wearing a black suit with a black shirt, which was unbuttoned at the neck. It was the first time I had ever seen him without a tie. It was totally sexy.

"Hi, Ashley," Greg said politely.

"Hello," she said, sounding a little breathless. She clearly thought he was sexy, too, and the realization sent a little thrill of pride through me. How had I managed to get the sexy one?

"Emily's right here." Ashley moved away from the door, gesturing Greg inside.

"You ready?" he asked me without moving. "I'd come in, but we have reservations."

"Sure." I picked up my purse and tried not to feel put out. I had spent half an hour after work straightening the apartment, hoping that Greg would come in for a drink. I really wanted Ashley to get to know him.

As I stepped to the doorway, Greg held out a hand and placed it lightly on my shoulder, stopping me. "You look amazing."

I blushed once again, suddenly not caring about whether he came in or not. "Thank you," I said, feeling shy. He smiled at me, and I blushed even harder. I looked over my shoulder at Ashley, who was smiling at me broadly. "Bye."

"Have fun!" she called out. Then Greg was shutting the door behind me and we were off.

***

After an hour or so in the high-roller room, I realized that I wasn't feeling nervous anymore.

Bored was more like it.

At first I had been totally blown away by the surroundings. Greg had been met by a personal concierge, Travis, at the entrance to the casino. After Greg told him I had never been to a casino before, Travis offered to give us a tour before taking us upstairs. I felt a little hum in my veins as he led us around the floor. Something about the noise, the lights, and the happy anticipation palpable in the air made me feel excited.

Eventually Travis led us to a private elevator to take us up to the fourth floor where the high-stakes gambling took place. "I thought we'd hang out and play some craps," Greg said, wrapping his arm around my waist and pulling me close to his side. I felt a rush of pleasure and smiled at him.

"Sounds good."

Travis led us to a VIP room, and I had to fight to keep my jaw from dropping. It was very swanky, the type of place I would have thought you'd only find in Vegas. Scantily dressed waitresses were plying the high rollers with drinks and food. With the low lighting and posh furnishings, the atmosphere was cool and downright sexy.

"What minimum would you like, sir?" Travis asked.

"I'll start at one hundred."

"Very good, sir." Travis led us to a table, where Greg was welcomed by the dealer as he sat down. I wasn't quite sure what I was supposed to do, but Greg once again wrapped his arm around me and pulled me close, so I figured he wanted me to stand next to him.

For the next twenty minutes I watched as Greg played craps. He tried to explain the game to me, but I felt completely lost. I was picking up on the fact that Greg, and the other players at the table, were betting huge amounts of money on each hand. Like, pay my rent for a month type of money. It made me feel a little sick, and very much out of place. But since all I had to do was stand there, I tried not to let my face show how I felt.

"Ready to mingle a little?"

I was caught off guard by Greg's question, as my mind had been wandering for the last several minutes. "Sure," I replied, trying to refocus my attention on him.

He stood up from the table, his arm still tightly

wrapped around me, and led me to the end of the room, where a bar and seating area was busy with players apparently taking a break.

"I don't actually play all that often," Greg said in my ear. "My firm has club privileges up here, but I mostly use it for networking."

"Wow," I said, not really sure how to respond to that. Fancy clubs and networking were so far beyond my realm, it was hard to make conversation on the subject without sounding stupid. "Do you play any other games?"

"I like craps the best," he said. "But sometimes I'll play a hand or two of poker."

We had reached the bar now, and Greg ordered us each a glass of wine. I tried not to feel envious of the woman beside me with a bright purple cocktail. I wasn't sure what it was, but it looked delicious. When Greg handed me my red, it was hard to feel grateful, but I thanked him all the same.

"That's a great vintage," he told me. "Let it breathe for a minute and then give it a try."

"Do you know a lot about wine?"

"I've been learning," he said. "I find it very interesting. Maybe one day we can go to a tasting and I can teach you a few things."

A wine tasting sounded like the most boring day I could think of. I liked wine, sure, but the extent of my knowledge was that white should be chilled and red shouldn't. Ashley and I usually just picked up whatever was cheap from the grocery store.

"Cook, is that you?"

Greg spun around to face a middle-aged man. He was wearing a three-piece suit and had what appeared to be a full jar's worth of gel in his hair. At his side was a busty red head in a skimpy dress with a huge swath of diamonds at her neck. She would have been pretty if she weren't wearing so much makeup.

"Jeremy, great to see you!" Greg's whole face lit up. You would have thought this Jeremy guy was his best friend. "And Kari, how are you?" He shook hands with Jeremy and leaned forward to kiss Kari's cheek.

"This is my date, Emily," he said, giving my side a little squeeze and smiling at me.

Jeremy smiled at me before turning back to Greg. "I thought you were going to call me about that Carter deal." He shook his finger at Greg. "Are you holding out on me?"

Greg laughed. "My client wants to get a feel for all of their options first," he said. "But don't worry, I'll give you a call."

"Well, I'm glad I ran into you. I wanted to give you a heads up on the MacArthur acquisition. Things are really heating up."

It went on and on like this. For the next fifteen minutes, Jeremy and Greg talked shop while Kari and I stood there, looking around the room. She seemed perfectly content to stand there and look pretty (or was she just drunk?), but I felt boredom creep over me almost immediately. When the two men finally shook hands, promising to talk more on Monday, I was so relieved I thought I might cry.

"Having fun?" Greg asked, smiling at me.

I looked at him, confused. Did he really think this was fun for me? "Um, I think your networking is a little over my head, to be honest."

Greg laughed. "Consider yourself lucky. You get to look around, enjoy the atmosphere, and drink your wine. I have to bullshit with a bunch of smarmy executives." The look on his face was so adorable, I couldn't help but laugh.

"I guess you're right."

He stared at me intently for a moment. "You really do look amazing tonight," he said, leaning a little closer to me. His proximity seemed to set off a million little tingles all across my skin.

"Thank you," I whispered.

He was watching my lips now, and his eyes seemed to darken slightly. *He's going to kiss me,* I thought, with a little leap of my heart. Before I could decide if I was excited or scared, another man came up next to him and tapped his shoulder.

"Greg!"

"Matthew!"

And off they went again. This time I tried to take Greg's advice. I sipped my wine and looked around the room, taking it all in. I saw men and women dressed to the nines, jewels and perfectly white teeth sparkling in the dim lights as they drank and talked. On the far side of the bar, I watched as that Kari woman pounded glass after glass of champagne. Seriously, she must have had four in the ten minutes that Greg was engaged with Matthew. I could already see her start to tip slightly on her stilettos.

"You ready to get out of here?" Greg asked in my ear.

"Already?" On the inside, I was practically cheering. I didn't want my time with Greg to end, but I also had no desire to stand in this room while he schmoozed either.

"I have tickets for the show downstairs." He grinned at the surprise on my face. "I thought you might enjoy it."

"Wow! Thank you, Greg! What's the show?"

He shrugged. "I'm actually not sure. But the tickets were really hard to get, so it must be popular.

And we have great seats. Shall we?"

He pulled my arm through his and led me to the door. As if by magic, Travis appeared to take us back downstairs. Once we were seated in the theater (front and center, just like Greg said), he let us know he'd be sending a waiter our way momentarily.

"Did you like that wine?" Greg asked, taking my hand in his.

"Um, yes, it was very good," I said, thinking that the cheap stuff from the gas station was nearly as good. Apparently, I wasn't much of a wine aficionado.

When the waiter arrived, Greg went ahead and ordered both of our drinks again—more wine. I tried not to feel disappointed that I was still missing out on the mystery purple cocktail. I would probably be too embarrassed to drink something so froufrou in front of Greg anyhow. I wondered what it had tasted like…

Once the lights went down, Greg wrapped his arm around my shoulder, and the feel of him, so big and solid against me, made me forget my complaints at once. He was so handsome, seemed so worldly and sophisticated. I felt giddy just being with him.

The entertainment was a magician. At first I thought it would be cheesy, but he turned out to be really cool. He brought a bunch of audience members up on stage and did a funny bit where he tried to read their minds. Then he made one lady's necklace and ring disappear. When they somehow ended up in her husband's pocket, I decided I was fully impressed.

By the time the show was over, I was feeling exhausted. I'd had three glasses of wine, my shoes hurt, and I had spent a good portion of the evening trying to keep myself entertained. It had been a long night. On the way home, Greg played some soft classical music; between the mellowing affect it had on me and the comfort of his heated leather seats, I had a hard time keeping my eyes open.

"You okay?"

I looked up at Greg, trying to rouse myself a little. "Sure." I smiled. I looked out the window behind him and realized we were outside of my apartment. "Wow, I must have dozed off. I'm sorry."

"Don't worry about it." Greg leaned closer to me, picking a strand of my hair off of my shoulder and rubbing it between his fingers. "I like that you feel safe and comfortable with me."

"I had a really nice time tonight." I was hyper aware of his proximity, of his finger tips gently rubbing on my hair. It felt like such an intimate gesture, it made my stomach flip in a really good way. Like riding a roller coaster.

"I love your hair like this," Greg said softly, letting the strand slip through his fingers. He leaned closer to me, practically whispering into my ear now. "It's very sexy, all sleek and soft. You should wear it like this more often."

"Okay," I whispered, feeling completely overwhelmed by the nearness of him. His voice was husky in my ear, the smell of his cologne practically overpowering my senses. How could any man be this attractive?

"Emily," he whispered, moving even closer to my ear. "I really like you."

"I like you too." I wished, at this seemingly pivotal moment, that he was looking at me, instead of staring at my hair. But when he leaned in to kiss me, I forgot about any objections.

Greg's mouth was warm, his lips soft against mine. It was a lovely kiss, gentle and sweet. It made me feel nice and warm inside, like I had just had a mug of hot tea. It was nice.

Okay, so there weren't any fireworks or choruses of angels singing in my head. Time didn't stand still when he kissed me. *But there's plenty of time for that kind of thing later*, I thought, as I climbed out of the car and headed up to my apartment.

If that kind of thing even existed.

Chapter Fifteen

"So what's this I hear about your new boyfriend?" Brooke asked the moment I picked up the phone.

"Hello to you too."

"Yeah, yeah. Hello, how are you, I miss you. All that crap. Now get to the good stuff. Who's the guy? And why the hell is this the first I'm hearing about it?"

"I didn't want to make a big deal out of it." I leaned back on the couch, putting my feet up on the opposite arm. "It's still pretty new."

"Well, according to my sources, it *is* a big deal. Like, see each other every single night kind of deal."

"You've been talking to Chris, I presume?" I said.

"Yes, I had to resort to asking Chris about my best friend's love life because *someone* didn't feel the need to tell me herself."

"Sorry, Brooke," I said, feeling a little guilty. "I just didn't want to turn it into some big production. I want to see how things go first."

"Were you worried I would disapprove?"

"Why would you disapprove?"

"Chris says you're moving too fast."

I threw my hands up in the air and looked around the room, wishing there was someone there to share in my incredulity. "Chris is getting mighty opinionated when it comes to my dating, isn't he?"

"He was just telling me what he thought." Brooke was quiet for a moment. "So. *Are* you moving too fast?"

"I haven't even slept with him!" I cried.

"That's not what I mean. Actually, I would be less concerned if you *had*. The fact that you're waiting means it must be serious."

"Which is something you should be concerned with?"

I couldn't believe I was having this conversation. I had been dating Greg for three weeks now. Yes, we had been seeing an awful lot of each other. But what was the big deal? He continued to be nothing but a gentleman to me—he treated me better than any guy I had ever been with. Plus, he seemed determined to show me a good time and expose me to new things. Why *shouldn't* I want to be with him as much as possible?

"That's not what I meant," Brooke was saying. "I just feel like maybe there's something you're not sure of, since you haven't told me anything about it."

"I'm sorry." I blew out a gust of air. "What do you want to know?"

"Well, tell me about him!"

"Okay, let's see. His name is Greg Cook. He's twenty-nine, and he works in real estate. He sells all those big mansions up in Bloomfield Hills, remember that time you visited and we drove around up there?"

"Yeah, I was trying to find Eminem," she said, and I laughed. As soon as Brooke found out I was going to be living near Detroit, she became convinced I would run into Eminem one day.

"Yeah, around there. So yeah, that's what he does. And he's pretty successful. He's got a great apartment in Birmingham, and he's always taking me out to really nice places." I felt a flicker of pride, which I knew was ridiculous, so I tried to squash it. "And he's very, very nice to me and really seems to like me. So it's going great."

"Okay, but what's he *like*?"

"I thought I just told you."

"You gave me his stats," she said, and I could practically feel her rolling her eyes the way she did when someone wasn't following her. "I want to know about *him*. What does he like, how does he make you feel? What kind of sense of humor does he have? What's his taste in books and movies?"

"Jesus, Brooke. I've only been dating him for three weeks."

"Don't you think all those things are important in getting to know someone?"

"Of course." I sighed. Why was it that Ashley was completely over the moon about Greg, convinced I was going to marry him, while Brooke had to give me the third degree? Why couldn't there be some happy medium for my friends to agree on—like normal people would.

"We're still getting to know each other," I told her. "But from what I can tell, Greg is very cultured and sophisticated. He's different from most of the people I know. It's ... it's nice. He's taking me to a vineyard out in the middle of the state in a few weeks for a wine tasting. I'm really excited about it."

"You are?" Brooke didn't sound convinced. "That doesn't really sound like your thing."

I felt a prickle of defensiveness. "Maybe because I've never tried it before."

"Don't get mad," she said. "I'm just worried."

"Really, Brooke? I couldn't tell. Maybe you should try to be a little more obvious." I knew my tone was sarcastic, pissy even. But I didn't care. Why did she have to try and bring me down? Couldn't she tell I was excited about this?

"Emily." Her voice was calm; apparently she had

chosen to ignore my obvious annoyance. "I just don't want you to rush into something. Take your time and get to know him, that's all."

"That's exactly what I'm trying to do," I shot back.

"Good," she said brightly. "Then I'm really excited for you, and I hope you'll keep me updated."

I sighed. Brooke may be pushy, but it was impossible for me to stay mad at her.

"So what's new up north?"

"The ice is finally starting to melt," she said. "There is talk of getting some boats out on the water soon."

"I'm totally jealous right now, you know," I said. "Do you know how long it's been since I've been out on the water?"

"Why don't you get your ass up here then? Bring your new fancy man and let us all meet him."

I tried to picture Greg up in Alpena, but for some reason the image wouldn't form in my mind. "Maybe I will," I said. "But I think I'll wait until the ice has *actually* melted. Have you forgotten about the traditional March storm?"

She groaned. "I'm trying to forget it, believe me." She was quiet for a minute. "Your dad would probably love to see you."

I felt a surge of guilt. "God, I'm a terrible daughter, aren't I?"

"No, you're not." Her voice was soothing. "But you will be if you wait much longer."

I laughed. "Good point. Okay, I should probably get going. I have a date with my fancy man tonight."

"Okay. Well, have fun. And maybe try to expose him to some of the stuff *you* know about. You might not be super sophisticated, but you are a pretty cool girl, you know."

I snorted. "I'll keep that in mind."

Once I was off the phone with Brooke, I closed my eyes and leaned back against the couch cushions. I should be getting up to get ready. Greg was cooking dinner for me at his apartment that night. But talking with Brooke had created a little seed of worry inside me. The fact that Chris was worried—worried enough to actually go to Brooke with his concern—had thrown me. Was I moving too fast?

I thought back over the last weeks with Greg. It all seemed like a whirlwind to me, from our dramatic meeting, to that perfect first date, to all the time spent since. Greg made me feel special. How could I not, with a guy like him showing so much interest in me? He was everything that I had always seen as being out of my reach—worldly, charming, wealthy, and seriously good-looking. It still surprised me that he would want to spend time with me.

Okay, maybe it was true, what Brooke had hinted at. We rarely spent very much time doing things that were very "me". Outside of our now typical Saturday morning jogs, everything we had done together had been completely Greg activities: dinners in fancy restaurants, nights out at posh clubs, playing tennis with his co-workers, networking with wealthy potential clients. I couldn't see a lot of myself in our activities.

But that made sense, didn't it? Greg was just more experienced than I was. What was I going to expose him to? Was I supposed to have him come hang out at the clinic while I chatted with Frank and ZiZi? Was I supposed to drag him along to the weekly Brew and View with Ryan and Chris?

Actually, maybe that wasn't the worst idea in the world. Maybe I could ask him to spend some time with my friends. Not at the Brew and View, that was totally not his scene. But why couldn't we all go out to dinner together, or something like that? Maybe if I could incorporate my friendships into my new relationship, everything wouldn't seem so foreign to me.

I smiled as I jumped up from the couch. I only had about forty-five minutes to shower and get ready, and suddenly I was looking forward to the evening a whole lot more.

***

"Pass me that garlic, would ya?"

I leaned over the counter to grab the bulb, handing it to Greg.

"Thanks." He smiled at me as I settled back on my stool.

"Where'd you learn how to do all this?" I asked, looking around at the various cooking odds and ends scattered around the stove where Greg was stirring something in a pot. He put a little bit on the wooden spoon, holding it out for me to taste. It was a sauce of some kind, and it smelled delicious. I took a taste and closed my eyes; it tasted even better.

"I've taken some classes," he said. "Mostly while traveling. I enjoy it."

"Well, you're pretty damn good at it." I thought about my kitchen at home, where the only appliance to get any use was the microwave. I couldn't even identify half the ingredients Greg had spent the last half hour dicing and sautéing.

"You don't cook?" He paused in his stirring to look up at me.

"Not a bit. I am culinary challenged."

"Maybe we should sign you up for some lessons." Greg raised his eyebrows at me, a teasing smile on his face.

"I'm perfectly content to let you do the work." Greg's smiled slipped a little bit.

"You'll want to be able to cook for your family one day, won't you?"

I shrugged. My mom had never been much of a cook; I figured I got my saucepan scorching from her. Usually our meals were cooked on the grill by my dad. We were big meat and potato people.

"I'm almost done here," Greg said. "Wanna set the table?"

"That I can handle." I stopped to kiss his cheek as I passed, and his face seemed to light up. Greg was really big into casual displays of affection like that. It was one of the sweetest things about him. He had told me once that his mom and dad had always been that way, holding hands, kissing each other, even after twenty-five years of marriage.

The first time I had been in Greg's apartment I had felt very out of place. For starters, it was huge. Bigger than my dad's entire house. There were three bedrooms, each with its own bathroom, and everything in the place was top of the line. Granite counters, crown molding, flat-screen TVs, polished wood floors, stainless steel appliances. Unlike Ryan's apartment, which was similarly high-end, but very modern, Greg's place had a homier feel. It was the kind of apartment you could imagine a young family living in—if that young family had the money to live in one of the nicest apartment buildings in a wealthy town like Birmingham.

I brought the stack of plates that Greg had gotten out over to the dining room table. I had learned pretty quickly that Greg insisted on a properly set table. He had shown me the correct way to lay out dinner, salad, and bread plates, as well as the right silverware to use for each course. I went back to kitchen to get wine glasses—two each, for ice water and wine. Then I went in search of a lighter for the tall taper candles. I didn't have to look far; it was in the cupboard, exactly where it should be.

Once the table was set, Greg enlisted my help to bring out the serving dishes. I felt my stomach grumble as I sat down. The food smelled amazing.

"Hand me your plate," he said, holding out his hand. I did so, and he served me out a portion of some vegetable pasta concoction and a cut of some kind of meat, smothered in the mushroom sauce he'd had me sample earlier. It looked really tender, if a bit under done for my taste.

"It looks great," I told him, reaching for the salad bowl. "Thanks."

"I was able to get the veal for a really good price this morning," he said. "It can be hard to find the good stuff."

"Veal?" I asked, looking down at the plate. I had never had veal before. Wasn't veal production supposed to be really cruel?

"Don't you like veal?"

"I've never tried it," I said, feeling a little squeamish. I was no vegetarian. I came from a town where hunting was an all-seasons pursuit. Venison and wild game were standard fare. I pretty much considered steak, burgers, and fish to be three of the major food groups. But something about the thought of those baby calves, trapped and unable to move, made my stomach turn.

"You'll like it," Greg said, his voice dismissive as he turned his attention back to his own meal. "It's very tender."

It would be rude not to try it, I told myself. *Just don't think about it too much...*

"Are you excited for our winery tour?" Greg asked.

"I am. I haven't spent much time in that part of the state."

"It's very pretty." Greg reached for my wine glass, filling it from a bottle of Merlot. I wasn't crazy about Merlot, but I had learned very early with Greg that wine pairings were important to him. If he had selected that wine to go with this meal, he had a very specific reason for doing it.

"Thank you," I said as he handed my glass back.

"The wineries we'll see are pretty nice," he continued. "Of course, they have nothing on the Traverse City area. Someday we'll do a tour up there, and you'll see the difference."

I felt a little flutter of pleasure. It was nice when Greg talked that way—like the future of our relationship was a given.

"That would be great," I said. "Traverse City is beautiful."

Greg nodded. "Then again, once you've been to Napa and France, any winery in Michigan is going to pale in comparison. But they're still worth seeing."

"When did you go to France?"

"I spent three months there, actually, my senior year of college. Study abroad."

"Wow." The only other country I had ever been to was Canada. As it was about twenty minutes away from my apartment with Ashley, that was hardly an exotic trip. "I've never been abroad. That must have been an amazing experience."

"Oh, it was," Greg said, his face lighting up. He started to tell me a long story about the cities he had visited, the vineyards he had toured, and the restaurants where he had dined. I struggled to stay focused. Sometimes when Greg told me stories about his experiences, they seemed a little impersonal. He hardly ever talked about memories or anecdotes or people he had met. It was more like listening to someone recite a list they had checked off on an itinerary of Must-See-Places-in-Tuscany, or whatever.

It wasn't that he was boring. I mean, look at all the things he had seen and done. I probably just had a hard time keeping up because I hadn't really had any experiences myself.

That reminded me that I had wanted to talk to Greg about hanging out with my friends. By the time he had finished talking about his study abroad, we had both finished eating and were drinking our second glasses of wine.

"You know, Ryan spent some time in France after we graduated," I told him. "I think he was mostly in Paris though."

Greg nodded. "Paris is a beautiful city. One of the best in the world." He smiled at me, his expression so intimate it made my stomach swoop. "Perhaps we could take a trip there. I'd love to show you the sights."

My mouth dropped open. Casually mentioning a visit to Traverse City was one thing, but practically inviting me to Paris?

"That would be amazing," I whispered.

Greg leaned toward me. "There are so many amazing things in the world I want to show you, Emily. You have no idea."

"Like what?" I felt like my head was spinning. Brooke's warning about moving too fast flashed through my mind, but I squashed it down. What was I supposed to do, when a man like this was offering me the world?

Greg took my hand. "Let's go sit."

He led me over to the couch, pulling me down next to him. I snuggled into his chest, feeling small against his large frame. I had spent so much of my life feeling freakishly tall amongst my friends, feeling gawky and awkward. Being with Greg made me feel girlish in a way I had never imagined was possible. It might sound silly, but I loved it.

With a remote control from the side table, Greg turned the gas fireplace on in front of us. He pressed another button and the soft strains of classical music could be heard from some unseen speaker.

"This is the Madrid Symphony Orchestra," he told me, resting his chin on the top of my head. His voice was low, somehow soothing and exciting me at the same time. "I saw them perform when I was in Spain." He kissed my hair. "I can see us now, walking through *el Parque del Buen Retiro*, stopping somewhere for tapas, sitting in a café in Plaza Mayor, drinking wine and people-watching."

"That sounds beautiful," I breathed.

"You're beautiful, Emily." He tilted my chin up so I was looking into his face, so close to my own. His words, the nearness of him, had already sent a blush to my cheeks. "So very beautiful. You deserve to see all the beauty of the world. Though none of it will compare to you."

Wow. He was good. I mean, I know it was just a line, but still.

"Thank you," I whispered. Greg only shook his head, a slight smile on his face. Then he was kissing me.

As he wrapped his arms around me, and later, as he led me to his bedroom, his words kept running over and over around in my head. He thought I was beautiful. He wanted to show me the world.

"Emily," he whispered in the darkness, leaning over me on the bed. "I think I'm falling for you."

I looked up into his dark eyes. The spinning in my head, the swooping of my stomach, the mad beating of my heart, all threatened to overwhelm me. Maybe that's what I was feeling right now. Maybe I was falling for him too.

"Me too," I whispered, rising up to kiss him. "Me too."

I hadn't slept with many guys in my life. Brooke sometimes teased me about it, about how I took the whole matter way too seriously. Now, with Greg, I was glad I had been choosey. No one else had ever made me feel so special, so cherished. And even though I didn't feel the earth shattering around me, as Brooke so often claimed happened to her, it was one of the sweetest, nicest experiences of my life.

It wasn't until much later, lying in the warmth of Greg's arms as he slept behind me, that I remembered that I was going to ask him to spend time with my friends. *Oh well*, I thought, snuggling closer to him, my heart practically bursting with happiness. I had plenty of time for all that. I had a feeling this man was going to be around for a long, long time.

Chapter Sixteen

"What the hell are you so chipper about?"

I had been heading to the storeroom to get more resistance bands when I passed Kelly Lee, another therapist in the practice. Kelly was one of my least favorite people to work with. She had a crappy attitude and a tendency to be short with the patients, especially the elderly ones. But today, not even she could bring me down. I'd had yet another fantastic night with Greg the night before, and our winery trip was only days away.

I smiled at her. "It's a beautiful spring day," I said. "And I have fifteen minutes until my lunch break. What isn't there to be chipper about?"

"Whatever," she muttered, heading back to the therapy floor where I could hear Mrs. Z loudly opining about what she would do to "that handsome Brad Pitt" if only she could get him in a room alone. I smirked and continued to the storeroom.

At the back of the clinic, I saw that the door to the storeroom was already open, the light inside clearly on. I walked in and found Sam, the owner of the clinic, with a clipboard. He appeared to be taking inventory of the equipment.

"Hey," I said, surprised to see him. Sam's company ran an entire system of health care practices—from clinics like this to a nursing placement center to equipment and supply retail stores. He was usually far too busy to stop by, leaving the day-to-day running of the place to Michael.

"Oh, hi, Emily," he said, looking up at me. He seemed distracted, anxious almost.

"I didn't know you were here today," I said, passing him to get to the shelf that held the extra resistance bands. "How are you?"

"Fine, fine." He turned back to his clipboard. "Just trying to get a feel for the current inventory."

I frowned to myself. Sam tended to complain whenever we put in a requisition form for new supplies. Maybe Michael had placed an order recently. I hoped Sam wouldn't be a jerk to him about it. It was hard to run a clinic without the basics like stretchy bands and clean towels.

"Well, better get back out there," I said, holding up the package of bands. "These keep breaking on us. One stung Mr. Taylor's leg pretty badly when it snapped.

"Uh huh," Sam said, clearly not listening to me as he studied his clipboard. I took my bands and walked back out to the therapy floor to find Michael. He was standing in the back of the room at the dryer, folding fresh towels.

"Hey," I said softly, looking around to make sure Kelly wasn't in hearing range. "What's Sam doing here?"

Michael looked up at me, his expression clearly stressed. "He's still here?" He peered over my shoulder, as if he'd be able to verify that Sam was back there. "He came in this morning for a meeting, I thought he'd be gone by now."

"He's taking inventory of the storeroom."

Michael sighed. "Just great," he muttered, picking up a stack of towels.

"Is something going on?" I asked, narrowing my eyes.

Michael looked at me for a minute. "Nothing to

worry about," he finally said.

"Michael. Come on. I can tell something's up. Are you in trouble with Sam?"

"No, no, it's nothing like that," he assured me. "I promise." When I didn't look reassured, he went on. "Look, I swear I'll tell you if it gets serious, but right now there's just some talk of restructuring the company. Nothing has been decided so there's not much point in worrying about it."

"But—"

"And," he lowered his voice. "I would rather not talk about it with Kelly here, okay?"

I could understand that. The last thing anyone would want was that girl on their case. "Okay," I said. "But you better tell me about it if you hear anything else."

"I promise," Michael said, putting his hand over his heart.

"Emily," Frank bellowed from the front of the room. "Are you coming back or am I allowed to leave now?"

I shook my head at Michael. "Duty calls."

Frank was sitting on the edge of Mrs. Z's table. She actually appeared to be working today, for once. She was much more accustomed to leaning against her pillows with a heat pack, complaining about how her medicines made her too groggy for exercise. I usually reminded her that if she actually did some work we could probably get her off her meds a lot faster, but my recriminations typically fell on deaf ears.

"Quit your yelling," I said to Frank, grabbing his arm and pulling him up off the table. "If you're in such a hurry, you could have always jumped on the bike or gotten started on your weights."

"I never do anything without your express

permission," he said, grinning at me. "I know what you women are like. As soon as a man exerts any free will, you squash it right down."

"I'll squash something," I muttered, grasping his shoulders and pushing him toward the standing leg station. I opened the resistance band package and removed the lowest level band. It had the least amount of resistance built in, and would be perfect for Frank's next exercise.

"Stay still," I ordered, kneeling down at his side and wrapping the band around his ankles, tying the ends together so it was loose enough for him to walk. "Okay," I said. "Take a few steps and let me see how that fits." He did as I asked, and I stood up. "Looks pretty good. Okay, I want you to take nice slow steps from one side of the room to the other."

"How many sets?"

"Just keep going till I tell you to stop."

At the front of the room, a bell rang, signaling someone opening the door. I looked over to see Elliot entering the clinic, his lunch bag in hand. I smiled. It had been a while since we'd had lunch together. I was doing a lot of shopping on my lunch breaks these days, trying to keep my wardrobe up to par with the consistently fantastic string of restaurants and clubs Greg took me to. I had never worn so many dresses in my life—and I had finally just about mastered walking in heels.

"Hey, stranger," Frank called out. "Long time no see."

"What are you still doing here, old man?" Elliot asked, joining us. "Aren't you any better yet?"

"I'm getting there," Frank said, puffing up his chest. "I could give you a run for your money, that's for sure."

"Yeah, yeah." Elliot slapped him on the back. "I'd love to see that."

"Frank," I said, my voice firm. "Quit stalling."

"You see what I put up with?" he asked Elliot.

"Frank..."

"I heard you the first time." Frank got started, and I watched him for a moment, checking his form.

"Hey, buddy, looking good," Michael called from Mrs. Z's table.

Frank chortled. "You know what this reminds me of? This is just like when I left my girlfriend's house last night." He looked up at me. When my face remained blank, he went on, "She got stroppy when I called her by the wrong name, and I had to high tail it out of there with my underwear down around my ankles."

"Oh dear God," I muttered, turning away as Frank laughed uproariously at his own joke. Out of the corner of my eye, I saw Michael quietly cracking up. Even Elliot looked like he was trying not to laugh. "You want to take over with him?" I called to Michael. He nodded, still laughing. "Then I'm officially on lunch." I turned to Elliot. "Gonna join me? Or did you want to stay here and make crude jokes with this dirty old man?"

"Sorry, Frank," Elliot said. "I'm with Emily on this one."

Frank was still laughing as I made my way to the back hallway. I noticed the light to the storeroom was off, the door now closed. It seemed like Sam had finally left. My stomach dipped a little. Frank had kept my mind off of it, but now I was wondering again whether I needed to be worried about the clinic.

In the office, I pulled my Tupperware container out of my bag, taking the top off before popping it in the microwave. From my bag, I pulled my bottled water and an orange. When the microwave dinged, I took my food and sat down next to Elliot, who was already munching on his sandwich.

"What's that?" he asked, peering into the container. "Some kind of take-out?"

"No, actually," I said, smiling at him a little smugly. "It's leftovers. From the dinner I made last night."

Elliot made a big show of gasping and falling off his chair. I rolled my eyes at him, but grinned all the same. "I never thought I'd see the day," he said, shaking his head. "You actually cooked?"

"I've been practicing," I told him proudly. "I can already brown meat, sauté veggies, and boil pasta."

"Wow," Elliot said. "I'm impressed. What's brought on this new-found dedication to the culinary arts?"

"Greg enrolled us in a class," I said, stirring the rice and veggie dish in front of me. "We've only had one session but it was pretty fun, actually. He knows all the ins and outs already, but he's very patient with me. He says I'm actually not half-bad."

"Well, I'm glad you're trying something new." Elliot crumpled up his sandwich bag and pulled his bag of carrots closer. "So, are we ever going to meet this mystery man?"

"Probably." I frowned. It hadn't really occurred to me to bring Greg by the clinic. Though he'd picked me up from work a few times, he had never shown any interest in coming inside. "He works so much though, I don't know when he would have time."

Elliot nodded and went back to his food. It was quiet for a few minutes as we both ate. There seemed to be a bit of tension in the air, and I wondered if it was my fault. I wasn't overly concerned about what Michael had said, but maybe I was sending out some worried vibes.

"Oh, I meant to tell you," Elliot turned to me, his face eager. "The Adventurers Club is going camping this weekend. I think you should get Chris and Ashley and Ryan and come along."

I wrinkled my nose at him. "I cannot imagine Ryan camping. I mean, would he have to sleep outside? That is so not happening."

"The rest of you then," Elliot said, waving his hands dismissively. "Come on, I bet you and Chris know more about the outdoors than the whole club combined. I would think you'd be eager to get back to your roots a little bit."

"It does sound fun," I said, suddenly remembering the real reason why I couldn't go. "But I actually have plans with Greg."

"You see him, what, every night?" Elliot said, and there was definitely a little irritation in his voice. "You couldn't reschedule?"

"We're going away," I said, shrugging. "Sorry. It was going to be just a one-day thing, but we decided to take the whole weekend. Greg just booked a B&B."

Elliot was quiet for a moment. "Where are you going?" he finally said.

"Wine tasting, out in the western part of the state. I guess there's a bunch of wineries out there. Who knew, right?"

Elliot looked at me for a moment, a strange expression on his face. "What?" I finally asked, self-conscious.

"Nothing," he muttered, looking back down at his food. "I'm just remembering that time you told me that wine snobs were some of the most pretentious people on earth."

"I never said that!"

"I think your exact words were 'whenever someone talks about the undertones of a wine, I want to laugh in their face'."

I blushed slightly. That actually did sound a little bit familiar.

"That was before I knew anything about wine," I said.

"So Greg's been teaching you how to be a true connoisseur?"

Something about his tone made me feel defensive. "You can enjoy good wine without being a snob, you know."

Elliot just shrugged. "What do I know about it? I only drink cheap beer." Suddenly he stood up, though his carrots weren't even finished yet. I gaped at him in surprise. "I better get back. Lots of work to do."

"Hey," I called out as he reached the door. "Are you mad at me?"

He looked back at me, his expression unreadable. "Why would I be mad at you?"

Without another word, he walked out, leaving me with a feeling of discomfort in my stomach, though I had no idea why.

Chapter Seventeen

"So, what's this surprise?" I asked Greg, for about the tenth time since he had mentioned it on the phone that morning.

He laughed, starting the car. "You'll see in a minute."

Greg pulled out of the parking lot of my apartment building and headed north. Traffic was heavy, being rush hour, so I relaxed back into my seat, not knowing how long it would take us to get to wherever we were going. "Music?" Greg asked.

"Sure."

He leaned forward and turned on the radio. Not surprisingly, it was tuned to a classical station. Greg pretty much listened to classical music exclusively. Sometimes he added a little jazz, and, on rare occasions, the Beatles. Usually I found his taste to be relaxing, if not altogether exciting.

"Long day at work?" he asked, noticing how quiet I was.

"Yeah, pretty long. Glad it's almost the weekend."

"Me too." He took his eyes off the road to smile at me. "We're going to have a great time."

"What's the B&B like?"

"It got very good reviews on TripAdvisor," Greg said, signaling and changing lanes. Good reviews were important to Greg. "And one of my work associates has been there, said it's the best inn on the west coast. Oh, that reminds me. A friend of mine, Tom Johnson—we work together?"

"Oh, yeah." The name sounded vaguely familiar to me.

"Well I was telling Tom about our trip, and he said he and his wife had been meaning to get away for a while. He thought it would be nice to surprise her with a weekend away. What would you think about them joining us?"

"Um..." I had no idea how to respond. Would it be rude to say no? I didn't want him to think I wasn't interested in meeting his friends. At the same time, this was our first weekend away together.

"We wouldn't be together all that very much," he said, taking my hand across the gearshift. "I want you all to myself as much as possible. But I thought it might be nice for us to have some company for dinner one night, and maybe on one of the tours. What do you think?"

"Well, that sounds fine," I said. When he put it that way, it didn't sound like all that big of a deal. It would be silly to make a thing about it.

"Good," Greg said, kissing my hand. "Tom's wife is Angie. And she's really great. I think the two of you will have a lot in common. Maybe Tom and I can squeeze in a game of golf and you girls could go to the spa."

"The spa sounds nice," I said, smiling at him. "It would be nice to get a massage instead of always being the one to give them."

Greg laughed. "You poor thing. Maybe I'll give you a massage later." He wiggled his eyebrows at me, making me laugh. A moment later, I realized where we were going.

"Somerset?" I asked. "The big surprise is the mall?"

"Not the mall!" he laughed, pulling straight up to

the valet line. "It's what's inside the mall."

The valet approached Greg's window, handing him a ticket and taking his key. Before I even had my seatbelt off, a second valet was at my side, opening the door for me. I thanked him and got out of the car. From the curb, I could see several open spots within quick walking distance, but I knew better than to say anything. Greg always used valet.

"So, what's inside the mall?" I asked Greg as he came around to my side of the car to take my hand. "The suspense is killing me!"

"Patience," Greg said. He pulled me through the glass doors. Somerset was bustling and crowded, a mass of well-dressed people walking around on their cell phones, loaded down with carrier bags. Greg propelled me along until we reached the glass front of the BCBG store. Standing there was a stunningly attractive young woman, about my age, dressed in a smart black suit, a broad smile on her face.

"You must be Greg and Emily!" she said, reaching out to take my hand. "I'm so excited to meet you both!"

I looked up at Greg, totally confused, and he grinned at me. "This is your surprise!" he said. "Your own personal shopper for the afternoon!"

I stared at him. A personal shopper? What was he talking about? Seeing that my confusion had not abated, Greg laughed. "This is Laura." He gestured at the woman, who was still smiling at me. "I've hired her to help you pick out clothes. For our weekend away!"

"Wow," I said, feeling totally shocked by this development. Of all the presents I had ever received, this seemed like the strangest. How was I supposed to react to this?

"We're going to have so much fun," Laura gushed. "What a lucky girl you are, I would just die if my boyfriend did something like this for me!"

"I'm very lucky," I stammered. "Um, Greg, could I just talk to you for a minute in private?"

"Sure," he said, still grinning like he was beyond pleased with himself. "Laura, will you excuse us?"

"Of course," she said, the smile never faltering. It was starting to creep me out a little bit. "Take your time."

I led Greg a few feet away and looked up at him, not sure what to say. How could I tell him how weirded out I was without being rude.

"This feels like too much," I told him finally. "It must be really expensive."

He waved his hands dismissively. "Don't worry about it," he said. "It's something that I want to do for you."

"But...why? I mean, I have plenty of clothes. And it's nice that you thought of a personal shopper, but it's...I mean, I think I can pick out my own stuff, you know?"

Greg's smile didn't alter, but a certain steeliness seemed to come over his face, almost like his features had hardened. "I know you're capable of picking out your own clothes," he said, and his voice sounded ever so slightly strained. "But a personal shopper can help take you to the next level."

"What...what does that mean?"

"Emily," Greg sighed. "You dress very nicely. I can tell that you always put forth an effort, and I appreciate that. But you're on a budget. I thought it would be nice for you to get a few pieces that would really serve you well. I really enjoy your company, and I want you around as much as possible. That means I'm going to be asking you to go to nice places, maybe even work functions. I just think you'll be more comfortable in more appropriate clothes."

I felt color flood my cheeks. Was he saying that he was embarrassed to have me around?

"Take this weekend, for example," Greg said, squeezing my hands. "We're going to be staying at a very nice inn with lots of classy people. Don't you want to look and feel your best?"

"Of course," I said, feeling absolutely mortified.

"So why don't we go over and meet with Laura and have her help us pick out some nice things! It will be fun! Doesn't every girl want to go on a fancy shopping spree? Honestly, I thought you would be jumping up and down at the mere mention of it."

Was I being totally spoiled here? It was very nice of him, what he was offering. The clothes in that BCBG boutique were bound to be more expensive and stylish than anything else I owned, even the nicer things I had taken to buying recently. To put up money like that, just for me, was really very sweet.

As he took my hand and led me back to Laura, I tried to forget about what he had said about my clothes. *More appropriate.* It didn't matter, really, it wasn't like he was critiquing me. He probably just wanted to make sure I was comfortable. And, like he had said, what girl wouldn't want an all-expenses-paid shopping spree?

Me, a little voice said in my head. *I don't want one.*

But as Laura led me into the store and gushed about what looks she thought we could try to best suit my height and figure, I did my best to ignore the voice of protest in my head.

***

"Oh. My. God." Ashley said, staring at me with her

hands over her mouth. "I can't even believe this. You are so lucky!"

"Do you think so?" I asked, setting my bags down and plopping onto the couch. "I felt a little bit weird about it, to be honest."

"Weird?" she asked, sitting next to me. "Are you crazy?"

I didn't know how to describe it to her. The embarrassment I had felt, coupled with the uncomfortable feeling that Greg was dressing me up like a doll. None of it had sat well with me, though I tried to act grateful and not show my discomfort.

"So what all did you get?" she asked when it was clear I wasn't going to elaborate. She peered into the closest bag. "Oh, shit. Is that Donna Karan? Oh my God. I have to call Ryan. You're going to try all of this on for us. I am so totally and completely jealous."

She jumped off the couch and went to fetch her cell phone. I heard her jabbering in the hallway and closed my eyes. It had been a really long night. I wasn't sure exactly what I was feeling, or how to tell my friend about it, but I knew something was wrong here.

"He's on his way," she said. "He did a U-turn in the middle of traffic. I think he's almost as excited as I am!"

"I'm gonna go make a drink," I said. "Want anything?"

"Sure," she said, distracted. She was still peeking into bags. "I can't believe I promised him I would wait till he got here to look. What was I thinking?"

I went into the kitchen and pulled a bottle of rum out of the freezer. I found a couple of diet cokes in the fridge and poured them out into glasses, adding a splash of rum to each. I looked down at mine for a moment, then added another splash. A big one. I took a big gulp, letting the heat of the rum burn my throat on the way down. I leaned my head against the cool fridge door and stood that way for a moment, my eyes closed.

"Emily?"

I looked up and saw Chris standing in the doorway, a worried look on his face. "You okay?"

I forced a smile onto my face. "I'm fine," I told him. "Just tired." I held up my glass. "Want a drink?"

"Sure." He still looked worried, but he joined me at the kitchen table. "So Ash is out there freaking out about those clothes. She said Greg bought them for you?"

I nodded, taking another drink. "Isn't it sweet?" I tried to keep my voice light, happy. "He surprised me with a shopping spree. He even hired a personal shopper to help me."

"Wow." Chris was still looking at me closely. "That sounds very nice of him. Did you have a good time?"

"Of course," I said, taking another long drink. "What girl wouldn't love a personal shopping spree?"

"True." Chris took a sip of his own rum and Coke. "Most girls would." He was quiet for a moment, watching me. "But I never thought of you as much of a shopping girl. In fact, I thought you hated shopping."

I shrugged my shoulders. Chris was right. Shopping had never been my thing. Since I had started dating Greg and letting Ryan and Ashley dress me up, I had found the whole fashion thing to be a lot more fun. I really did enjoy the expression that would come into Greg's eyes when he thought I looked particularly nice. And it did give me a little boost of confidence when I left the house looking good. But still...in the master list of surprises that would make my day, a shopping spree would be pretty far down on the list.

"He was just trying to be nice," I said, wrapping my hands around the cool glass in front of me. "He thought I'd get a kick out of it."

"Does he know you don't really dig shopping?" I could tell Chris was holding back, that he was choosing his words carefully. I thought about what he had told Brooke and wondered what he really thought about Greg and me.

"I guess not," I said. "I mean, the subject has never really come up."

"The subject of what your interests are? Hmm. I would have thought that would be one of the first things you covered in a new relationship."

I stared at Chris' controlled face and felt a little dart of fear. His meaning was clear—Greg didn't know me. But that was silly, wasn't it? We had been spending nearly every day together for the last five weeks. Of course he knew me.

Then why did he think you'd want to spend a whole day shopping?

Before I could respond to Chris or to that annoying voice in my head, the front door banged open, and the sound of Ryan's voice drifted back to the kitchen.

"Get out here!" he called. "I've got to see this, you lucky little brat!"

I forced a smile for Chris. "Don't worry, okay? I had a good time with Greg, and I think it was really nice of him." I stood and pointed at Chris' drink. "That one was for Ash. You better pour her a new one."

I turned and walked out of the kitchen, leaving Chris sitting behind me. I could practically feel the excitement radiating out from the living room where Ashley and Ryan were waiting. Maybe if I tried very hard, I'd be able to feel a little bit of it myself.

Chapter Eighteen

"So, what do you think so far?"

"It's all very beautiful," I said, peering out the window at the rolling fields of vines around us.

"What about the wine?" Greg asked, taking his eyes off the road to glance at me. "Isn't it fascinating, seeing the process like this?"

"Uh...yes. I mean, absolutely."

Fascinating wasn't exactly the word I would have used to describe our tours of the wineries. It was possible that I was actually a little bit bored.

Ready to pull my hair out, bored out of my mind was more like it.

Okay, so maybe I wasn't having the best time of my life. I just never realized there were so many different kinds of grapes. Or so many different components that all had to be perfect in order for those grapes to turn into wine. Or so many different ridiculous, pretentious adjectives to describe wine. Woody undertones? Seriously? Who says crap like that?

"I'm glad you're enjoying yourself," Greg was saying, and I immediately felt bad for my negative thoughts. He really had done everything within his power to make this a nice trip for me. After we had arrived at the B&B, he took me out to a lovely, fancy restaurant, just the two of us. And the room he had booked for us was really nice, with a giant king-sized bed and the most comfortable mattress and linens I had ever experienced. Seriously, it was like sleeping on a cloud.

This morning, we had woken up early to start our winery tours. At first, I did think it was interesting. And the vineyards really were beautiful, row after row of grape vines stretching off as far as the eye could see. It was just, well, how much could you really talk about wine?

A lot, I discovered. It was now three p.m., and we had only seen half of the total number of wineries Greg had scheduled for us. Luckily, we were heading back to the inn to meet up with Tom and Angie. Greg was looking forward to his golf game, and I was eager to be doing anything that wasn't listening to some old dude with white hair and a tweed jacket drone on and on about the characteristics of his favorite vintage.

"I really think you're going to like Angie," Greg said, as we pulled into the circular drive in front of the inn. "She reminds me of you quite a bit."

"I'm sure we'll get along very well," I said. Greg had asked Angie to plan an afternoon of treatments at the spa for us. To be honest, I was pretty excited about it. I had never really experienced any kind of pampering. I hoped the company would live up to what I was sure would be a great experience.

Greg handed his keys off to the valet and came around to open my car door. I reminded myself that it was a polite thing to do. There was no reason to feel so antsy that he wouldn't let me open my own door once in a while. He had been raised as a gentleman, and I was lucky to have him.

"Ah, here they are," Greg said, smiling as he looked up to the front porch. "Tom! Good to see you, man!"

I followed his gaze to catch sight of an attractive couple standing at the top of the stairs. The man, whom I assumed was Tom, looked like the fair version of Greg. They were equally tall, equally well built, and finely dressed in khakis and sport coats. The only real difference I could make out was Tom's blond hair. Next to him stood a drop-dead gorgeous woman, a good six inches shorter than me, with highly teased blonde curls. She was smiling broadly as we approached, a heavy-looking sapphire necklace glinting in the sunlight on her neck.

"Hi," she called out. "You must be Emily!"

"Hello," I responded, smiling politely and holding out my hand. Angie didn't take it. Instead she pulled me into a tight hug. "I'm so glad to meet you," she whispered in my ear. "We've been waiting for Greg to find someone like you for ages!"

A bit caught off guard, I did my best to smile at her as I pulled back. "We're going to have such a great time this afternoon," she said, putting her arm around me and smiling at the guys. "Though I have to say, I'm a little angry they won't let us play a round with them."

Greg smiled at her. "Emily doesn't golf," he said. "But maybe next time."

"You don't?" Angie looked at me with an almost comical mixture of shock and pity. "But you really must learn. You'll love it! And it's such a good way to stay active."

"Emily's very athletic," Greg assured her. "Once I get her started, I'm sure she'll pick up the game in no time."

"Then there's hope yet," Angie said, squeezing my shoulders a little. "Until then, we'll have to satisfy ourselves with the spa."

"Sounds good to me," I said, feeling a little embarrassed by all the attention.

"Though I have to tell you," Angie said, pulling me

along to the doorway and whispering conspiratorially in my ear. "The spa isn't quite up to standards. I had a peek when I went to make our reservations. I do hope you won't be disappointed."

"I'm sure it will be just fine."

"I guess we should all head up to change," Greg said, taking my hand and pulling me away from Angie. "Should we meet back here in fifteen?"

"Great," Tom said, taking his wife's hand. It was only then that I realized Greg had never introduced me to his colleague. It struck me as a little odd, but I didn't have time to think about it much, with Angie squeezing my other hand and telling me that she couldn't wait for our afternoon to start.

***

"She seems, uh, nice," I said to Greg as we walked up the steps toward our room.

"I told you you'd hit it off," he said.

I wasn't exactly sure I would qualify five minutes of completely one-sided conversation as hitting it off, but I didn't belabor the point. I had something else on my mind. "Why do we need to change?"

Greg looked at me with a strange expression on his face. "What do you mean?"

"Well, what am I supposed to put on?" I asked, looking down at the Donna Karan khaki Capri pants and Michael Kors navy boat-neck tank I was wearing. When I had gotten dressed that morning, Greg had frowned at me and said something was missing. He dug around in my bag until he pulled out a white and navy striped cashmere sweater, which was now wrapped around my shoulders in a way I was sure would make Brooke shake her head in disgust.

"You can't go to the spa in that," Greg said now, an

almost incredulous tone in his voice. "And do you expect me to go golfing in this?"

I looked him over. To be honest, he was wearing the kind of outfit I totally imagined a golfer to wear, but I didn't say so. Clearly I had no idea what appropriate fashion was for a situation like this.

Back in our room, Greg took off his sport coat and carefully hung it in the closet. Then he turned to me. "Okay, spa wear." He walked over to my dresser and pulled open the second drawer. "I usually see the women in something like this." He pulled out a white cashmere sweater and laid it on the bed. Next came a matching pair of lounge pants. It had seemed strange to me when he insisted I buy it the other day. Why would I dress up so much for lounging around? Now I got it.

"Thank you," I said, feeling slightly stupid that I needed my boyfriend to pick out my clothes for me.

"No problem," he said, kissing the top of my head as he walked by. For some reason, the act made me feel ever so slightly worse.

Greg pulled off his sweater, and the sight of his chest beneath his Ralph Lauren undershirt momentarily distracted me. He really was a beautiful man. I turned to the outfit he laid out and began to dress, pulling my own sweater off and reaching for the button on my capris.

"You're so beautiful," Greg said, coming up behind me and wrapping his arms around me. "I wish we had an hour to just stay in this room."

"We could always be late," I said, turning around in his arms so I was facing him. I smiled up at him and wrapped my arms around his neck. "I wouldn't mind a little alone time with you myself."

Greg smiled and kissed the tip of my nose.

"Unfortunately, we need to get going."

"Oh, come on," I said, pressing up against him. "They can wait a few minutes."

Greg's face seemed to tighten a little, and he released me. "We won't be rude."

My embarrassment returned full force as he turned away and continued getting dressed. I felt silly and rejected, standing there in only my bra and capris. I quickly picked up the cream sweater and pulled it on. Once I had changed my pants, I headed to the closet to find some shoes.

"Probably sandals would be best," Greg called from the bed, where he was putting his golf shoes into a shoe bag. "You might get a pedicure. And maybe your hair in a ponytail?"

I looked over at him, the urge to tell him to go screw himself practically overwhelming me. Did he have to treat me like a child?

"Perfect," he said, once I was ready. He looked me over and smiled before coming toward me and taking my hand, bringing it to his lips to kiss it gently. "What a lucky man I am to have you on my arm."

I tried to smile, but the action felt wooden. As he led me out of the room, all I could think was that this weekend wasn't turning out at all how I thought it would.

***

After a few hours in the spa, my mood improved considerably. I had never felt so pampered in all my life. I had some kind of body scrub treatment done, before being all wrapped up in a mud and seaweed wrap. My skin felt amazing afterward, so smooth and soft I could hardly believe it was my own. After that, a nice woman named Denise came in to give me a hot stone massage. As she pressed the hot stones firmly into my muscles, I decided I could learn to like this kind of lifestyle just fine.

The other nice thing about the treatments was that they were done in a private room. Which meant no Angie. It wasn't that she wasn't pleasant, or anything like that. It was just that she was kind of...stupid. I know that sounds mean, but there was just no other way to describe her. I was used to celebrity gossip from Ryan and Ashley, but man, Angie took it to a new level. During our pedicures, she prattled on and on about Jennifer Garner and Ben Affleck and the new baby they were about to have. To hear her talk, you'd think she knew them both personally.

When I finally managed to get a word in, I asked her what she did for work, thinking maybe a more serious topic would make her more relatable to me. Instead, she stared at me as if she thought I was joking. "Work?" she asked. "I haven't worked since Tom and I got engaged."

"Oh," I said, not sure what to say to that. My own mom hadn't worked when I was little, choosing to stay home with me and take care of the house. I had a feeling though, looking at Angie, that she didn't take care of too much at all.

"I stay busy, of course," she said. "Don't think you have a life of boredom to look forward to when it's your turn!"

"My turn?"

"With Greg!" she said, as if I should know exactly what she was talking about. "When you guys get married!"

"Oh!" I was caught off guard. "Greg and I...well, we only just started dating."

"Sweetie," she said, giving me an even look. "I

have known Greg for two years now, and I can assure you he's never been this way with any other girl. He's rarely brought anyone to a work function before, let alone planned a weekend away like this, with such close friends. This is his way of telling you he's comfortable with you in his inner circle. He's crazy about you."

She smiled at me, the look on her face clearly indicating that I should consider myself immeasurably lucky. Instead, I felt something akin to terror.

This is too fast, I thought, over and over again. *Too fast*. I thought it as Angie talked about the cast of Jersey Shore for a solid fifteen minutes as we got French manicures. *Do I even want this?* I wondered as I returned to the room and took a long, hot bath before Greg came back. *Too fast*, I thought again as I blew my hair perfectly straight, the way Greg liked it, and got dressed in the clothes he suggested I wear for dinner. *This isn't right,* I thought, as I watched him pull a small blue box out of his suit pocket and approach me.

"I wanted you to have something, so you know how much I care about you," he said softly.

"Greg," I stammered, feeling the sudden urge to bolt from the room.

"Wait," he said, taking my hand. "Let me finish." He stared intently into my eyes, his handsome face close to mine. "I know we've only been seeing each other for a short time. But I also know how I feel. You're an amazing woman, everything I ever dreamed of. I've fallen for you, Emily Donovan."

He smiled, a little sadly. "My mother used to always say that when you care for a woman, you should give her something special, something that will last, to prove to her that you'll always be around." His gaze seemed to bore into mine. "You remind me of her so much. You have no idea." Greg opened the box, and I immediately recognized the diamond bracelet Chris and I had seen at Tiffany's. *Holy shit.*

"Please accept this from me," he said, his face open and eager. "It would mean so much for me to see you wear it."

"I can't," I whispered, staring at the bracelet. "It's too much, Greg. It's way too much."

"No," he said, placing his thumb gently over my lips. "It's nothing compared to you. Ever since our first date, I've been hearing my mom's words in my head, every time I look at you. It's like she's talking to me, Emily." He smiled sheepishly. "You probably think that sounds crazy, but it's true. It's like she's been telling me to show you, to prove to you that I care."

"Greg," I said, not knowing what to say. How could I argue with that? How could I tell him he was wrong? How could I refuse a man who was so good to me, who clearly cared for me so much? I wondered what my mother would try to tell me, if she were here right now. Would she tell me to refuse his gift, to make him feel terrible and unappreciated? Of course not—my mother put kindness and appreciation above all else.

Suddenly, all of my complaints and worries of the last few days seemed incredibly petty and childish. This wasn't some stupid high-school romance where everything had to go the way I wanted it. This was a serious, grown-up relationship. And Greg was perfect; anyone would have to see that. What had I been thinking?

"Thank you," I whispered, looking up at him with tears in my eyes. "It's beautiful."

Chapter Nineteen

The following Friday, I bustled around the office, trying to get my paperwork done so I could go home for the weekend. I was feeling disproportionately excited about my evening plans. I had arranged for a rare night out with my friends in celebration of Ashley's birthday. I felt as if I had been neglecting them, what with all the time I had been spending with Greg, and I really missed them. The idea of going somewhere casual and being able to wear a ratty old pair of jeans—or maybe even yoga pants!—sounded so good I almost wanted to cry.

Greg, however, was not quite so pleased when I told him. We were heading home from dinner on Thursday night when I mentioned it. Since we hadn't made set plans, I figured he wouldn't mind much. I was wrong.

"I had tickets for us to attend the symphony." He frowned. "Several of my work colleagues will be there with their wives." I felt a flash of irritation that he hadn't even asked, that he just assumed I would be free, but I tamped it down.

"I'm very sorry," I said. "But I haven't really seen my friends in ages. And Ashley's birthday is this weekend. I really need to spend some time with them."

Greg didn't respond, just stared out the windshield, the frown never leaving his face.

"I really am sorry," I said, once we had pulled up to my apartment building. I waited for him to respond or, at the very least, turn off the car so he could walk me up. After a moment, it dawned on me that he had no intention of doing so. Since our first date, I didn't think there had been a single instance where he hadn't walked me safely to my door. He must be really pissed.

For a second, I considered changing my mind and telling him that I would go after all. I was sure Ashley wouldn't mind too much. But something in me refused to back down. Why shouldn't I spend time with my friends?

"I'll call you tomorrow," I finally said, leaning over to kiss his cheek. Greg still didn't respond, staring stonily ahead. Suddenly, I wanted to laugh. It was so childish, the way he was acting. But I managed to control myself, instead getting out of the car without another word.

***

"Hot date tonight?"

I looked up to see Elliot standing in the doorway, his appearance snapping my thoughts away from the tense memories of the night before. It had been ages since he had been by, and I suddenly realized how much I missed our lunches.

"Hey!" I said, grinning at him. "How are you?"

"Not bad." He leaned against the doorway. "So, what's the rush?"

"Just want to get out of here," I said, shoving the last file into the cabinet. "It's Ashley's birthday tonight, and we're going out to dinner."

"That sounds nice. Where you eating?"

"Royal Oak Brewery."

Elliot closed his eyes and whimpered. "They have deep fried Twinkies there."

I laughed. "That they do. One of the best features of that place. That and the beer."

"Well, have fun." Elliot opened his eyes and smiled at me. "I'm totally jealous, by the way."

"You should come," I said impulsively. "There's gonna be a big group of us. Michael and Sarah are coming, too. It should be pretty fun."

"Yeah?" he asked, his face lighting up a little. "I might take you up on that. I didn't have plans tonight." He paused for a moment. "So, uh, will I finally get to meet the famous Greg?"

I shook my head. "Nope. He has a work thing. It's just me and my friends tonight."

"Well, I am honored to be considered in that category." Elliot winked at me. "What time?"

"Eight."

"Sounds good." He grinned, and it struck me again how much I had missed seeing him. "I'll see you there."

I grinned back. "I'm glad to hear it."

***

By eight thirty, I was well on my way to being drunk. I hadn't had much more than a glass or two of wine with dinner for the past month and a half. It was almost like I had forgotten how much I loved beer. The atmosphere of the Royal Oak Brewery was great, very relaxed and fun. With all of my friends there, and good food on the menu, I was feeling practically giddy.

"You're happy tonight," Ryan said, bumping my shoulder with his. "You must be in love."

I frowned a little. For some reason, I had no desire to talk about Greg that night. "I'm happy to see *you*," I told him. "I miss the crap out of you. Tell me what's new and exciting in the world of Ryan West."

Ryan snorted. "It's majorly exciting, let me tell you. Let's see. I go to work. I come home. I have no man waiting for me. I go out. I meet men. I fail to convince them to come home with me. They really should make a movie about me."

I giggled and leaned into him. "Oh, Ryan. One day you will meet the most perfect, wonderful guy, and he will fall head over heels in love with you."

"Yeah, that will be the day."

"I wasn't finished," I said, holding up my hand. "After he falls for you, you will dismiss him for not dressing well enough, or something equally stupid."

"Some pep talk!" Ryan shoved me away from his shoulder, but he was smiling.

"You know I'm right," I said. "You are way too picky for your own good. And you always seek out the totally wrong guy. You go after the slick, shallow ones just 'cause they're cute. Who knows what you might be missing."

"Oh God." Ryan sighed dramatically. "I've created a monster. Listen to you giving dating advice."

I laughed. "I just call it like I see it, buddy."

"How *is* the hot man?" Ryan asked. "You changed the subject before."

"He's good. Busy, of course."

Ryan looked at me closely. "You know, Chris said something last week, while you were away on your trip. I think he's worried about you."

I sighed. Since Greg had given me the bracelet, I had managed to put all those pesky doubts out of my head. But now, in the company of some of my oldest and best friends, I could feel them rearing up again.

"I just don't know," I said. "Sometimes I wonder if Greg really knows me, or if he wants me to be someone else. But then he goes and does something completely sweet and wonderful, and I feel like I'm being stupid." I thought about the bracelet, hidden in my jewelry box.

For some reason, I hadn't wanted to show it to anyone just yet.

"Have you told him any of this?" Ryan asked.

"No," I said, watching Elliot and Sarah across the table. Elliot was telling her some story, probably about hiking or something, and she was laughing her head off. "I just don't know how to bring it up without sounding stupid."

"Maybe you don't have to make a big deal about it," Ryan said. "Why don't you just casually drop hints about stuff you like? Or invite him to go do something you want to do."

I smiled at him, a little surprised. "That's exactly what Brooke said."

"Smart girl. Why didn't you do it?"

I frowned, trying to remember. "I'm not sure. But I think you guys are both right. I think I need to try to bring more of myself into the relationship."

"Exactly. You can't really blame him for not knowing you if you never tell him who you are."

"Right."

"And he should know who you are," Ryan continued, leaning his head on mine. "Because you're a pretty kick-ass girl. Even if you totally bruised my ego about men."

I laughed, and kissed him on the cheek. "Thank you."

For a moment, we sat in comfortable silence, watching our friends. Chris and Ashley were sitting together at the far end of the table. She was even tipsier than I was, her face flushed, clearly happy, as she sat on Chris' lap and gestured widely at a co-worker.

"You're running low there," Ryan said, pointing down at my beer. I glanced down and saw that he was correct; my glass was nearly empty. "Want me to get you a refill?"

"Naw," I told him, patting his arm. "I'll stretch my legs."

As I stood, I felt the room sway ever so slightly.

"Drunker than you thought?" Ryan asked, grinning at me.

"Sitting is deceptive." I steadied myself and headed to the bar, where the bartender was clearly rushed off his feet. Figuring it might be a minute, I hopped up onto a bar stool to wait.

"Having fun?" Elliot asked, sliding onto the stool next to me.

"I am." I smiled at him, a feeling of general well being settling over me. "There's nothing like a good bar with good friends."

"Very true. Whatcha drinking there?"

"I'm actually not sure," I told him, glancing at his glass. "I just ordered whatever Ryan got. What was that?"

"The Porter. It's fantastic, you should try it."

"Aren't porters really dark?" I scrunched up my nose. "I don't think that's my thing."

"This one has a bit of a chocolate flavor," Elliot said, winking. "I know how you feel about chocolate-flavored drinks. I have not forgotten the Mudslide Extravaganza that was your last birthday."

"That's a nice change," I murmured, without thinking.

"What?"

I looked up at him, realizing I should have kept my mouth shut. "Uh, nothing. Just, you know, nice that you're recommending something because you know I like chocolate. Instead of just because you think it's good."

Elliot looked at me for a moment. I had a feeling he wanted to say something, but the bartender appeared at that moment to take our orders. I decided I would try the Porter, and Elliot was right. Even though it was a tad more bitter than I usually went for, I could definitely taste the chocolate. It was delicious.

"So what's new with you?" I asked as we sipped our beers. "I feel like I never get to see you anymore."

Elliot shrugged, looking a little uncomfortable. "Not much. The store is pretty busy, which is a good thing. But I've been having trouble filling the afternoon shift, so I'm working a lot."

"And how are the Birdwatchers?"

"It's the Adventurers Club," he said, shaking a finger at me. "Which you totally know."

I grinned. "Sorry. Have you guys been having fun? What was it last weekend—a study of field mice?"

"You are just so funny, Emily Donovan," he said, taking a sip of his beer. "If you must know, we went rock climbing. And had a really good time."

"I'm sure you did. So, are there any outdoorswomen in this group of yours? Any prospects there?"

Elliot's ears colored slightly. "Uh...yeah, actually. There is this one girl."

I stared at him, feeling surprised for some reason. In the two years that I had known him, I had rarely heard Elliot talk about any girl. I had to admit, it threw me.

"Wow," I said. "What's her name?"

"Heather. She's...well, she's nice. And we have a lot in common. We've gone out a few times." He seemed to be having a hard time meeting my eyes.

"That's great, Elliot." I was aware of a little hollow feeling in my stomach, which made no sense at all. It wasn't like I should be jealous of a friend meeting someone—didn't I have the most perfect boyfriend? Even if he had been a little baby about me coming out with my friends.

"How about you?" Elliot asked, finally looking at me. "How's it going with Greg?"

"Oh, great," I said, making my voice bright. "He's wonderful. We had a really nice time on our trip. He even bought me this amazing bracelet. It was totally gorgeous, and way too extravagant." I knew I was babbling, and I forced myself to stop. Elliot just nodded and turned back to his beer. We each sat in silence for a moment, drinking.

"Wanna do a shot?" Elliot asked finally, breaking the tension that had seemed to settle over us.

"Sure," I said, grinning. "You pick."

Elliot waved the bartender over and ordered us each two shots of Jameson. "Holy, hell," I muttered, staring at the glasses in front of me. "It's been a while since I've done this."

"You can always back out," Elliot said. "I promise not to judge or ridicule you."

"Nice try." I picked up the first shot and held it up to clink against his. "Ready?"

Elliot nodded, and we both downed our drinks. The whiskey burned like fire down my throat, and I gave a huge shudder. Elliot laughed next to me. "You okay?"

"I'm fine," I told him firmly. "I finished it, didn't I?"

"That you did."

The atmosphere seemed to lighten a little after that. Elliot started talking about great whiskies he had tried over the years. I had forgotten how good he was at telling stories. He could somehow make you feel like you had been right there with him. Before long, I was laughing at the antics of people that I hardly knew. By the time we had the second shot, my buzz had deepened and I was feeling warm and happy.

I felt slightly annoyed when my cell interrupted us, but my happiness doubled when I saw the name on the screen.

"Brooke!" I shouted happily into the phone. "I miss you!"

"Wow," she said drily. "Just how drunk are you?"

I giggled. "Oh, I'm a little bit drunk. It's Ashley's birthday, you know. And we are having a parrr-ty." Next to me, Elliot started to laugh, and I stuck my tongue out at him.

"Where are you?"

"We're at the Brewery. Do you know they have deep-fried Twinkies here? Doesn't that sound amazing? It should, because it is."

"Emily," she said patiently. "Try to pull it together. I have news."

"Oooh," I said, clapping my hands together, which caused me to drop my phone. Elliot, still laughing, picked it up for me.

"Brooke?" he said. "This is Emily's friend Elliot. She's a little tipsy right now."

"Give me that," I said, swatting his arm. "Brooke!" I yelled loudly. "Brooooke!"

Elliot handed me the phone, smirking. "Control yourself, you lush."

I took a deep breath and nodded. "I'm better," I promised. He handed me the phone back, and I held it up to my ear.

"Who was that?" Brooke asked. "He sounded sexy."

I giggled, picturing Elliot that night at the party in

his black shirt and dark jeans. Hell, even tonight he looked pretty damn good in a crew neck sweater, the white of the button-down underneath contrasting with his tanned skin. Must be from all that time outside being nature boy. I shook my head slightly, trying to get control.

"You know Elliot," I told her. "He works next door."

"Oh yeah, vitamin man," Brooke said, her tone appreciative. "Not bad."

"What's the news?" I asked, impatient.

"Oh, yeah. So, there was a little fire at the inn yesterday."

"A fire?" I yelled, practically falling off my barstool. "Are you okay?"

"Everything's fine," she said calmly. "We stopped it before it really damaged much. But we had the fire department come in, and it turns out we have some wiring issues."

"Oh, no," I muttered. Brooke would just be approaching the busy tourism season in northern Michigan. She so did not need these kinds of problems.

"Apparently it's nothing all that major, and they can fix it in a matter of days," she went on. "But it means we have to close up for a while. Which in turn means I don't have to work. And since I don't have to work..."

"Are you coming down here?" I yelled, and this time I really did fall off the stool. Elliot caught my arm before I could hit the floor, and pulled me back up, rolling his eyes at me. I mouthed a silent thank you as Brooke answered.

"Yup! That is, if you'll have me."

"Oh my God! Brooke that would be awesome! I

miss you so much!"

On the other end of the line, my best friend laughed. "I miss you too, you crazy drunk. Now make sure you ask Ashley first, I don't want to impose on her."

"I will, but I know she won't mind. Oh, this is gonna be awesome. When can you come? I'll try to get some time off. We can go out and drink and watch movies and stay up all night talking…"

"Take a breath," she instructed.

"Right, sorry. I just really miss you!"

Her voice softened. "I really miss you too."

After I hung up, I turned to Elliot, unable to keep the smile off my face. "My best friend is coming to visit!"

"I gathered," he said drily. "That sounds exciting. Are you guys close?"

"So close," I said emphatically. "She's like my sister. You'll love her, she's the best." Suddenly, it felt like the whole room was spinning. "Ugh," I said, putting my hand to my head. "Maybe I'm too excited."

"Let's move back over there, and I'll get you a water," Elliot said, taking my arm and pulling me down from the stool. He led me back over to the long table and deposited me on a regular chair. It felt better to be a few inches closer to the floor than I had been on the stool. "I'll be right back."

I watched as he headed over to the bar for my water. *Such a nice friend*, I thought.

"Hey, Em, you have a minute?" I looked up and saw Michael sliding into the seat across from me.

"Hey," I said. "What's up?"

"Not too much," he said. "I just wanted to run something by you."

"Shoot," I said, trying to focus my eyes. I'd

definitely had one too many drinks. Wordlessly, Elliot appeared at my side and pushed a glass of water toward me. I grinned at him gratefully.

"Okay, so you know how I told you Sam was considering selling?"

"Yeah," I said, eyeing him suspiciously. "And you said you would tell me right away if it turned into anything serious."

"Well, yeah," Michael said, rubbing the back of his neck. "I think it just got serious."

"Wow." I pushed the water away, my head reeling. What would happen if the clinic was sold? Was I about to lose my job? "Why is he selling?"

Michael shrugged. "I guess the company wants to focus on retail right now. Apparently they're doing really well with the supply stores, and they want to expand, but they don't think they can do that with the nursing placement center and the clinics. So they're going to unload."

"Crap," I muttered, suddenly feeling a hell of a lot more sober. "What's going to happen?"

"Well, that's what I wanted to talk to you about." Michael leaned forward across the table, his face serious. "The clinic is probably going to get purchased by the same type of bullshit company that only cares about the bottom line. People who wouldn't know the first thing about PT best practices, you know?"

"God, you're really cheering me up here, Michael," I muttered.

"What would you say about working for someone that *does* know PT?" he asked. "Someone with experience who's willing to try new things and put the patients first?"

"I would say, sign me up," I said. "But where are we going to find someone like that?"

"You're looking at him."

I stared at him for a minute, not understanding. Suddenly, it dawned on me. "Oh my God," I gasped. "You? You want to buy the clinic? Oh, Michael, that sounds totally amazing—"

"No, no, no." He held up his hands. "Not just me. Us."

"Us?"

"Us, as in me and you."

I gaped at him, speechless.

"I think that sounds like an awesome idea," Elliot said fiercely. "You guys should totally go for it."

"Why me?" I asked, still shocked by Michael's suggestion.

"You and I are the best therapists in that place, hands down," Michael said. "I have experience running the practice, but you are key with those patients. I've never seen someone as good as you, I mean that, Em. You have, like, a sixth sense about what they need."

I felt my face color with pleasure. Out of the corner of my eye, I saw Elliot grinning at me broadly.

"Thank you," I stammered.

"I don't want to do this by myself," Michael went on. "It's way too much work for me alone. But I think the two of us could be a really good team. I think we could make the clinic into exactly what we want. A little smaller, a lot more patient focused—"

"More emphasis on preventive care," I added, starting to feel excited.

"Exactly." Michael pointed at me. "See, you know what needs to be done. You're the best partner I could think to have."

"Michael, I don't know what to say."

"You don't have to decide anything," he said. "Just

think about it."

I sat in silence for a moment, but found I couldn't contain myself. The idea of owning and running the clinic was just too exciting. "What would we need to do?"

"First, obviously, we would need some capital. Which would mean a loan. I have some savings I'd be willing to put down, but we'll need quite a bit more than that."

My mind flashed immediately to my own savings account, the money from my mom that I'd saved for all these years. I had always imagined I might buy a house with it, or pass it down to my own kids. But if it could help me to own my own practice....

Michael was still talking. "To get a bank loan, we'd need to go in with a good business plan. I don't have a whole lot of experience with putting that type of thing together—"

"Brooke," I said immediately. "Brooke could help us. She's a whiz at business stuff. And she's coming into town next week."

Michael nodded, looking happy. "So, you're on board?"

My mind was rushing, my whole body felt feverish. I was so excited, I could barely sit in my chair. But I forced myself to take a deep breath. I'd had a lot to drink tonight and was in no shape to make this kind of decision on the spot. "I should talk it over with Brooke and my dad first," I said. "When do we have to decide by?"

"We have some time," Michael said. "They haven't made the final decision to sell yet. From all accounts, it's a done deal, but they're still studying the market and having meetings."

"Okay," I said, nodding. "Then I'll get back to you

ASAP."

Michael grinned at me, and raised his glass. I smiled back and clinked mine against his. "I want in on this," Elliot said quickly. I looked over at him and found that he was still grinning from ear to ear. He seemed so excited, and I realized that was for me. He was happy because he could tell that I was happy. I felt a surge of affection for my old friend, and I raised my glass to toast with him as well.

Chapter Twenty

I was worried Greg might still be grumpy with me, but when I told him about Brooke coming in the next day over lunch, he seemed pretty excited.

"We should throw a party," he said. "A chance for our friends to all meet. What do you think?"

"That sounds great," I told him. *See?* I told myself. *Look at what a great boyfriend you have.*

"This actually works out nicely," he continued, pulling out his Smartphone to open his calendar. "I have to be out of town on business this week. There's a conference in Chicago. So it will be nice for you to have your friend with you while I'm gone."

I felt a little annoyed that he hadn't mentioned anything about his trip, but I was too excited about Brooke to care very much.

"Should I plan the party while you're gone?" I asked.

"You don't need to do that." He shook his head and started punching the keys on his phone. "I'll let my secretary know right now. She can handle everything, and you can just spend time with your friend."

It wasn't until after I was back home that I realized I hadn't said anything to him about Michael and the clinic. I had already called Brooke back to tell her about it, and she promised to meet with both of us to give her opinions and advice. I had even called my dad already, and he seemed very excited for me (or, at least, as excited as my dad ever got). I decided not to try to analyze the reasons why I hadn't felt compelled to tell Greg. It was probably just an oversight.

By Sunday night, I was so excited for Brooke to come that I parked myself in front of the living room window so I would have the best view of the street below. It had been way too long since I had seen my best friend.

"She's here!" I finally squealed as I saw her familiar Ford pick-up pull into the parking lot of our building. Brooke had had that truck since we'd been teenagers. Even though she was making pretty good money these days, she saw no need to get rid of it. "It's classic, Em," she would always say. "Practically indestructible. Why would I give that up?"

Watching it pull in now, I couldn't even sit still. I ran out of the apartment and down the stairs, throwing open the front door of the complex just as she opened her own door. "Brooke!"

She saw me running for her and laughed, jumping out of the car to pull me into a big hug. We had never been the touchy feely types, so I hid my genuine need to feel her arms around me with a big production of pretending we hadn't seen each other in years.

"I can't believe it's really you!" I cried, sniffling loudly into her shoulder.

"You look so different," she fake-sobbed. "The last time I saw you, you were in pigtails. Is this a bra I feel under your shirt? How could you have grown so much?"

"You guys are nuts," Chris said from the doorway of the building, where apparently he had followed me. "Can't you just hug like normal people?"

"Chris!" she cried, pushing me aside and running toward him. "Oh my God, it's been years! You're practically a man!"

"Shut up," he muttered, but hugged her tight all the same. "How was your drive?"

"Pretty good," she said, dropping the act. "I made good time. Wanna grab my bags for me?"

"As ever, I exist only to serve you," Chris said drily.

"Thanks, hon," she said, throwing her arm around my shoulder. I led her up to our apartment, feeling giddy that she was finally there.

"Hey, Brooke!" Ashley called, sticking her head into the living room. "I'm just getting dinner finished, I'll be out in a minute."

"Hi, Ash!" Brooke plopped down onto the couch. "God, I'm tired. It's been crazy up there, trying to get everything out of the kitchen and dining room so the electricians can get in there to do their work. I didn't get home until two a.m. last night."

"Then you were up early to make the drive," I said, sympathetically, sitting next to her. "Poor little Brooke. Seriously, I can't believe you're letting your dad handle the whole thing."

"I wouldn't, if I didn't know the electrician so well." She raised her eyebrows at me, and I slapped my hand to my forehead, feeling stupid.

"My dad? Why didn't you say so?"

"I assumed *you* would assume I would go with him. I mean, who else would I call?"

"Good point. So...how's he doing?"

"He seems good," she said. "That cough finally went away."

I felt a guilty pang. I knew he had been sick, and I still hadn't gone up to see him. I'd totally let this thing with Greg take over my life. "I'm coming up there at the end of the month," I said firmly, making up my mind. "I can get a Monday off and make it a nice long weekend."

"You should," Brooke said, never one to placate me or try to assuage my guilt when she knew I was in the wrong. Sometimes it could be an annoying trait, but tonight I was grateful for it.

"Where do you want all this crap?" Chris asked, appearing at the open front door with Brooke's bags.

"Bedroom," I told him, pointing behind me.

"No, don't get up," he said sarcastically. "Please stay right there on the comfy couch, I've got this."

"Sweet of you," Brooke said, giving him her most wicked grin. Chris rolled his eyes and made a huge production of dragging the bags back to my room.

"So, am I gonna meet the new boy tonight?" Brooke asked.

"Nope, he goes out of town for business tomorrow," I said. "But he'll be back Thursday for your last night. And we're throwing you a big old party."

"A party? For me? You shouldn't have."

I snorted. "Nice try. I know that you secretly harbor the belief that everyone should be celebrating your presence on a daily basis."

"Don't you?" she asked with a totally straight face. "I mean, I would expect you to do it discreetly, but I do fully assume some kind of internal celebration is happening every day."

"Dinner's ready!" Ashley said, coming into the living room. Brooke stood up to give her a hug. "It's so good to see you!"

"You too," Brooke said. "Thanks for letting me stay."

"Of course," Ashley said, waving her hands. "You're always welcome."

"Is Ryan coming for dinner?" I asked, looking up at the clock.

"Yeah, he's on his way, but he said not to wait for him."

We headed to the kitchen table, which Ashley had taken the time to set with our nicest dishes and a vase of daisies. She had made a pig pot of spaghetti, with salad and garlic bread—not bad for a girl who had just gotten home from her own mini vacation to Port Huron. I always got the feeling that Ashley was slightly intimidated by Brooke. Not that I could blame her—most girls were. She always seemed to go out of her way to be extra nice and welcoming to her.

"This looks awesome," Brooke said. "I'm starving. Thanks, Ash."

"No problem." Ashley beamed at her. "I thought you might want a nice meal after being on the road all day."

"You had a bit of a drive, too, didn't you?" Brooke asked, helping herself to salad. "Did Emily tell me you guys were out in Port Huron last night?"

"Yeah, Chris took me for my birthday." Ashley smiled at him. "It was very sweet, and a total surprise."

"Wow, Chris, I'm impressed," Brooke said, smirking at him. "Who knew you had such a way with the ladies?"

"Don't make me regret being happy to see you," he warned, pointing his fork at her.

She laughed, and I felt my heart swell. There was nothing like having my two oldest friends together in the same place, teasing each other just like nothing had ever changed. Add to that the imminent arrival of Ryan, and Ashley sitting right across from me, and I was feeling happier than I had in a long, long time.

***

I had managed to get both Monday and Tuesday

off work. Michael agreed to cover for me under the condition that I talk to Brooke about the business proposal for the bank. We spent both mornings working hard. Brooke insisted we research the other clinics in our area and dig up the going rate for rent in the shopping plaza. She also wanted access to our billing information and Michael's expense reports. We promised she could come in on Wednesday morning, when I did have to work, to poke around.

This left our afternoons and evenings free, and I was determined to squeeze as much fun into our time together as I possibly could. The party would be Thursday night, and Brooke had to leave first thing Friday morning to get back to the inn for the weekend crowd.

So I dragged her around town to my favorite restaurants, stores, even the Art Institute downtown. At night, the five of us went out to my favorite bars, then Brooke and I would curl up in my double bed and chat until our exhaustion won out. It was perfect.

On Wednesday, Brooke came into work with me. I had clients to see, and she wanted to get a feel for the finances of the clinic. I wasn't exactly sure how Sam would feel about that, so I was glad that Michael was the one to show her the records while I worked with patients.

"Who is that?" Frank whispered to me, staring at Brooke with naked awe on his face.

"She's my best friend," I told him, familiar with this kind of reaction from men of all ages. "That's Brooke."

"Think she might be interested in an older man?" he asked, winking at me. "I could show her the benefit of experience."

"Frank," I said firmly, pushing him toward the

exercise bike. "Believe me when I tell you that you don't want to go there. Brooke would eat you for breakfast."

"That sounds like fun," he said wistfully. I laughed and left him at the bike.

Around noon, Michael shooed Brooke and me out of the clinic. "You've done enough for today," he told her. "Go have lunch with your friend. I really can't thank you enough."

"It's no problem," she assured him. "I have a lot of notes now, I think we have what we need to put the proposal together tomorrow."

"You're a life saver," he said.

It was a perfect day outside, the sky cloudless and blue, and the air warm and breezy. We'd had a few days that reminded me it was spring, but nothing quite like this yet. "This is gorgeous." I said, closing my eyes and tilting my head up to the sun.

"Speaking of gorgeous," Brooke said. "Who's that?"

I turned in the direction she was pointing and saw Elliot sitting on a picnic table in the small dirt-covered area next to the parking lot. He waved at us.

"That's Elliot." I told Brooke. "You know, vitamin man. Wanna go meet him?"

"Yes, please," she said, licking her lips. I shoved her.

"Be good!"

We walked over to the picnic table. "Hey, Elliot!" I called as we approached. "Whatcha doing?"

He held up his brown paper bag in response, and I briefly wondered if this is where he had been eating lately, without me.

"This is my best friend, Brooke," I said. "Brooke, this is Elliot."

"We talked on the phone Friday," she said, her throaty sex-kitten voice on full display as she gave him her most inviting smile. "It's so nice to finally meet you." I glared at her, but Elliot just smiled back in his easy way.

"Nice to meet you too," he said. "I've heard so much about you. Here, sit down you guys."

Elliot moved over to the edge of the table so Brooke and I could join him. I made sure to sit in between them. Knowing Brooke, she'd probably be resting her hand casually on his knee before he had finished his sandwich.

"Isn't this a gorgeous day?" I asked, looking around. "I had forgotten what summer felt like."

"It's pretty perfect," Elliot said. "Makes me glad I'm done with work."

"Me too."

"I don't know," Brooke said, looking wistfully across the expanse of cement. "How do you guys live here? I mean, I can see nothing green, anywhere in my line of vision."

I laughed. "Brooke, seriously? You make it sound like this is some huge city. We're in a suburban town, okay? People have lawns and trees and gardens. You're exaggerating."

"Yeah, a suburb that is next to another suburb, that's next to another suburb. There's nothing in between! No fields, no farms, no woods. Where do you take walks?"

I shrugged. "On the sidewalk?"

"This from a girl who grew up within walking distance of some of the best wooded areas in the state." Brooke sighed. "It's sad."

"That's what I keep telling her!" Elliot chimed in. "I'm always trying to get her to come to some of my

Adventurer Club meet-ups. When she told me about her hometown, I was shocked that she never spends any time in nature now."

"I spend time in nature!" I said, wondering why they were ganging up on me over something so trivial. "I jog outside every single day, for God's sake."

"That's not the same," Brooke said. She turned to Elliot. "When we were in high school, we used to go hiking on a weekly basis. Sometimes we would find a clearing in the woods and just like, lie there, on a blanket, looking at the sky. I bet she hasn't done that in years."

Elliot nodded sadly. "She just can't enjoy being still and quiet."

"You guys are ridiculous," I muttered. "I'm still and quiet all the time."

Brook snorted. "Yeah right. She used to be so outdoorsy too. Would you believe that this girl knows how to sail? And snowshoe?"

"It's sad, really," Elliot said.

"All right, that's it," I said, standing up and picking up my purse. "Let's go."

"Where?" Brooke asked.

"Let's go find something to do in nature," I said, looking down at the two of them. "If I'm so lacking, now's your chance to do something about it."

"Really?" Elliot asked, looking excited.

"Yeah. Let's go find some woods. Show Brooke that we're far from the concrete jungle."

"Awesome!" Elliot said, looking like a little kid on Christmas morning. It was kind of cute, really. "Come on, I'll drive."

Elliot's battered Jeep Wrangler was a far cry from the leather-seated luxury I had become accustomed to with Greg. When I climbed into the front seat, I had to push aside a stack of CD cases, and the door stuck when I tried to close it.

"Just slam it really hard," he advised, buckling his seat belt.

"So where are you taking us, oh great master of nature?" I asked, as Elliot pulled out of the parking lot and headed north.

"Have you been to Kensington?"

I shook my head. I had heard of the recreation area, but had never made it up there.

"It's pretty good," Elliot said. "I'm sure it's nothing like what you guys have up north, but I love it. And it's only about twenty minutes away." He smiled at Brooke in the rearview mirror. "We're not quite as far from the great outdoors as you might think."

"We need some music," Brooke said. "What have you got up there?"

"Mostly Motown," Elliot replied, gesturing to the pile of CDs now resting near my feet.

"Sounds good to me," I said, reaching down to pluck one up at random. It appeared to be a mix, but Elliot hadn't included a track listing in the case. I slipped the disc into the CD player and sat back.

"Stevie Wonder," Brooke said approvingly as the strains of *Signed, Sealed, Delivered* filled the car. "Nice."

Elliot immediately began bopping his head along to the music. I allowed myself a small smile as I glanced at him out of the corner of my eye. There was something so appealing about the way he did his own thing at all times, never seeming to care if anyone was watching him. After a moment, Brooke started singing along. Elliot grinned at her in the rearview mirror, then turned to look at me momentarily. He winked, then joined her, his surprisingly strong tenor loud in the enclosed space.

I laughed, and he winked at me again. "Come on, Donovan," he said. "You can't fight the power of Motown for long!"

He had a point there. I looked in the rearview mirror and saw Brooke, happily singing, her eyes closed, the breeze from her open window blowing her hair around in a mess of brown curls. It was so familiar to me, a sight I had seen a thousand times over the years as we cruised around town, looking for something to do. In that moment, I was so happy that she was there with me, driving along in search of adventure with Elliot, that I did the only thing that made sense. I took a deep breath and started to sing.

Chapter Twenty-One

The recreation area was really beautiful. Thousands of acres of woodlands nestled right off the highway. There were hiking trails, little ponds, wetlands, bike paths, an education center—all of it centered around a thousand-acre lake.

Elliot parked near the kayak rental place and looked at the two of us. "You up for it?" he asked.

"Heck, yeah," Brooke said.

"Oh God, don't let her convince you to race," I warned him. "She rowed crew in high school."

"Why'd you give me away?" she asked. "Now he'll be too scared to try."

We rented three single-seat kayaks and got fitted out in life vests. Elliot offered to haul our boats, but Brooke and I just rolled our eyes, picking up the end of our respective kayaks and dragging them the few feet to the launch. "We've done this before," I reminded him. "Many, many times."

Once we were all situated in the water, Elliot took the lead. "If we head over this way, we can get into the Huron River," he told us. "The current can get a little strong in places, but the scenery is perfect."

As we paddled across the open water of the lake, I felt myself fall into a familiar rhythm. Brooke had actually had a good point—it had been ages since I had done something like this. The lake was almost deserted, being the middle of the day and all. On the far side, there was a nice-looking beach area. I could just make out two women, sitting at a picnic bench, while three little kids ran to the water's edge, squealed at the cold, then ran back, only to repeat the entire process seconds later.

The water was a deep cobalt, contrasting with the lighter baby blue of the sky above us. The green of maples, oaks, and evergreens stood out boldly against the sky along the tree line. The colors, the sights and smells, were well known to me, as familiar as if I was at home. There was something so appealing about being out on the water of a lake. I had been to the ocean a few times and had liked the spray of saltwater and hugeness of the crashing waves, but give me a freshwater lake in the woods any day.

After a while, we left the openness of the lake behind us as we moved into the mouth of the river. Elliot was right about the current being strong, so we moved closer to the shoreline as we paddled through.

"This is gorgeous," Brooke said, her voice soft.

"Yeah," I answered, not really knowing what else to say. Gorgeous kind of covered it. Trees covered the shoreline as far as the eye could see, their branches spreading a riot of green across my vision. Even the water here seemed more green than blue, reflecting the leaves above it. The only noises I could hear were the gentle rush of water, the singing of birds high above. It was perfect.

We kayaked for about two hours. By the time we pulled back into the boat launch, my arms and shoulders ached, and I was starving. "Crap," I said, rubbing my biceps. "I had no idea how out of shape I was."

"You're out of practice," Brooke reminded me. "Yet another reason you should do stuff like this more often."

"Okay, okay." I held my hands up. "You guys are

both right. I have been neglecting my roots and the nature that I love. I promise never to do it again. Are you happy now?"

"Very," Elliot said, grinning at me. "And also starving. Let's go find some food."

"You're one to talk," Brooke grumbled. "At least you had lunch."

We piled back into Elliot's car, the mood happy and mellow. "There's a pub I like pretty close by," he said, looking over at me. "They have pretty good burgers. You up for it?"

"That sounds like heaven," I sighed, rubbing my belly.

"Beer and a burger?" Brooke asked. "Hell yeah."

Elliot grinned at me and put the car into gear. "Burgers it is."

Brooke's cell phone rang, and I heard her curse. "Can the man do nothing without me?" she muttered, then held the phone up to her ear. "Hello, Dad," she said, sounding exasperated already.

While she was occupied, I tapped Elliot on the shoulder. He took his eyes off the road to look at me. "Thanks for today," I said softly. "It was exactly what I needed."

He held my gaze for a minute, then turned back to the road. "It was my pleasure, Emily," he said, his voice equally soft. "Completely my pleasure."

Chapter Twenty-Two

I spent an hour getting ready for the party on Thursday. I was feeling slightly nervous that Brooke and Greg wouldn't hit it off. I loved her, but I knew how she could come off to strangers. Greg didn't do bold and brassy very well.

"You look hot, sister," she said, coming into my room. "Are you actually putting makeup on?"

I looked over at her and sighed. It didn't matter what I did, I could never compete with Brooke. Not that I would actually try, but still. She was simply gorgeous, no getting around it.

"I wear makeup all the time now," I told her. "And I do my hair. Your little girl is all grown up."

I expected her to laugh, but she just squinted her eyes at me, as if in deep thought. "Really? Because I don't remember you wearing makeup once the whole time I've been here."

"Really?" I asked, trying to remember. That didn't sound right. I got dressed up on a daily basis lately—surely this wasn't the first time she had seen me in makeup.

"Anyhow." She bent down to fasten the buckle on her heels. "You about ready?"

"Yup," I said, standing up from my dressing table and fluffing out my hair. I had styled it straight and sleek, the way Greg liked it. I had thought about wearing one of the dresses he had bought me, but fell in love with this one while out shopping with Brooke earlier in the week. It was black with brightly colored flowers splattered across it, cut straight across at the top with tiny spaghetti straps and falling to an asymmetrically cut skirt. It was different from anything else I owned—much more colorful and wild. I hoped Greg would like it as much as I did.

My fingers lingered over my jewelry box. I knew he would like to see me in the bracelet, but I couldn't bring myself to put it on. The questions Brooke would fling at me if she saw it—well, I just didn't feel up for it. Besides, it didn't exactly go with my wild dress.

"Alright," I said. "Let's head out."

Ryan, Chris, and Ashley were waiting for us in the living room. "Wow," I said, looking them over. "This is definitely the best this group has ever cleaned up."

"We're all a little nervous to go over to your rich boyfriend's house and meet his rich friends," Chris said, tugging on the sleeve of his suit coat uncomfortably. I tried to remember the last time I had seen Chris in a suit. Graduation, probably.

"There's nothing to be nervous about," I assured them. "We'll all have fun."

I didn't admit that I myself was feeling pretty damn nervous. I said a silent prayer as we all headed down the stairs that everything would go well.

We decided to take two cars so no one had to squash their party clothes, Ryan and Brooke coming with me while Chris and Ash drove together. Ryan and Brooke kept up a steady stream of gossip about hot celebrities, for which I was grateful. My stomach was churning, and I didn't think I was up to small talk just then.

"Okay," I said, pulling up to Greg's building. "Here we are."

"Holy, crap," Brooke said, looking up at the towering stone façade. A valet rushed over to take my keys.

"Welcome, Miss Donovan," he said politely.

"The valet knows your name?" Brooke hissed.

I nodded, feeling stuck up. This particular valet had taken Greg's car on a number of occasions, yet I had no idea what his name was.

We waited on the sidewalk for Chris and Ashley to arrive. Once the valet had taken Chris' car and we were all together, I turned to the glass front door. "Here we go," I murmured.

My friends were silent as we walked through the ornate lobby and climbed into the elevator. I could tell that they were trying to play it cool. They could barely look at each other, probably for fear that they might curse or start laughing or something.

A doorman met us at Greg's apartment. *A doorman*, I thought, trying hard not to roll my eyes. Did he have to be so over the top?

"Welcome," the man said, smiling at us. "Please come in, and enjoy your evening."

We all filed into the foyer. From here I could see hints of Greg's apartment, the glass wall of windows in the living room, the marble abstract sculpture resting on the hall table, the polished wood floors. Thinking about it from my friends' perspective, I was struck anew by how large and fancy everything was. I chanced a glance at them—with the exception of Ryan they were all wide eyed. Chris whistled softly under his breath, and I had to fight to keep from laughing.

"Emily!"

Greg strode down the hallway toward us, his face alight. I couldn't help but smile back, my tension melting away.

Just before he reached me, I noticed his eyes flicker down over my dress. His expression instantaneously seemed to close up a little, but he took me in his arms all the same, kissing the top of my head as he pulled me to his chest. "I missed you."

"I missed you too," I said, pulling back. "Greg, I want you to meet my friends. You know Ashley and Ryan, I think, but this is Chris and Brooke." I pointed them out and they both nodded at him, smiling. "They're two of my closest friends from home."

"It's wonderful to meet you," Greg said formally. I once again saw his eyes flicker down over Brooke's dress as he shook her hand. Was I crazy, or was there just the barest hint of coldness in his voice? "Please come in. There are drinks and hors d'oeuvres through there."

He took my arm. "Sweetheart, can I talk to you for a minute?"

I smiled at my friends, hoping they got the hint to go ahead into the party. They walked ahead, and Greg led me to the laundry room just off the hall. Right before we walked through I caught sight of Brooke, looking over her shoulder at me. Her eyes met mine, and I thought I detected a hint of worry.

"Hi," I said, turning to smile at Greg—but he was frowning at me. "What?"

"What are you wearing?" he asked, disapproval clear in his voice.

"What do you mean?"

"I assumed you would wear one of the dresses Lauren helped you pick out," he said, looking me up and down. The disapproval in his eyes seemed to grow. "I thought that was the whole point of our shopping trip."

"But I...I thought..." I knew I was stammering, but he had caught me so off guard. "I saw this shopping with Brooke and really liked it. Is there a problem?"

"No," he said, shaking his head. "I just wish...my boss is here, Emily. I thought you might wear something a little more appropriate. Don't you think that dress is a little...loud?"

I felt like he slapped me. What right did he have to criticize my clothes?

"I didn't think you controlled my wardrobe," I said, crossing my arms. "I like this dress."

Greg just shook his head. "You're in an adult relationship, Emily, and you need to think about my position."

Before I could respond, he turned to the shelf above the washing machine. "You left this here last week," he said. "Maria had it dry cleaned. Please put it on."

He held out a black cashmere cardigan. I just stared at him, not really believing he could be so rude.

"Emily," he said, his voice sharp. "I'm asking you to put this sweater on, while you are in my house with my boss. Please don't be a child."

All of a sudden, all of my anger left in a rush, leaving embarrassment behind. The expression on his face made me feel small and silly. Had I really messed up here? Greg's business was so important to him. For him to get worked up like this, I must look really inappropriate. I took the sweater without a word and pulled it on.

"Thank you," he said, leaning down to kiss my head. "I need to get back out there." Without another word, he turned and left.

***

The party seemed endless to me. Endless and painful. I could see Ashley and Ryan trying to make an effort with Greg and his friends, trying to mingle and be social. But Brooke and Chris seemed perfectly content to stand off alone and not talk to anyone but each other. I couldn't really blame them. With Greg's arm constantly around my waist, I was stuck listening to the most boring stream of real estate shoptalk I could imagine. And when they weren't talking about work, they were talking about *stuff*. Cars, toys, electronics, clothes. I stood there in near silence, a vague smile plastered on my face.

Sometime later (I was so bored it was hard to keep track of time), Tom and Angie approached us. Tom wanted to see Greg's new sound system, so he left me to chat with Angie.

"Where's your bracelet?" she asked the second Greg was out of earshot. "I was dying to see it. Tiffany's! Why on earth aren't you wearing it?"

"It, uh, didn't go with my dress," I said.

"Yes, your dress is, uh, lovely, dear. So unique."

I looked up and saw Brooke standing a few feet away from me, her eyes locked on me. Suddenly, I was struck with the most uncontrollable urge to burst into tears.

"Will you excuse me, Angie?" I asked, backing away. "I need to use the restroom."

"Sure, sure," she said waving me away. "But I want to hear all about that bracelet when you get back."

I just barely made it to Greg's bedroom before the tears started to sting my eyes. What was wrong with me? I'd had such high hopes for the night, for Greg and Brooke to meet. Instead, I had barely said two words to my best friend all night, and Greg had said even fewer.

I went over to his bedside table to get a Kleenex, pressing it firmly against my eyes. I couldn't cry tonight, not here. Everyone would be able to tell. I looked down at the table, trying to distract myself. Greg kept a silver framed photo of his mother there, right next to the bed. I picked it up and looked at her face. She really had been beautiful, tall and blonde with blue eyes.

You remind me of her, Greg had said, more than once.

Feeling weepy all over again, though I barely knew why, I set the picture down and pressed the Kleenex back to my eyes, taking deep breaths.

"Em?"

I spun around and saw Brooke closing the bedroom door softly behind her. "What's the matter?"

"Nothing," I said quickly. "Just tired."

"You don't look tired. You look really upset."

I shook my head. "I'm fine, Brooke. Really."

"What are you doing here, Em?"

I gestured to the table behind me. "I just needed a Kleenex—"

"Not in the bedroom," she said, clearly exasperated. "Here. With that guy."

"Greg? Greg is wonderful—"

"No he's not," she said, her voice flat. "He's rude and judgmental, and he's trying to turn you into something you're not."

"Excuse me?" I felt immediately defensive. How dare she talk about Greg like that?

"What's with the sweater, Em?" she asked pointedly.

"Look, Greg has a lot of important work people here tonight. He needs me to look a certain way..." I quelled under the fiery look in her eyes. "I mean, to look appropriate. It's not a big deal."

"Not a big deal? It's a huge deal."

"You don't know what you're talking about," I

said. "You've never been in a serious relationship, you don't know how this works."

"I know exactly how this works," she said, her lips turning up in a sneer. "You think you're not good enough for the guy, so you let him control you."

"He doesn't control me!" I spluttered. "You don't know what you're talking about. In fact, I think you're just jealous!"

She laughed without humor. "Do you know what I think, Emily Donovan?" she asked, her eyes flashing. "I think you are fooling yourself." She shook her head. "In fact, I'm not even sure I know who the hell you are right now."

"What are you talking about?" I asked, the heat rising to my face.

"I'm talking about this," she waved her hands around the room. "I don't know who this person is, but it sure as hell isn't my best friend."

"What, because he has money? Don't you think you're being a little bit judgmental?"

"It isn't about money!" she cried, looking downright pissed now. "Why would I care about his money? It's about you."

"What about me?"

"Can't you see how you act around him?" she asked. "I mean, do you have any idea? When Chris told me about the romance project thing, I just thought it was stupid, harmless, and silly. But *this*. Jesus, what happened to you?"

I felt a momentary flash of embarrassment that Chris had told her about the project, but I pushed it down. "I don't know what you're talking about," I said, defiant. "Greg makes me very happy."

She snorted. "You seem real happy. God, I haven't seen you smile once since we got here."

"I've been smiling all night," I cried, throwing my hands up in exasperation.

"Not your real smile," she said, and I rolled my eyes. Before I could respond, she went on. "You know what you've been doing? You've been smiling the way you do whenever someone comes up to you and tells you how much you look like your mom."

I felt the air leave my lungs. Brooke knew how hard it was for me when people at home would accost me, wanting to tell me some story about my mom. How dare she bring it up now, here?

"Em," she said softly. "I just mean I know what it looks like when you're trying to convince people that you're fine, even though you really aren't. That's how you look when people bring her up. And it's how you look here, with him."

"You're wrong," I told her, my voice shaking. "You haven't seen me much lately, you know? How do you know what my expressions mean? For all you know, you've been seeing my totally real, blissful smile all night long."

She shook her head. "It doesn't matter how long it's been, Em. I know you. And I know when you're really happy. I saw it yesterday, remember? When we were out with Elliot, you were happy all day long. God, I haven't seen you look like that with Greg once."

"Shut up," I whispered. I didn't want to hear this anymore. I had so wanted her to like Greg, to be happy and impressed when she saw this place, when she saw how far I had come. And she was tearing it all down, casting everything I had worked for into shadow. It wasn't fair. I was about to tell her so when I heard the bedroom door behind us open.

"Emily!"

The voice was firm, disapproving. I looked up and

saw Greg standing in the doorway. "I can hear raised voices from outside. What's going on?"

I immediately felt guilty. "Nothing," I said quickly. "Sorry, we were just...just..."

"Whatever you're doing, it's inappropriate," he continued, his voice flat. "We have guests. You shouldn't be hiding away in here arguing."

I lowered my head, the guilt growing. "Sorry," I said softly. "We'll be right out."

Without another word, Greg left the room, shutting the door quietly behind him. The room was silent for a moment. I finally looked up and saw Brooke staring at me, the look on her face impossible to read.

"That," she whispered, and I suddenly realized what I was seeing in her face. It was disgust. "That is what I'm talking about. You're like some wet dish cloth around him. He calls all the shots, and you act like you're just lucky to be in his presence."

"I am lucky," I shot back. "I'm lucky to have him. He's—"

"No," she said firmly. "You're not. He makes you someone different, someone weak. Of all people, Emily Donovan, controlled by a man. I never thought I'd see the day."

I wanted to argue with her, to tell her that she was wrong, that she didn't know what she was talking about. Tell her that she was jealous. But the words got stuck in my throat. Brooke stared at me for a long moment, her breathing heavy, the way it always got when she was worked up. When I didn't respond, she shook her head and brushed past me, toward the door. When she had gotten a few paces away, she turned back.

"You know," she said, the anger gone from her

voice. Now she just sounded sad. "I knew your mom for eight years. Loved her like she was my own family. She would be so sad if she could see you right now."

Her words hit me like a physical blow. I actually took a step back, as if she had slapped me. But I had no argument for her, no way to refute her. I could do nothing but watch her as she turned without another word, leaving me alone in the room.

Chapter Twenty-Three

The next morning, I cowered under my blankets, listening to Brooke gather her things. She had slept out on the couch last night, apparently too disappointed in me to be in my room. When I got home from Greg's after midnight, she was already asleep on the couch—or pretending to be.

After she had left Greg's bedroom, she and Chris had left immediately—gone before I had even come back out to the party. Ashley and Ryan were waiting for me, clearly bewildered.

"Don't worry about it," I told them, my voice emotionless. "They're mad at me. You guys can go if you want, I probably won't be good company. Take my car."

They left a few minutes later, casting me worried looks as they thanked Greg and said good night.

Greg hadn't said another word about my fight with Emily or our argument over the dress. Instead, he carried on as he usually did—charming to everyone, attentive to me. Even when he drove me home and we were alone in the car, he was simply his normal, polite self. I wondered if he even noticed how quiet I was.

Remembering the previous night sent a blush to my face, even though I was alone. Even though I was angry as hell at Brooke for what she had said, I had the terrible feeling she might be... I closed my eyes and buried my face in my pillow, feeling the knots in my stomach double as I tried to banish that thought from my head.

"I guess you're too chicken to come out and say goodbye," Brooke called out suddenly from the living room. I froze under my blankets. How did she know I was awake?

"Whatever, Emily," she said, her voice dismissive. "See you around."

I heard the front door slam and felt like bursting into tears. She was right—I was a chicken. Too cowardly to face her. Too afraid she would be able to see in my eyes that I knew she was right.

No, I told myself firmly. *She's not. She doesn't know the first thing about your relationship with Greg.*

I told myself that over and over again throughout the day, as I got ready for work, as I treated my patients, as I ate my lunch alone in the office. *She's wrong, she's wrong, she's wrong.*

"Emily?" Sarah said, peeking her head into the office. "Sorry, I know you're on break. I just wanted to let you know that your twelve thirty was here."

Philip. Great. He would be as grumpy as ever. Just what I needed.

I threw my mostly uneaten lunch away and headed out to the therapy floor. I might as well get it over with.

"Good afternoon, Philip."

He grunted in reply, hitching himself up onto the table without assistance. I was pleased to see that he was showing some improvement, finally, though he still had a long way to go.

"How's it feeling today?"

"Little better," he said. "Sore last night."

I nodded, making a note on his chart. "The rain probably didn't help."

I looked up from the chart, ready to apply his

ultrasound therapy, and realized that he was staring at my face. "What?"

"You look like hell."

"Well, thanks a lot for that, Philip," I said, feeling even grumpier than before. I'd be giving him a run for his money soon if he didn't watch it.

He didn't respond, but he also didn't avert his eyes, instead holding his gaze steady on my face. "You okay?"

I stared at him, shocked. Philip had never once shown any interest in me, or anyone else in the clinic for that matter. It caught me off guard.

"Yeah," I said. "I'm, uh, fine."

"Boy problems?"

Okay, seriously? Was I about to have a heart to heart about my dating life with *Philip*?

"You could say that." I sighed, feeling like I might as well tell him. "My friends hate my boyfriend."

"Should they?"

"I...I don't know. I really don't. I thought he was perfect but now..."

Philip snorted. "If you don't know, he's not. I got forty-five years with my Beverly. It wasn't long enough. I knew from the moment I met her it would be me and her. And I never doubted that once."

To my surprise, I felt tears prick my eyes. The love in his voice was palpable, transforming him from a grumpy old man to someone softer, somehow.

"If this guy was the one, you'd know it. And if he is, it's worth losing all the friendships in the world. I can promise you that. If you're really in love, your friends will know it. If they don't, they weren't worth being friends with in the first place."

I couldn't speak for a moment. Philip was so sure of himself, so certain. The certainty of a man who had known true love.

"So," he said eventually. "Are we gonna get on with this or do you need to go cry in the bathroom like a little girl?"

"There you are," I said. "I wondered what happened to the gruff old grump I've come to know." But I smiled at him as I helped him roll over onto his side, and, unless I was very much mistaken, he gave me a small wink in return.

***

My chat with Philip had made one thing clear to me: Love was important enough that I needed to be sure about Greg before I made any rash decisions. When he called me after work and asked me to have dinner with him at his place, I readily agreed.

Feeling like this could be our chance to start fresh, I took special care getting dressed. I wore a Diane von Furstenberg black and white wrap dress that I knew he loved. I styled my hair straight and, for a finishing touch, slipped my diamond bracelet onto my wrist.

"You look beautiful," Greg said, meeting me at the door to his apartment. He kissed the top of my head. "Just beautiful." He caught sight of the bracelet and grinned at me, taking my hand to lead me into the apartment.

"Thank you," I told him, trying not to remember the scene that had taken place the night before as we passed the laundry room and entered the kitchen. "This smells good," I murmured, peeking into a sauce pan on the stove.

"Red wine reduction for veal chops," he said proudly. "Your favorite."

I stared at him. "No, it's not."

Greg looked at me in surprise. "What do you

mean?"

"Veal is not my favorite." I don't know why I was making such a big deal about this, but just then it seemed very important to me that he knew my favorite food.

"Okay," he said, giving me a bemused smile. "What is your favorite then?"

"Lasagna," I said firmly.

"Then next time I shall make you lasagna."

I suddenly felt much better. Maybe it wouldn't be so hard to let Greg know the real me.

I heard a buzz from my purse and peeked down at my phone. It was a text message from Michael. *Brooke just sent me the final proposal,* it read. *I've emailed it to you. Take a look and let me know what you think.*

So Brooke had emailed him the final proposal, huh? I was torn between irritation with her for going straight to Michael, and gratitude that she hadn't let our fight get in the way of her helping us.

"Can I use your computer for a minute to check my email?"

Greg looked up from the stove, frowning. "We really need to get you a Smartphone."

I shook my head vehemently. "I love my old, sadly outdated phone."

He shook his head, but waved the wooden spoon in his hand toward the office. "Go ahead, it's on."

I slipped out of the kitchen and settled myself behind Greg's big desk. He had one of those awesome, plush leather executive chairs—it was more comfortable than my couch at home. I clicked on the Internet browser and loaded my email account. The email from Michael was right there at the top. I opened the document and scanned over it. Everything looked really good, just the way Brooke and I had discussed it. The proposal was thorough and professional; I felt a little leap of excitement. We had to get this loan. How could any bank refuse us?

"That was quick," Greg said when I had rejoined him in the kitchen. He was dishing out the veal onto a serving platter. "Ready to eat?"

"Sure," I said, picking up the salad bowl and water pitcher and following him to the dining table. The room looked spotless, despite the number of people that had been here the night before. I was sure Maria and a whole team of cleaners had been here first thing to get it into this shape.

Greg and I ate in silence for a few moments. The veal was very good, but I had never quite gotten over my squickiness about it. Maybe I would tell him that, tell him that I much preferred beef or chicken—

"So, what was the email about?" Greg asked, pouring himself more iced water. "Anything important?"

"Actually, yes," I said, sitting up straighter with excitement. "There's a business opportunity I'm considering."

Greg put his fork down, frowning. "Business opportunity?"

"Yes. The company that owns our clinic is considering selling. Michael—you know, my manager Michael? He asked me if I would consider going into business with him and trying to buy the place."

"You want to own the clinic?"

I nodded. "I think it would be amazing. There're so many things I want to do with it, I have a ton of ideas. And Michael is such a good manager; he'd be so good to have as a partner."

"Emily," Greg said, a slight smile now playing on his lips. "Owning a business is a huge undertaking. It's not something you jump into because you think it'd be 'amazing'. It's a lot of hard work."

"I know that." I felt stung. "We're taking this very seriously. We've been working on a business plan to present to the bank so we can try for a loan."

"You've done a business plan?" he asked, frowning again. "Without talking to me about any of it?"

I shifted, uncomfortable. "It's really just come up in the last week or so," I said. "You were out of town."

Greg just watched me for a minute, then picked up his fork again. "I don't think it's a good idea." Maybe I was imagining it, but I thought I heard a note of finality in his voice. It pissed me off.

"I think it's a great idea," I said, knowing I sounded defiant.

"You realize owning your own clinic means lots of late nights, don't you? Lots of weekends, taking your work home. Why would you want to get involved in all that?"

"To do something I love? To create something that's mine?"

"You don't have any concept of how much work it would be," he said firmly. "Seriously, Emily. It's a bad idea."

I wanted to tell him he was wrong, that I was well up to this job. I wanted to tell him to go to hell, to be honest. But I found I couldn't speak. He took my silence as acquiescence. "Besides," he said, "you won't have time for any of that once we're married."

I could hear a dull ringing in my ears. Had he seriously just said what I thought he said?

"What?"

"When we're married," he said patiently. "You won't need to work. I can take care of you, of course."

I felt panic building in my chest. I had the

strongest desire to get up and run, as fast as I could, away from there.

Greg was watching my face. "I mean," he continued, "you're not going to want to spend all your time working when you're a mom, will you? My mom stayed home with us, and I'm so grateful for it to this day."

"No," I whispered.

"Good," Greg said, misunderstanding me. "That's settled then. Why don't you email Marcus back after dinner and tell him you're not interested after all." Greg returned to his meal, spearing a piece of veal with a satisfied expression on his face. All was once again right in his world, under his control.

"No," I said again, louder. "It's not settled, not at all."

He looked at me, clearly beginning to get irritated now. "Emily—"

"No! I don't want to quit my job and get married. I don't even want to think about babies yet." I looked down at Greg's carefully set table, his beautiful dishes, feeling the blood rush through my ears. "And I don't want to eat this stupid veal anymore!"

I stood up quickly, knocking over my chair behind me. Greg stared at me, speechless, clearly shocked by my outburst.

"I'm sorry," I said. "I just...this is way too fast for me. And I don't know what I want."

"Emily, sit down!"

"No." I shook my head. "I'm sorry. You've been wonderful to me, you really have. But I don't think this is me." I spread my arms out wide, as if to encompass the whole room and the lifestyle it represented. Out of the corner of my eye, I saw the diamonds of my bracelet flash in the candle light.

"This isn't me," I repeated, pulling the bracelet off and setting it next to my plate. "I'm sorry, Greg. I just…I need to go."

I turned and headed to the door, but Greg was up and out of his chair before I could get more than a few steps away. "Wait," he said, grabbing my arm and spinning me around. "Emily, what on earth has gotten into you?"

"I'm sorry," I said, feeling tears start to well in my eyes. "I think I've been fooling myself this whole time, fooling you too, into thinking I belonged here. I don't."

"You do," he said, dropping my arm. "Of course you do. I love you."

"No, you don't. You don't really know me. And that's my fault."

"This is ridiculous," Greg said. "Of course I know you. Now come and sit back down and finish your meal. You don't throw a fit and stalk off when you're at the dinner table."

Of course. Leave it to Greg to be more upset about my violating proper dinner behavior than my telling him he didn't know me.

"I don't want to finish dinner, Greg," I said softly, wiping at the tears in my eyes. "I'm sorry, but I'm going to go now."

I turned again and got as far as the door this time before he caught me.

"Emily," he said, his face scared now. "Why are you doing this?"

"I'm trying to tell you," I said, the tears falling freely now. "This isn't working for me. I don't think you really know me, and I don't think I fit here."

He shook his head. "You're just upset because we quarreled at the party last night. You're probably tired. Go home and get some rest, and we'll talk about this tomorrow."

"I will rest," I said. Even I could hear the sadness in my voice. "And I'll call you tomorrow. But I don't think anything will have changed."

"No," he said, putting his thumb over my lip. He had done that once before, and I thought it was the height of romantic. Now, it just made me want to push his hand away. "I'm not going to accept that, not yet. You'll feel better tomorrow. Just promise me you'll call me."

"Okay," I said, wiping my eyes. I knew nothing would have changed by tomorrow. "I'll call you."

I reached for the door handle, and he caught my hand. "Emily," he said, his voice panicked. "I really love you. I do."

I just looked at him, feeling so guilty and so, so sad. This was all my fault.

"Good night, Greg."

Chapter Twenty-Four

I did call Greg on Saturday, but I told him I wasn't ready to talk. He seemed to take my refusal as good news. "Time is all you need," he said confidently. "Time and a nice rest."

He was right about the rest part. I felt exhausted, like I had just run some kind of race or something. The second I got home from his apartment I went straight to my room, saying a silent prayer of thanks that the apartment was empty. Once in my room, I unzipped my dress and let it fall away from my body, leaving it to pool on the floor. I knew Ryan would be horrified if he could see what I had done to a precious piece of high fashion, but I couldn't care less.

I climbed straight into bed, in nothing but my underwear, and didn't leave it for more than a day.

My body felt hot and tingly, like I had a fever of some kind. My arms and legs ached and my head pounded. I fell asleep almost immediately.

I woke in the morning to the sounds of Ashley and Chris in the kitchen, making breakfast and laughing. I considered getting up to join them, but decided I was still too tired to move. I rolled over and went right back to sleep.

Sometime after noon I heard a knock on my door. I sat up, feeling disoriented and confused. "Come in," I called, pulling the comforter up over my chest.

"You okay?" Ashley asked, sticking her head around the door. "You've been asleep all day."

"I'm pretty tired," I said, yawning.

I saw her eyes flick to the dress on the floor. "Everything go okay last night?" she asked, and I could hear the concern in her voice.

I sighed, not really wanting to have this conversation yet. I was still feeling so muddled up inside. But Ashley took my response as an invitation. She came in and sat on the side of my bed, peering at my face with a worried expression.

"You never told me what happened at the party," she said. "Chris wouldn't tell me either, but he and Brooke both seemed so upset."

"We got in a fight," I sighed. "Brooke thinks I let Greg control me. She doesn't think he's good for me."

Ashley frowned. "Really? Does she know about all of the nice stuff he does for you?"

I nodded. "I guess...I guess she thinks I'm not myself with him." I felt a little nervous to tell her the next part, so I studied my comforter instead of watching her face. "And then, last night, Greg and I had a fight. And I think...I think it might be over."

"Oh, Emily!" Out of the corner of my eye I could see Ashley slap her hands over her mouth. "Are you okay? I'm so sorry! Oh, Em, are you sure?"

I nodded. "It just...it doesn't feel right. It hasn't for a while."

She didn't say anything, so I chanced a look at her face. Her expression was very concerned and also...was it doubtful? Skeptical?

"What?" I asked.

"I just wonder if you're really sure that you can't work it out." I watched as she twisted her fingers together.

"He wants me to be someone I'm not," I sighed. "It's like, he doesn't really know me, or something, you know?"

"Have you tried to tell him that? He seems like such a reasonable guy, I'm sure he'd listen. Maybe he really wants to get to know the real you and you're just not letting him."

I frowned. Was it possible that Greg would still be interested in me if I showed him who I really was? God, did I even know how to go about doing that?

"I don't know, Ash," I said. "I just don't see it working."

"Emily, I'm only going to say this once, and please don't get mad, okay?"

"Okay," I said, feeling apprehensive. "Go for it."

"I know you love Brooke and everything, and you respect her opinion, but I don't want you to make this decision just because she doesn't approve. She doesn't understand your relationship with Greg. How do you know she isn't jumping to conclusions?"

I stared at my friend. Her words had sent a brand new worry into my already confused mind. Was I seriously just trading in one form of control for another? Was it possible that I was now making my decisions based on what Brooke wanted, instead of what Greg wanted?

I suddenly felt so frustrated I could scream. I buried my head in my hands, clutching at the roots of my hair. Why the hell was it so hard for me to just figure out what *I* wanted for a change?

"I'm sorry," Ashley said quickly. "I've upset you even more."

"No, it's not your fault," I said. "I'm just all muddled up, Ash."

"Why don't you get out of bed?" she suggested. "We can hang out on the couch and eat ice cream and talk it all through."

The idea of having a drawn-out conversation

about the way I was feeling made me feel tired all over again. "No, thanks. It's really nice of you, but I just want to lie here for a while more."

"Are you sure?" she asked, clearly skeptical.

"Yeah," I said, already moving to lie back down. "I just need some more sleep."

***

I woke up again a few more times throughout the afternoon, even managing to get up to use the bathroom once or twice. I called Greg, as promised, around five. The brief conversation left me so exhausted that I promptly fell back asleep, not getting up again until the following morning, when Ryan pounded on my door and demanded I take a shower before he called protective services.

"This look," he said, pointing at me, "is not attractive on you. You've been in bed for like, thirty-six hours. You're starting to smell."

I sighed, and sat up. "Fine," I said. "You're probably right."

"Good girl." He sounded relieved. "I'll go start the shower."

I did feel better after my shower. The sun was shining outside, and Ashley had thrown open most of the windows to let some air in. As I pulled my wet hair up into a ponytail, I actually felt awake and rested.

"She lives," Chris said when I entered the living room.

"Nice to see you too," I said, plopping down onto the couch. "So what'd I miss during my mini-hibernation?"

"Not much," Chris said. "Ash has just been trying to convince us that you're making a huge mistake breaking up with Greg."

I squirmed a little, not sure where I myself fell on that issue.

"Of course, I told her she's insane," he continued. I looked at him in surprise. "Oh, come on, Emily. That guy was totally wrong for you."

"You think so?"

"Of course," Chris said dismissively. "He didn't get you at all. The way you've been dressing and the shit you've been doing—I mean, wine tastings? Shopping sprees? I was worried I was dealing with an invasion of the body snatchers situation here."

I had to laugh at that, but Ashley sighed. "He seemed so perfect though," she said wistfully.

"Yeah, if it's perfect to treat someone like crap." Chris sounded annoyed now, and I saw him throw her an angry look.

"He hardly treated her like crap," she argued, clearly not having noticed his irritation. "I don't call romantic weekends away and expensive shopping sprees treating someone like crap."

"You know what, I'm gonna take off," Chris said, standing suddenly.

"What?" Ashley looked up at him in bewilderment. "What are you talking about?"

"I don't need to sit here and listen to you make it any more clear how lacking you find me as a boyfriend."

Ashley stared at him for a minute, then burst into laughter. It was the wrong reaction.

"Oh, sure, laugh. Laugh at the stupid guy who can't make you happy no matter what he does. That's just great, Ash."

She stopped immediately. "What on earth are you talking about?"

"Ever since you guys started this damn research

project, all I've heard is romance this and romance that. Could you be any more obvious that you're disappointed in our relationship? Maybe it would be better for you if I just stepped aside and left you to find that great romance of your life."

I caught Ryan's eye across the room. His mouth was wide open in shock. I wondered briefly if we should leave them alone, but found I couldn't really tear myself away from the fight.

"Chris, this is ridiculous!" Ashley cried, the exasperation clear in her voice. "You *are* the great romance of my life. How can you not see that?"

"Sure," Chris sneered. "Which is why you spend so much of your time mooning about the guys in those movies you always watch. How am I supposed to compete with that?"

"You don't have to!" She looked close to tears now. "Because there is no competition, don't you get it?"

He looked like he wanted to argue, but Ashley jumped up from the couch, holding up her hands to stop him. Her face was ablaze in color, transforming her normally sweet features with harsh passion.

"I think we have the perfect love story," she went on. "I loved you for years. Years! Every guy I went out with couldn't compare with you, no matter how much I tried to convince myself that they did. You've always been the one for me. And finding out that you felt the same way? I don't know any movie that could top that." Ashley was crying now, impatiently brushing the tears from her eyes. "If you don't see things like that, if it's not the same for you, then maybe *I* shouldn't be with *you* anymore."

Chris was silent for a moment, staring at her. "Do you mean that?" he finally said. "Do you really feel that way about me?"

"Of course I do, you stupid idiot!" she cried.

Chris burst into laughter, then rushed forward, gathering her in his arms and kissing her head. "Stop crying, you silly girl. I love you too."

"Are you sure?" she asked, her voice muffled against his chest, still somewhat bitter. "Are you sure I'm not too silly and sentimental for you?"

"You're perfect for me," he said, tipping her chin up so she was looking at him. "You're perfect. And I love you."

Her face, finally, broke into a smile, then she was kissing him. I looked at Ryan, sure I would see him making a disgusted face, so I was shocked to see his eyes looking a little moist.

"They really are perfect for each other," he said quietly. "I never realized it."

"You sap," I said, hitting him on the shoulder. Across the room, Ashley and Ryan were still kissing, completely oblivious to us. "Come on, crybaby," I said, grabbing Ryan's hand. "Let's get out of here. I'll buy you breakfast."

Chapter Twenty-Five

I don't know how I managed to get through the next morning at work. In spite of all the sleep I had gotten on Saturday, I still felt wiped out, like I was recovering from a violent illness. When my lunch break finally came, I retreated to the office in relief. I had barely sat down when Elliot appeared at the door.

"Hey," he said, smiling. "Just wanted to see if you were still sore from your afternoon of kayaking."

I looked up at his friendly, familiar face, and suddenly found that I was crying.

"Emily!" he cried in alarm. "What's the matter?"

"I'm sorry," I gasped, burying my face in my hands. "Don't look at me Elliot, please."

"That's silly," he said, coming over to sit next to me. Without a word he wrapped his arm around me and pulled me into his chest. It felt nice there. Cozy and warm. I felt my tears abating almost instantly.

"Sorry," I said again, my voice stronger now as I pulled away. "I don't know what my problem is."

He reached over and grabbed a Kleenex from the box on the desk. I blew my nose and tossed the tissue into the garbage can, taking the moment's distraction to try and get a hold of myself.

"Better?" Elliot asked. I nodded. "Good. So what the hell is the matter?"

I laughed weakly, then sighed. "God. I don't even know."

"Missing Brooke? It must have been hard when she left."

"Actually, Brooke and I got in a pretty big fight," I admitted.

"I'm sorry. Want to talk about it?"

I was silent for a moment. Part of me wanted to forget that any of it had ever happened. I was still angry with Brooke, angrier than I had ever been with her in all of our years of friendship. Regardless of my current confused status with Greg, I couldn't believe that she'd had the gall to question my relationship. She barely knew him! She certainly had no right to assume she knew how I felt.

But at the same time...My confrontation with Greg on Friday night was chasing around and around in my head, along with all the resulting doubt. What I really wanted was someone I could talk to.

I looked up at Elliot, at his kind and open face. If there was anyone in my life who would listen, really listen, to me, it might just be him.

"Things are kind of weird with Greg," I said. I watched his face closely, but didn't see a response, so I continued. "I guess we kind of broke up. I'm wondering if...well, Brooke called me out on a lot of stuff there, and it's kind of got me messed up in my head."

"What kind of stuff?"

"She thinks I'm not myself when I'm with him," I said, feeling a tingle of shame run down my spine. "She thinks I'm trying to be someone different so I'll fit in with him and his scene better."

"She's known you a long time, hasn't she?" Elliot asked. I nodded. "Do you think she knows you well enough to make a judgment like that?" I didn't respond. "I know she has your best interests at heart," he went on. "She loves you very much, that's obvious. But the truth is, no one knows what happens in a relationship unless they're the one in it, you know?"

"True," I said softly.

"From the outside, we can't really tell how the two people work together, how they feel. So no matter how well she might know you, her opinion is just that—an opinion."

I didn't say anything for a long time, mulling over his words. He had a point. But at the same time, the little pit of discomfort in my belly hadn't dissipated in the slightest. Finally, Elliot said, "Do you think she's right? Because you're the only one who can really say."

"She is," I whispered, horrified to find another tear slipping down my cheek. I did not want to cry in front of Elliot again, so I hurriedly wiped it away. "I just feel so much pressure when I'm with him," I said.

"What kind of pressure?"

"Pressure to be what he wants, I guess. Pressure to fit in, to get it right."

"Emily," Elliot said firmly, and I looked up into his face. "You don't need to be anything for anybody. You only need to be you. If he wants more than that, he's wrong. Way wrong."

"That's the problem though," I said, feeling the frustration well up inside of me again. "I don't even know who that is anymore—who I am. I feel like I've been changing myself to adapt to what's going on around me for so long I can't even tell what's real anymore."

"Changing like how?"

"Like, when my mom died. I knew my dad wasn't up for all the girly stuff from a teenager, so I just opted out. I went for sports and fishing and all the things he could relate to. I mean, I enjoyed that stuff. But how do I know how much of it was really me and how much of it was just for him?"

I took a deep breath. "And then there was this whole mess with Ashley and Ryan."

"The romance research project?" he asked, a slight smile playing at his lips.

"Yeah," I said, rolling my eyes. "I mean, what was that? I was freaking out because of what happened with Dylan, thinking there was something seriously wrong with me because of it. So I let them convince me I was making all these mistakes with men and the only way to change was to go along with what they thought I should be."

"And that's when you met Greg."

I looked at him, surprised. In my mind, the two things had been so separate. There was the silliness with Ashley and Ryan and those two disastrous dates. And then there was Greg, the answer to all my problems. Had he only been an extension of what was wrong in the first place?

I leaned forward, resting my elbows on my knees and burying my head in my hands. "I'm such an idiot," I sighed. "Seriously. Who on earth thinks that their problems will be solved because they watch a couple of silly romantic movies with their friends?"

Elliot chuckled softly beside me.

"You're laughing at me," I said, raising my head to give him a rueful smile. "Don't worry, I don't blame you."

"I'm not laughing at you," Elliot said quickly. "I swear I'm not. I'm just thinking how strange it is that we can both look at the same person and see something completely different."

"What do you mean?"

"Em, when I look at you, I don't see someone who's fake, or someone who's trying too hard. I don't see a girl who can't fall in love or be loved back. I see someone who is loyal beyond belief to her family and friends. Someone who genuinely cares for her patients. A girl who wants to get out and experience everything she can in life."

His voice had gotten lower as he talked, so that I had to lean forward slightly to hear him as he finished. "None of that makes you weak or a mess. It makes you someone really, really cool."

His words sent warmth deep inside me, drowning out the sick feeling I'd been struggling with ever since the party. Somehow, I felt better, much better than I had in a really long time.

And somehow, in that moment, I felt more sure of myself, of who I was, than I had been in years.

The sound of my ringing phone startled me. I glanced down at the screen and felt a jolt of surprise. Brooke. My anger resurfaced and for a minute I considered ignoring it. But something, some unknown sense of premonition, stopped me.

Looking back, I guess it's silly to think I could have known what was coming. But still, a small knot of fear had lodged itself in my stomach before I even heard the sound of her voice.

"Em," she said, and the fear immediately grew by a degree. Something had happened, something was wrong. I knew it.

"It's your dad. He had a heart attack."

Chapter Twenty-Six

The next half hour passed in a blur of panic. It was clear to Elliot that I was in no shape to drive. Without asking, he took my keys and ushered me out to my car, barking a quick explanation to Michael as we passed.

As we sped across town to my apartment, I couldn't make my mind focus. I knew I needed to be thinking of what had to be done next. Packing, getting gas, finding Ashley to let her know what was going on. But each time I tried to focus on one of those necessitates, the panic in my chest would take over, forcing coherent thought from my mind.

Please, I thought to myself. *Don't let him die. Please, please, please.*

When we reached my apartment, I looked down to unbuckle my seatbelt and saw that my left hand was firmly in the grip of Elliot's. Funny, I hadn't even noticed him taking it.

He followed me as I rushed inside, calling out to Ashley as I went. It took me a minute to realize that it was the middle of a weekday and Ash would surely be at work.

"Emily," Elliot said behind me, his voice firm and steady. I spun to face him, and he grasped me by the shoulders.

"You need to focus," he said. "I know it's the most impossible thing in the world right now, but you need to try and calm down."

It was funny. Looking into his familiar brown eyes, so steady on mine, calm suddenly didn't feel quite so impossible. I took a deep breath, then another. Elliot smiled.

"Better. Okay, what do you need to do? Pack?"

I nodded. "I should get a few things."

"Will you be okay by yourself for a minute?" he asked. "I could go put gas in the car."

"You don't have to—"

"Emily," he said, holding up his hand. "It's fine."

I merely nodded. He squeezed my shoulders briefly, then turned to go. I watched him for a minute, feeling suddenly unfocused without him there. *You have to get to Dad,* I told myself firmly.

I headed to the bedroom, finding my gym bag at the foot of the bed. I emptied it out onto the floor, then opened the top drawer of my dresser, trying to keep my head clear. It wouldn't serve much purpose if I ended up in Alpena with a suitcase full of T-shirts and no socks.

I managed to get my bag packed, even remembering to grab my toothbrush and my favorite facial cleanser. There was still no sign of Elliot, so I sat down on the couch, figuring I may as well call Ashley now. I was relieved when her voice mail picked up immediately—she must have had her phone off at work. It was going to be hard enough to tell her what was happening, let alone have to hear her reaction.

"Ash, it's me," I said, my voice sounding strange in my ears, too calm, almost fake. "My dad...my dad had a heart attack this morning. I have to head up to Alpena, right away." I took a deep breath. "I'm not sure..." Now the emotion was starting to creep into my voice. "I'm not sure how long I'll be, but I'll call you when I know more."

I ended the call, feeling my heart start to race again. While I had been packing, while I had a task, I had been able to block out the horrible panic, the reality of what was happening. Brooke had said he was in surgery. Apparently the heart attack had been massive. The doctors hadn't been able to say how much damage there was. I closed my eyes. My dad, alone, five hours away. In a hospital. Hurt, afraid. Maybe dying.

"Please," I whispered aloud, burying my head in my hands. "Please."

"Emily?"

I looked up to see Elliot standing there in the doorway, my keys in his hand. "Are you ready to go?"

"Yeah," I said, standing. I felt awkward that he had probably heard me talking to myself, but Elliot didn't seem thrown. "Thank you for your help," I said, picking up my duffle bag from the floor. "I'll drop you back at the store on my way."

"I'm not going back to the store," he said, coming over to take the bag from me. "I already called and let them know."

"What—?"

"I'm going with you," he replied. "You're in no shape to drive."

"You don't have to do that," I said quickly. "Really."

"Don't be silly," he said. "You have what, a five hour drive ahead of you? You could use the company."

I just stared at him. I felt like I should argue, tell him I would be okay. But the truth was, the thought of him being there made me feel better somehow, calmer. I *wanted* him to come with me.

"Come on," he said, placing his hand on my lower back and gently pushing me toward the door. "I have coffee and snacks in the car. We should get going."

"Okay," I agreed. "Let's go."

***

Under perfect weather and traffic conditions, without stopping, it takes about four and a half hours to get from Royal Oak to Alpena. Somehow, Elliot managed to get us there in four hours, and we even stopped twice along the way to use the bathroom and get fresh coffee.

Even though we made excellent time, four hours seems endless when you're as terrified as I was.

After we were on the highway, I called Brooke to let her know I was on the way. She and her parents, along with my Aunt Barbara, were waiting at the hospital while my dad was in surgery. She still didn't have any news, but promised to call me the second they heard from the doctor.

"Brooke," I said, my throat closing up. "Thank you so much for being there. I just want to say...about the other night—"

"Not worth mentioning," she said firmly. "Don't give it another thought. Just be safe and get up here, okay? I'll be here."

"Thanks," I said again. We had never been big on the sappy stuff, but the occasion seemed to call for it. "I love you."

"Love you too," she said, her voice even more throaty than normal. "See you soon."

After that, there wasn't much to do but wait. Elliot put a CD on, something quiet and unobtrusive with a lot of strummy guitar in the background. We sat without talking for a half hour or so. Outside my window, I watched as the scenery slowly changed from suburban sprawl to wooded areas and fields, leaving the shopping centers and high-rise buildings behind.

"How you doing over there?" Elliot asked eventually. "Warm enough?" His right hand flitted over to the temperature controls.

It felt weird to be in the passenger seat of my own car, but at the same time, I was relieved to not have to worry about driving. "I'm fine," I told him. "Thanks." We lapsed back into silence for a minute. "And thanks for coming with me," I said eventually. "I really appreciate it."

"I'm happy to," he said. "It's what friends do, right?"

"I hate this feeling," I said, directing my attention back to the window. "The not knowing. It's the worst part."

"I bet," Elliot said.

"It was like this with my mom too. But for much longer. The whole time she was sick, it was like I was just waiting for the bad news to come, for the other shoe to drop."

"This might not be bad news," Elliot said firmly. "You have to try to stay positive or you'll go crazy."

"Have you ever lost someone?" I asked. I was surprised to realize that the subject had never come up. It seemed like we had talked about everything else over lunch in my little office.

"A good friend," he said softly. "Jeremy. Guy I went to high school with. He was hit by a drunk driver our senior year, coming home from work one night."

"Oh my God," I said, horrified. "Elliot, that's terrible."

"It was," he agreed. "We were so close to graduation, our whole lives ahead of us. Then he was just gone."

"Were you close?" I asked. He nodded, his face unreadable. "I'm so sorry."

"It's hard to talk about," he said, looking over at me briefly before turning back to the road. "People never know what to say, and you end up feeling like you're comforting them."

"I know the feeling," I said. I thought for a moment. "That's why you never ask about my mom, isn't it?"

He shrugged. "I figure if you wanted to tell me, you would."

And suddenly, I did. I wanted to tell him everything about her. Not about how she had left, and what had happened after, but all the good stuff of our twelve years together. The stuff that always got lost beneath the tragedy of her loss.

"My mom was obsessed with planning trips," I said quietly. "She always wanted to travel. She would make these big elaborate plans, no matter how minor the destination. We used to go over to Lake Michigan, just for the day, and she would spend weeks planning it all out, to the last little detail. What shops we would hit, where we would eat. It drove my dad crazy."

I thought it might make me feel worse to talk about her. I usually avoided it at all costs, and under the circumstance, I thought it might make me worry even more about my dad. But I found that it didn't. In a weird way, it kind of made me feel better. Elliot didn't say much, he just let me talk—about the way she would blast classical music while she cleaned the house; how she used to pay me to brush her hair at night while we watched TV; how she would come in my room after school and lie on my bed and we would talk, and talk.

"What did she look like?" he asked.

"Everyone always tells me I look just like her," I said. "And I mean seriously everyone. It used to drive me crazy, living in such a small town. I couldn't even go to the store without seeing someone who had known my mom, stopping me to tell me how like her I was getting."

"Probably not what you wanted to hear on a daily basis."

"No. I mean, I'm honored people thought I looked like her. She was gorgeous. But it was hard enough to keep my mind off it without the reminders."

"Probably makes it hard for you to go home as often as you might like."

I looked at him, surprised. It was funny the way he knew things about me without me even having to tell him.

"Do you want to tell me about Jeremy?"

Elliot sighed. "Not really," he finally said. He looked over at me and smiled. "But I will someday."

I smiled back, glad he could be honest with me. He started to say something else, but my phone rang, interrupting him. I pulled it from my purse and swallowed at the sight of Brooke's name.

"He's out of surgery," she said the moment I'd answered. "The doctors say it went well. They were able to put a stint in, and they say he's resting comfortably now."

The relief I felt was so great, I slumped back into the seat. I knew enough from my anatomy classes that he wasn't out of the woods yet. But coming out of surgery had to be a good sign.

"You okay?" she asked.

"Better now," I said. "Thanks, Brooke." I looked out the window at the approaching mile marker. "We should be there in an hour or so."

"Okay. Be safe."

I ended the call and turned to Elliot. He was smiling. "Good news?"

"Pretty good," I said, smiling back. "Pretty good."

Chapter Twenty-Seven

I was able to see my dad that night. The doctors wouldn't let me stay long, saying he needed his rest, and, in fact, he was very groggy. But he was able to open his eyes and tell me he loved me, and the strength in his hand when he squeezed mine was steady and firm.

Though everyone encouraged me to go back to the house for the night, I insisted on staying. Being so far away when he was in danger had been terrible, and I wasn't about to put any distance between us while he was still far from recovered.

"Can Elliot stay at the inn?" I asked Brooke.

Before she could answer he interjected. "I'll hang out here, keep you company."

"You don't have to do that," I said. "You've done enough already."

"No, really," he said. "I've never slept in a plastic chair before. It will be an adventure, good practice for the club." He winked at me, and my will to argue disappeared.

He did leave for a while, taking my directions to one of the few fast food restaurants in the area. He came back with bags full of burgers and fries. I realized I was starving, and Elliot must have been too, because he didn't even complain about the lack of nutrients in the food. We made a little picnic on the floor of the waiting room, using his hoodie as a blanket for the food.

"You kind of screwed yourself over, you do realize

that, right?" I asked as Elliot sipped his Coke.

"What do you mean?"

"Well, I'm gonna need to stay up here for a while. And you came in my car. How will you get home?"

He shrugged. "I have plenty of vacation time coming my way."

I snorted. "And I'm sure this is exactly how you wanted to spend your vacation."

He met my gaze and held it for a moment. "Actually, it is." His voice was serious and soft and sent a flock of butterflies straight into my stomach. "Besides," he went on, his voice more normal, "I hear there're lots of great features for a nature lover around here."

His lightness made it easy for me to forget the look in his eyes and the way it had made me feel. Almost.

***

Over the next few days, I settled into a pattern. I would spend all morning at the hospital, visiting my dad as often as I could. Then I'd leave for a few hours at lunch, only because my dad insisted. I would try to nap or visit with Brooke, but mostly I just counted down the minutes until I could get back to his side.

He was looking better every day, that terrible grey color fading slowly. He was able to sit up in bed now and talk to me, but still needed a lot of rest. I sat by his bed whether he was awake or asleep. While he slept, I tried to read, but when he was awake, I insisted that we talk. About everything.

We had spent so many years not talking about too much that was real, always hiding behind sports and fishing subjects. I was determined to put an end to that once and for all, no matter how uncomfortable it might be.

I asked him about mom, about their early years together before I came along. At first it was hard, for both of us, but soon we eased our way in, testing out the waters until we were both comfortable. I told him about how hard it was for me to be in town, about why I came home so seldom. He surprised me by saying he had figured that out long ago. He confided that he should have come to visit me more often, but it was easier for him to keep up the status quo.

One afternoon, after he had woken up from a nap, he asked me about Elliot.

"Is he the boy you had been dating? The real estate guy?"

I colored. "No," I said quickly. "That's, uh, over. Elliot is a friend. He works next door to the clinic."

"Pretty good friend, to come all this way," my dad said, a shrewd look on his face. "So, what happened with the real estate guy?"

"It didn't work out," I said, shrugging and looking down at his blanket. "It happens."

"Emily."

I looked up into my dad's face. I could tell he was concerned but, more than that, he really wanted to know. He wanted to be involved in my life.

So I told him everything. About Dylan and how small and insignificant it had made me feel. About how I had let Ashley and Ryan convince me that I was clueless about men and needed to change. About how I met Greg and *made* myself change. It was hard, to admit those things. But I knew, as I spoke, that they were true. Everything about me had been fake with Greg. Everything. I knew then, more than ever, that we were completely over. If my parents had taught me anything, it was that life was too short to waste time.

"I'm proud of you," my dad said, once I had

finished talking.

I looked at him in surprise. "Proud? That's not really the word I would use to describe my actions lately."

"But you figured it out," he said. "Before it went too far and someone got too hurt. That counts for a lot."

"I guess," I said, shrugging.

"Emily," he said, reaching over and placing his hand over mine. "It does. Believe me."

Chapter Twenty-Eight

I could tell that Elliot was trying to strike a respectful balance. He spent some time at the hospital, keeping me company when my dad was sleeping, or sitting with us watching Tigers games when he was awake. The rest of the time he took my car and explored the area. He would come back at night and tell us stories of the places he had seen. My dad and I would add our own stories, tell him about our own memories.

On the fifth day my dad was in the hospital, the doctors started talking about his release. I was terrified at the idea of him going home where they wouldn't be right down the hall to help him, but they assured me he was improving even better than they had hoped.

"You should get out of here for a while," my dad said to Elliot and me, looking out the window at the clear blue sky. "It looks like a great day for fishing."

He sounded wistful, and I laughed. "You'll be out there soon enough."

"I'm planning to take lots of time to go fishing," he said, meeting my eye. The night before, we had talked at length about him slowing down at work. He had even entertained the idea that he might retire. "Go out and see the world," he had said. I was keeping my fingers crossed that he would go through with it.

"Really," he said. "You heard the doctors. I'm doing good. So get out of here, enjoy the day."

Reluctantly, I agreed. As Elliot and I headed out to

the car, I called Brooke to see if she could get a few hours to join us.

"God, yes," she said. "We have a tour group of birdwatchers here this week. They've been showing slides in the dining room all morning. I feel like I might start pulling my hair out."

"Bird-watchers, eh?" I asked, grinning. "Sounds right up Elliot's alley." He shoved me into the wall, and I laughed. "We'll stop at home and get the trailer," I said. "Be there in twenty?"

It surprised me a little how comfortable I felt being back home. For once in my life, the familiarity of the setting didn't make me feel nervous, or panicked. I didn't even mind when my dad's neighbor, Mrs. Sterling, stopped me while we were hooking up the trailer to ask after my dad. She babbled on for about ten minutes about my parents, and what great neighbors they had been, and how much she loved my mom. I got through the entire conversation without even breaking a sweat—not bad for me.

We took my dad's truck, since my car lacked the horsepower, not to mention a trailer hitch, to tow the rowboat. Once we'd picked up Brooke, I headed west out of town. "You haven't been over to Lake Winyah yet, have you?" I asked Elliot.

"Nope."

"Fishing out there can be pretty good," I said. I cranked up the radio—CDs had not yet been invented when my dad bought this truck—and we rolled the windows down, the sunlight warming my skin.

Out at Lake Winyah, I expertly backed the trailer out into the launch. "Impressive," Elliot said, raising his eyebrows in surprise when I jumped out of the truck.

"I've done this more times that I can count," I told

him, heading around to help Brooke slide the boat down into the water. I threw Elliot the keys. "Make yourself useful and go park the truck."

Once we had our poles, Brooke's cooler (freshly filled with beer), and my old tackle box situated, Elliot and I climbed into the boat, Brooke pushing us off from the shore before jumping in. I sat at the back and started the little motor up, maneuvering us out to a far inlet. Brooke tossed the anchor down and we were set.

"Now what?" Elliot asked.

I stared at him. "What do you mean, now what?"

He looked a little sheepish. "I mean, what do we do now?"

"You've never fished before?" I was incredulous. Elliot shook his head.

"I don't believe this! Mr. Nature Boy, tells-everyone-else-how-stunted-they-are-by-the-city has never been fishing before. Unbelievable!"

"Here," Brooke said, taking pity on him. She took his line and showed him how to string a hook. We hadn't stopped for night crawlers, so we made do with my collection of lures.

It was silent out on the lake, the only other boat around on the far side. In the heat of the early afternoon sun, I could hear cicadas buzzing in the trees. I settled into a pattern: cast, wait, reel. I could almost feel the tension of the past week—the past several weeks, really—draining away from me.

"I love this," I said softly. "Being out in the woods, on the water. The quiet, the routine of it. I can't believe I let myself go so long without it."

"Once a country girl, always a country girl," Brooke said drily. She had abandoned her fishing pole and had spread out at the front of the boat, soaking up the sun.

But Elliot caught my eye and smiled, and I knew he understood.

After two hours, we had caught several trout and a pike. Well, I did most of the catching, but Brooke managed to reel in a pretty decent-sized trout. Even Elliot had snagged one just about big enough to be kept. Not bad for his first time out.

As soon as we were back in the truck, I called my dad's room. "Go home and cook that up," he instructed once I'd told him of our haul. "I'm fine. Your Aunt Barbara is here, keeping me company."

So we went back to the house, where I cleaned and fried up the fish, and Brooke dug up some more beer. "Wow," Elliot said softly, watching me as I flipped the trout in the pan.

"What?"

"I had no idea you were so good at this. It's...well, it's really impressive."

I looked up into his eyes and felt my stomach flip. He was watching me intently, his gaze dark. Was I imagining it, or was there something there, in his eyes...

"Almost done?" Brooke asked, coming up next to me. "I'm starving."

I tried to forget about what I had sensed in Elliot's gaze as we took our plates and our beers outside to the deck. Night was starting to fall, and I could hear the eerie cry of the whippoorwill in the trees as I settled back onto a lounge chair and put my feet up.

It had been years since I'd had freshly caught fish, and I practically whimpered as I took my first bite. It was just as good as I remembered. "You caught a good one," Brooke said, wiping her mouth and grinning at me.

"Hey, for all you know we're eating the one I

caught." Elliot said.

"We're not," Brooke and I said together.

After we finished our fish, I called my dad one more time. "Stay home," he said firmly. "I'm tired and I don't need any more company."

"You're tired?" I asked, feeling a shiver of fear. "Are you okay? Did you overdo it?"

He laughed. "I'm tired because your Aunt Barbara talks more than any woman I've ever met. Listen, there's a game on TV, and I'm just gonna lie here and watch it until I fall asleep. Stay with your friends. That's an order from your father."

"Fine," I said. "But you call me if you feel bad at all, you understand? Well, call the nurse first. But then you call me!"

"Em, you're getting bossy in your old age," he said, chuckling. "Night."

"Night, love you."

I hung up the phone and leaned back against my chair. I could just make out the first stars in the sky. From the open windows of the house next door, I could hear the quiet sounds of the baseball game on the radio.

"This is nice," Brooke said, sounding sleepy. "We haven't done this in a while."

"Yeah," I agreed, stretching out. "I've missed this."

We sat like that for an hour or so, not really talking, just listening to the quiet sounds of the woods and the neighborhood as night fell, watching the stars come out above us and drinking cold beer. Eventually, Brooke stood up and stretched.

"I should get going," she said. "The birdwatchers will be up early for their first day trip, and someone's got to make the coffee."

"Have fun," I told her, yawning. "I'd get up to see

you out, but I don't want to."

She snorted. "Nice. See you tomorrow. Night, Elliot."

After she was gone, I became hyper aware of Elliot in the lounger next to me. It was the polar opposite of how I usually felt around him. Normally being with Elliot was as comfortable as taking a warm bath. This feeling wasn't exactly unpleasant, but it was sure no warm bath.

"I had such a nice day," he said finally. "Thank you for teaching me how to fish."

"I had a nice day too," I said, my voice soft. "I could stay out here forever."

"Me too. Hey, do you know the constellations up there?"

"Not really," I said, looking up. I had forgotten how much brighter the stars were out here. Down by Detroit, I was lucky if I could make out the Big Dipper.

"That right there is Orion," Elliot said softly, pointing up. I followed his finger to a line of three stars. "And if you follow his belt out that way, you can see Sirius."

I followed his finger, mesmerized by the sound of his voice.

"Beautiful," I whispered.

"Yes, it is." I looked over and saw that Elliot was now staring at me, not the stars. I felt that same flipping in my belly. I decided I liked the feeling.

Just then, I yawned hugely. Elliot chuckled. "You've been running yourself ragged at the hospital. You should go to bed."

"Probably."

He stood up first, reaching down to pull me up from the lounge chair. His hands were strong and steady against mine, and I held on for just a second longer than necessary.

We gathered up the beer cans and went inside. The house was dark, and I didn't turn on any lights. It felt like I was moving through some kind of dreamy fog, and I didn't really want to disturb it just yet. In silence, we headed up the stairs. Elliot had been sleeping in the guest bedroom at the end of the hall, but he stopped when I reached my door. A tiny sliver of light shone through from the open door behind us, hitting him directly across the face so I could make out his eyes in the darkness.

"Good night, Elliot," I whispered.

"Good night." He leaned forward and kissed my cheek, and I closed my eyes, overwhelmed by the nearness of him. He smelled like beer and the lake and a little bit of sweat. I know it doesn't sound good, but let me tell you, it was very appealing and all Elliot. Before I could even think about what I was doing, I turned my face so his lips landed on my mouth. And then we were kissing.

I don't think I'd ever been kissed like that before. Elliot's mouth was hard against mine, as if he was determined to drink in every inch of my lips. I heard him release a little sigh of air, a happy, almost relieved sound that sent a thrill straight into my heart. I kissed him back, as hard as I could, until I was breathless.

Everything that had ever been missing from any of my past kisses was there with Elliot—sparks, heat, maybe even fireworks. Nothing with Greg had ever been—

Suddenly, I pulled away. "I can't," I gasped. "I'm sorry. Greg—"

Elliot's face immediately closed up. "I'm sorry," he said stiffly.

"No," I reached for his hand. "Don't be. I just...I

can't. Not yet."

He pulled his hand away from mine and, without another word, walked down the hallway, shutting the door to his room behind him.

Chapter Twenty-Nine

"You did what?" Brooke asked, her voice incredulous. "Wait a second, go back. You kissed him?"

"Yup," I said, smiling against my coffee mug. "And it was amazing."

"Holy shit," she said, staring at me across the little table at the inn. "I didn't think you had it in you. So what happened next?"

I frowned a little bit as I thought of what followed. "Well, I realized that I hadn't exactly totally ended things with Greg, and I told him I couldn't."

"Wow," Brooke said, her wide eyes. "Way to kill the mood."

I sighed. "I know. And I was too flustered from the kiss to really explain myself. So, you know, I'm gonna need to take care of that ASAP."

"You didn't see him this morning?"

"He left a note that he went hiking. He was gone when I woke up."

"He's pissed," she said shrewdly.

"Probably," I agreed. "But I'm hoping he'll get over it when I throw myself at him later."

I had expected Brooke to laugh at that, but she just frowned slightly. "What?" I asked.

"I just...listen, don't get me wrong, okay? I really like Elliot. I just don't want you to rush anything. There's a lot going on in your life."

"Yeah, but—"

"Just think about it. There's all this stress about

your dad, right? And you're just ending this really intense relationship. Plus there's the whole clinic purchase plan when you get home. It's a lot."

"I know," I said. "But Elliot is the one guy who actually supports me in all of that. I can't think of anyone better to have by my side."

"Just take it slow, that's all I'm saying."

I felt a little peeved, to be honest. I was more excited about what had happened last night than I had ever been about any guy. Until last night, I had never really understood what I was missing. I didn't really appreciate Brooke being a buzz kill.

"Well, regardless," I said. "I need to get on the phone with Greg and tell him nothing is going to change. It's done."

"Have fun with that," she said in a better-you-than-me tone.

Greg did not take the news very well. He had called me a few times since I had been home, but I refused to talk to him, telling him my dad was my only priority. Now he tried to convince me that I was speaking irrationally because I was upset about the heart attack.

"Greg," I said, as patiently as possible. "I'm telling you the truth. It is over. I'm not the one for you. I know that now. Nothing is going to change my mind."

"I just can't believe this," he sighed, but he sounded more resigned. I felt a little flicker of hope that this might be over soon. "I don't understand what I did wrong."

"It wasn't your fault," I said. "I was trying to be something I'm not because it's what you wanted."

Greg was quiet for a long moment. "Listen," I said. "I'm going to take those clothes back and send you the money. The ones I wore already, well, maybe I can sell them on eBay."

"Don't be silly," he said, the hint of disapproval back in his voice. "That would be totally inappropriate."

I sighed to myself, more sure than ever that I was doing the right thing.

"I'm sorry, Greg," I said, once more. "I truly am."

"I'm sorry too," he said, his voice sad. "I think I could have been really happy with you."

Maybe, I thought after I hung up, *but I would have never been happy with you.*

As I slipped my purse into my bag, I couldn't help but feel my spirits lift a little. That was out of the way now. And when Elliot came back, I could tell him.

***

But Elliot didn't come back, not all day. He wasn't at the house when I left for the hospital, or when I called home a few hours later. And he still wasn't there when I came home at lunch. I went back to the hospital and ate dinner with my dad, hanging out to watch the ball game, checking my phone every five minutes. What if something had happened to him?

When I got home, and Elliot still wasn't there, I started to panic. He didn't know this area. What if he fell and hurt himself somewhere out in the woods. I shivered a little, thinking of the wild animals one might encounter out there at night hurt.

I pulled out my cell and called him one last time, startled when I heard the ringing of his phone from the back deck. It had been there since last night, probably. Which meant he was out there somewhere with no way to communicate. I walked outside to get the phone and happened to glance down at the screen. Five missed calls. Four were from me. One was from

Heather.

There is this girl, actually…

Oh my God, how stupid could I possibly be? Elliot had told me there was a girl he was seeing from his club. What if I had misinterpreted everything? What if he had been upset, not because I pulled away, but because he was offended I would come on to him when he had a girlfriend.

He kissed me back, a voice in my head shouted defiantly.

Yeah, but he had also had quite a bit to drink. I closed my eyes. God, was he out there right now thinking I was a drunken, sleazy girl who would throw herself at a guy who was just trying to be a friend? The thought made my stomach clench with dismay.

My phone rang in my hand and I hurriedly held it up to my ear, thinking it might be him.

"So what's this I hear about you kissing Elliot?" Ashley sounded gob smacked.

"Who told you that?"

"Brooke told Chris," she said hurriedly. "What does it matter. Is it true?"

"Yes," I said, slumping into a kitchen chair. "And I think I screwed everything up."

"Em, it is way too soon for that," she said. "I know it's been a while since you had a serious relationship like Greg, but you don't want to just bounce around to the next guy. Especially when he's a friend."

Somewhere deep inside, her words set off a little flame. Was she seriously going to lecture me about dating right now? After everything that happened, did she still think that I needed her to be my romance guru?

"Actually, you're wrong," I said, my voice steady. "Elliot is different. The way I feel is different." As I said the words, I knew they were true. With Elliot, I never worried about anything—not about how I looked, or how I should act, or what he was thinking. He accepted me, he always had. Sure, we argued about stupid stuff, but I also felt comfortable enough with him to argue. Comfortable enough to make him mad and let him tease me.

In one crystal clear moment, I got it. Elliot saw me for what I really was. And I'd be damned if I let go of that so easily.

On the other end of the phone, Ashley was still talking, apparently oblivious to my breakthrough. "Come on, Em," she said. "Don't you think it's really soon to—"

"No, you know what *I* think?" I interrupted, standing up suddenly. I was fed up—like, really, really fed up. "I think I'm sick and tired of taking advice from everyone else about my life."

"Emily—"

"No, Ashley, I'm *done*. I'm done having people think I need to be taught or changed or exposed to things in order to be happy. I'm making my own decisions now, okay? You can go ahead and tell Ryan that, and tell Chris he can call Brooke up and tell her too."

On the other end of the line, Ashley was silent, but I could hear Chris in the background, and what sounded like clapping. "Good for you, Em!" he called.

"Now, Ashley, if you'll excuse me, I need to go find Elliot and tell him how I feel."

"Okay," she squeaked, sounding a little scared.

"Thank you for caring, Ash," I said, not wanting her to think I was mad. "I love you. And I'm telling you with love—butt out."

I hung up the phone and grabbed my purse,

determined to set out in the truck until I found him. I pulled out my keys and spun around—and stopped dead in my tracks.

"You need to tell me how you feel, huh?" Elliot asked. He was standing in the doorway to the kitchen, a little grin on his face. "And just how would that be, Emily?"

I took a deep breath, wanting to tell him, wanting to ask him to break up with Heather and tell him that I had broken up with Greg. But instead, I launched myself into his arms, kissing him on the mouth before he could say a word.

I was relieved to find that the kiss was every bit as good as the one the night before. A part of me had been scared that it had just been a spell of the moonlight and the beer. But as Elliot kissed me back, I knew that it was not. It was definitely, definitely not. He really was that good of a kisser.

"What did you want to tell me?" he said breathlessly, pulling back. "Come on, I want to hear you say it."

"I broke up with Greg," I said quickly. "Like, officially. That's why I had to stop last night. I wanted it to be right first."

He smiled, and kissed me softly. "God, you have no idea how glad I am to hear that. I really, really hated that guy."

I laughed. "You never even met him!"

"It doesn't matter," Elliot said firmly.

"So, what about you?" I asked.

"What do you mean?"

"Did you break up with that girl, that Heather?" I wrinkled my nose a little, hating the thought of the unknown girl. Elliot laughed.

"That ended ages ago. It wasn't very fair to her,

you know. To date her when I was so head over heels for you."

"You were?" I asked, delighted.

"Of course," he looked at me levelly. "I always have been, Em."

"I'm sorry it took me so long."

He leaned in for another kiss, smiling that Elliot smile I knew so well. "I think I can forgive you."

After a moment, he pulled back again. I was almost relieved—my head was spinning and I was out of breath. If I would have known kissing Elliot would have been like this, I would have done it a long time ago.

"So," he said, looking down at me with a twinkle of amusement in his eyes. "What guy am I?"

"What guy?" I asked, confused.

"You know. From your research. I know I'm not the high school sweetheart or the boy next door. So what is it? The guy with hidden depths? The bad boy?" He wiggled his eyebrows at me suggestively at that, making me laugh.

"Nope," I said, wrapping my hands more tightly behind his neck. "You're not any of those things. You, Elliot, are the guy I met in a totally normal, natural, every-day kind of way. You're the guy I took my time getting to know and becoming friends with. And you're the guy I fell totally and completely in love with without even realizing it."

"Hmm," he said in a mock-serious tone—the grin on his face kind of gave him away though. "I'm not sure if that's romantic enough for your friends."

I kissed him again before pulling back and grinning at him. "Somehow, I really don't care one little bit."

We stood in silence for a moment, just holding

each other. Finally, Elliot bent his head toward me once again. "Hey, Emily," he whispered in my ear, kissing my neck lightly and making me shiver. I could practically hear the smile in his voice. "Does this mean you're going to join the Adventurers Club?"

I laughed and pulled him closer. "Don't press your luck, buddy."

Chapter Thirty

"Emily, let's go!"

"Hang on a second," I yelled back, leaning in toward the mirror to check my mascara. Somehow I still never quite managed the secret technique of getting it clump free. Satisfied that I looked somewhat decent, I stood up from my dressing mirror and headed to the living room.

"It's about time," Brooke grumbled from the couch, looking up from her magazine as I entered the room.

"What's your big hurry?" I asked, picking up my purse. "We're just going to dinner."

"Yeah, your celebration dinner," she said, throwing the magazine aside and standing. "This is a big deal."

I rolled my eyes and she smirked. "You weren't this blasé a few hours ago. In fact, I think I remember someone begging me to pull off the road so she could throw up."

"Shut up," I said, walking to the door. "I was allowed to be nervous then. But this is supposed to be the nice relaxing part." Brooke followed me through the door, waiting while I stopped to lock it behind us.

"So are Ashley and Chris meeting us at the restaurant?"

"I think that's the plan." We headed down the stairs to the parking lot and climbed into my car.

"We'll be late," Brooke muttered, looking at the dashboard clock.

"Relax," I told her. "The restaurant is like, five minutes away."

She didn't answer, just stared determinedly out the window. After a moment, I saw her jump slightly. "Crap," she muttered, reaching for her bag. "I left my phone at the clinic this afternoon."

I looked over at her. There was something weird about her voice, like it was almost too casual. "No, problem," I said, signaling to turn. "We can stop by on the way."

"Sorry," she said, still not looking at me. "I don't want to make you late for your dinner."

As we neared the clinic, Brooke seemed to get increasingly anxious. She tapped her foot against the floorboard and crossed her arms, glancing at the clock over and over again.

"Okay, Brooke," I said as I turned into the parking lot of the clinic. "What's going on? You're acting all weird."

"I am not," she said, her voice high pitched. "I'm fine! Everything's fine."

I parked the car and turned to her, but she was already swinging her door open and hopping out. "Come on," she called over her shoulder.

I sighed and followed her. The clinic was dark behind the glass windows. As we reached the front door I heard a familiar voice.

"Emily!"

I looked up and saw Michael and his girlfriend approaching us. "What are you doing here?" I asked, confused. "I thought we were meeting at the restaurant?"

"Meg forgot something," he said, looking like he wanted to laugh. I looked at his girlfriend, but she was determinedly not meeting my gaze. I looked back at

Brooke and saw that she too had apparently become fascinated with the pavement. Something clicked, and I looked back at Michael. He grinned at me, and I knew he got it too.

"Well, by all means," I said, waving my hand toward the glass door. "Let's go inside."

Michael pulled out his keys and opened the front door. I followed him into the dark entryway and waited while he fumbled for the lights.

"Surprise!"

As the room filled with light our friends and family were revealed to us, grouped together on the exercise floor under a large banner. I had a fleeting glance of balloons and streamers before Ashley and Ryan were pulling me into a group hug.

"Congratulations!" Ashley said in my ear, kissing my cheek.

"Congrats, babe," Ryan said. As I pulled back, I saw Chris behind them, grinning at me.

"You did it!" he said.

Once my friends had released me, I could see more clearly the group of people there to celebrate with us. I caught sight of Michael's parents, Sarah, a few of our regular patients (including Frank and Mrs. Z, who appeared to be holding hands), Ryan's new boyfriend, Dean (an aspiring male model who Ryan was crazy about), and my dad.

"Dad!" I cried, throwing my arms around him. "What are you doing here?"

"Like I would miss this," he said into my ear, squeezing me tight. "I'm so proud of you, Em."

"Thanks, Dad," I said, feeling choked up all of a sudden.

"Everyone!" Brooke called out, standing up on a chair. The room immediately fell silent. Brooke tended to have that kind of effect on people. "I just want to say a few words." She looked down at me, smiling broadly. "First of all, we are so proud of Emily and Michael. As you know, they signed all the ownership and lease papers today, and this clinic is now officially theirs!" The room broke into applause and cheers at these words. I grinned at Michael and wondered if I looked as goofy happy as he did. Probably.

Brooke continued. "We want you guys to know that we understand you have a really hard road ahead of you—buying this place was the easy part. But we're all here to support you and help in any way we can." She smiled at us both, and I felt the lump return in my throat. "So anyhow, if you'll all join me." She held out her hand and Ryan handed her a plastic cup, which she raised in the air. "To Michael and Emily!"

"To Michael and Emily!" our friends and family echoed.

"There's plenty of food and drinks, so everyone have a great time!" Brooke jumped down off her chair, and I made a beeline for her, grabbing her and hugging her tightly.

"Alright, alright," she muttered, trying to pull back. "No reason to get all sappy on me."

"Nope," I said, holding on tightly. "You're not getting away that easily. I love you, Brooke. I can't thank you enough for all your help. This wouldn't have been possible without you."

She didn't reply, so I figured I'd tortured her enough and started to release her, but she surprised me by squeezing me back.

"I am so, so proud of you," she whispered, her voice breaking slightly. "For everything. Emily, you have no idea."

I felt tears prick my eyes, so I squeezed them

tightly shut and buried my head in her shoulder. It was so unlike Brooke to get emotional—

"Alright, now let go of me before I puke on you," she said, her voice returning to normal. I laughed and pulled back, grinning at her. She rolled her eyes at me and pointed over my shoulder. "Someone wants to talk to you."

I spun around and saw Elliot standing there, holding out a plastic cup of champagne.

"Hey," I said as Brooke squeezed my arm and moved away. "I didn't see you."

"I was at the counter, getting the food ready when you guys showed up." He made a face at me as he handed me the champagne. "I missed the surprise."

"That's okay." I kissed him briefly, smiling up at him. "I forgive you."

"You look happy," he said, wrapping an arm around my waist. "Are you happy?"

I rested my head against his shoulder, looking around at the clinic that was now half mine. I felt tired and exhilarated all at the same time. It had been a whirlwind of a day. Brooke had arrived from Alpena early in the afternoon so she could accompany Michael and me to the bank to sign the papers. In the moments leading up to the closing, I had been practically beside myself with terror. It had seemed like such a huge undertaking, way too grown up and scary for me.

But Brooke had squeezed my knee under the table while I signed the papers, and I had gotten through it. And now Michael and I actually owned this place.

I looked around at my friends and family. Chris was talking to my dad, both of them holding plates filled with food. I was pleased to see my dad had avoided the chips and burgers. He looked much better than he had when I left him a month ago—his color was back, and he had dropped some weight.

Ashley and Ryan were standing together next to Dean, who looked thoroughly bored and unimpressed by the scene. I smiled to myself, wondering when Ryan would get a clue about the boys he dated. Behind them, Brooke was perched up on one of the therapy tables, her legs crossed as she talked to one of Michael's friends. I noticed a lot of hair flicking and eyelash batting from that corner of the room. Next to them stood Frank and Mrs. Z, and the similarities between my friend and ZiZi were comically obvious. I laughed and turned back to Elliot.

"You still with me?" he asked, squeezing my waist.

"Yeah," I said, smiling. "I'm with you."

"You didn't answer me." Elliot kissed the top of my head. "I asked if you were happy?"

In response, I leaned up and kissed him, loving the feel of his arm around me, of his warm lips on mine.

"No, I'm not happy," I whispered against his mouth. He frowned slightly, and I went on, "Happy doesn't even begin to cover it."

THE END

Interested in reading more from this author? Check out the best-selling *Three Girls* series, available now in paperback and ebook.

Come along for the crazy ride as Ginny McKensie and her best friends deal with an unexpected pregnancy in *Three Girls and a Baby*.

Follow Jen Campbell as she struggles to plan the perfect wedding—and find her very own happily ever after in *Three Girls and a Wedding*.

Join Annie Duncan as she continues her search for the perfect leading role—and the perfect man to go along with it. The third and final book of the series, *Three Girls and a Leading Man*, is available now!

ABOUT THE AUTHOR

Rachel Schurig is the best-selling author of the *Three Girls* series, available now in paperback and ebook. Rachel lives in the metro Detroit area with her dog, Lucy. She loves to watch reality TV, and reads as many books as she can get her hands on. In her spare time, Rachel decorates cakes.

To find out more about her books, visit Rachel at rachelschurig.com

Printed in Poland
by Amazon Fulfillment
Poland Sp. z o.o., Wrocław